"We'll find your daughter."

Despite her words, Grant felt as if his limbs were weighted down with worry, grief and dread of what he might find in the woods. Or not find. He hesitated as he walked to the door, remembering something that sent a chill to his bones.

Failure and disappointment washed over him. "It was the last promise I made to my wife. To keep Peyton safe. And now—"

Amy stepped close and wrapped her arms around him, then rested her chin on his shoulder. She said nothing, but her embrace said more than anything she could verbalize.

Amy was there for him. She had come to mean so much to him in just a few days. Sure, he recognized his physical attraction to her for what it was, but he'd also grown close to her on a personal level that went far deeper than sexual chemistry. That connection scared him. He'd only had this sort of connection with one other person in his life.

He hoped he didn't lose Amy, too.

Dear Reader,

If you started the Mansfield Brothers series with *The Return of Connor Mansfield*, then you know the story of how Connor's older brother Grant lost his wife, a casualty of the war a crime family waged against Connor. The past year has been rough on Grant. He's mourned his wife deeply while trying to care for their two little girls. But life isn't through surprising Grant or throwing obstacles in his path. As a writer, torturing a character with emotionally gut-wrenching events is part of the job. Characters need challenges to grow and earn their happy ending. But poor Grant has really suffered, and he broke my heart.

Fortunately, fate has something special in store for Grant. Not what he expects, not what he wants... but what he needs—Amy Robinson. A daredevil smoke jumper with absolutely no domestic skills or proclivities for mothering is hardly Grant's idea of his ideal match, but sometimes fate—and the heart—knows best.

Grant's story wraps up the Mansfield Brothers series. I love these Louisiana guys and hope you have, too!

Happy reading,

Beth Cornelison

THE MANSFIELD RESCUE

Beth Cornelison

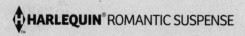
HARLEQUIN® ROMANTIC SUSPENSE

Recycling programs
for this product may
not exist in your area.

ISBN-13: 978-0-373-27897-8

The Mansfield Rescue

Copyright © 2014 by Beth Cornelison

All rights reserved. Except for use in any review, the reproduction or
utilization of this work in whole or in part in any form by any electronic,
mechanical or other means, now known or hereinafter invented, including
xerography, photocopying and recording, or in any information storage
or retrieval system, is forbidden without the written permission of the
publisher, Harlequin Enterprises Limited, 225 Duncan Mill Road,
Don Mills, Ontario M3B 3K9, Canada.

This is a work of fiction. Names, characters, places and incidents are
either the product of the author's imagination or are used fictitiously,
and any resemblance to actual persons, living or dead, business
establishments, events or locales is entirely coincidental.

This edition published by arrangement with Harlequin Books S.A.

For questions and comments about the quality of this book,
please contact us at CustomerService@Harlequin.com.

® and TM are trademarks of Harlequin Enterprises Limited or its
corporate affiliates. Trademarks indicated with ® are registered in the
United States Patent and Trademark Office, the Canadian Intellectual
Property Office and in other countries.

Printed in U.S.A.

HARLEQUIN®
www.Harlequin.com

Beth Cornelison started writing stories as a child when she penned a tale about the adventures of her cat, Ajax. A Georgia native, she received her bachelor's degree in public relations from the University of Georgia. After working in public relations for a little more than a year, she moved with her husband to Louisiana, where she decided to pursue her love of writing fiction.

Since that first time, Beth has written many more stories of adventure and romantic suspense and has won numerous honors for her work, including a coveted Golden Heart Award in romantic suspense from Romance Writers of America. She is active on the board of directors for the North Louisiana Storytellers and Authors of Romance (NOLA STARS) and loves reading, traveling, *Peanuts'* Snoopy and spending downtime with her family.

She writes from her home in Louisiana, where she lives with her husband, one son and two cats who think they are people. Beth loves to hear from her readers. You can write to her at P.O. Box 5418, Bossier City, LA 71171, or visit her website, www.bethcornelison.com.

Books by Beth Cornelison

HARLEQUIN ROMANTIC SUSPENSE

The Mansfield Brothers

The Return of Connor Mansfield
Protecting Her Royal Baby
The Mansfield Rescue

The Coltons of Wyoming

Colton Christmas Rescue

Black Ops Rescues

Soldier's Pregnancy Protocol
The Reunion Mission
Cowboy's Texas Rescue

Visit the author profile page at Harlequin.com for more titles.

To Doris Robinson, dear friend and plotter extraordinaire, for suggesting the perfect twist to get this book moving when I got stuck. You're a treasure to me! Thanks also to Teresa Hughes and her son, Payne, for the balloon release scene idea.

Prologue

Smoke jumper Amy Robinson squinted out the window of the Twin Otter jump ship at the massive smoke column billowing skyward from the forest below. A yellow-gray haze blanketed the Idaho mountain range. The fire was huge, a gobbler.

Anticipation spiked in her blood. Reaching into a pocket of her jumpsuit, she fingered the key to her father's old Mustang convertible. *Stella*. She walked her fingers up the key to the locket ornament on the key chain. One side of the locket held a picture of her father, taken two months before he died, and the other side was inscribed, Carpe diem. *Seize the day*. A bit trite, she admitted, but only a short motto would fit in the tiny locket, and the words were enough to remind her not to let her past define her or hold her back. The sentiment had kept her going as she worked to become the only female smoke jumper on her squad and only one of a handful of women smoke jumpers in the United States.

"All right, first stick, get in the door!" the spotter shouted.

Amy tucked the locket back in her pocket, scooped her shoulder-length dark blond hair into her helmet and waddled with her jump partner, Jim "Bear" Berolli, to the open side door of the Twin Otter. The roar of the

110-mile-per-hour slipstream was almost deafening, and the scent of wood smoke poured into the small aircraft. Her body hummed, her senses on full alert. She signaled thumbs-up. *Ready.*

Johnson, the spotter, chucked the last set of drift streamers out the door. Amy watched them unfurl in a swirl of red, yellow and blue, dancing and spinning as they caught every ripple and current in the air, blazing the trail before Amy battled the same winds.

"Looks like about three hundred yards of drift to the north. But things will get tricky down low. Lot of shifting winds and updrafts," Johnson shouted over the engine noise and rushing slipstream.

"Roger that." Bear gave his parachute strap a firm double-check tug.

"Right." Amy flipped down the screen mask of her helmet.

"Take us to three thousand!" Johnson called to the pilot.

Amy's heart drummed an eager cadence against her ribs as the jump ship circled. Climbed.

She braced in the open door. Waiting. Focused. Confident.

"Get ready!"

She tensed. Felt the slap on her shoulder. And launched herself out.

She savored the thrill as she careened through the air in a free fall for precious few seconds before going through her count. Jump thousand. Look thousand. Reach thousand. Wait thousand. Pull!

Amy checked her canopy. A perfect red-and-white rectangular canopy flew above her. Adrenaline-laced excitement swelled in her chest. "Woo-hoo!"

"Hoo-yah!" Bear answered, descending smoothly beside her.

Amy drew air into her lungs as deeply as she could with the straps of her gear cinched around her chest. She concentrated on her descent, finding the jump spot and toggling toward it.

Orange flames shot from the treetops. A crown fire. They had a big job ahead of them. She surveyed the landscape for the best place to lay a waterline to the nearby creek. The head of the fire had burned—

A sudden updraft interrupted her analysis and jerked her canopy, slinging her hard to the right. She adjusted, only to have another wind gust snatch her another direction.

Tricky, Johnson had said.

Amy scoffed as the wind shifted again and pulled her farther off target. *Tricky ain't the half of it.*

She lost elevation quickly and fought to get back to the jump spot. Damn it, she was headed for the trees!

Knowing she couldn't make her intended target anymore, Amy searched for a viable option. Anything but the trees!

She chose a rocky clearing about a hundred feet south of the jump spot. She'd have to play dodge the boulders, but the rocks still seemed her best option. And her choices were rapidly dwindling. She was coming in too fast.

Another sharp updraft jerked her off course, then spun her around. Now, rather than heading toward the rocks, she was dropping straight into the trees. Burning trees! A vile curse flickered in her brain even as her heart rate skyrocketed. If she crashed into the lodgepole pines and aspens, so be it. But landing behind the fire line was deadly.

She tried to toggle away from the crown fire. Nothing happened. She cut a sharp glance at her canopy and found one of her risers had got tangled in the last updraft.

"Robinson!" Bear's panicked shout reached her over the roar of flames and exploding trees. Her partner knew as well as she did she was on a lethal course.

She had precious few seconds to do something to avoid disaster. She tugged hard on the riser, praying she could dislodge it from the snag. She drifted closer to the trees, felt the searing waves of heat. Flames danced from the treetops like the tongues of demons waiting to gobble her up.

She refused to give up and simply drift into that cauldron of smoke and flame. She wasn't ready to die. Not today!

After she gave the riser another strong jerk, the tangle released. Choking on thick smoke, she cut hard and yanked the toggle for all she was worth. Another swirling wind current swept past, catching her canopy and carrying her hard to the east with a tooth-rattling snap. Her parachute straps knocked the breath from her. Before she could recalculate her location, thick, spiky branches swallowed her. Pine limbs snapped and clawed at her as she crashed through the lattice of branches. Her Kevlar-lined jumpsuit and face shield protected her from the smaller limbs as the trees grabbed at her chute. The canopy caught briefly in the upper branches, bringing her to a jarring halt.

Amy cast a wary glance—around, up and to the ground far below. She was hung up, but the trees nearest her were not burning. Yet. She could see the fire line approximately fifty to sixty feet west of her. That last gust of wind had saved her from getting cooked, but she wasn't out of danger yet. She still had to get out of this tree and—

With a loud crack, the branch her parachute had caught on broke. She plummeted again. The lower branches were larger than the ones at the top. As she crashed past these limbs her body was bumped and battered. She clipped one of the thick branches, and sharp pain ripped through her left ankle. She yelped, but the breath carrying the cry was slammed from her throat as her chest straps jerked taut a second time. Her canopy had snagged again but could tear loose anytime. Free-falling the final thirty or so feet to the ground would be fatal. She had to get busy, tying off to the tree and unhooking her parachute so she could rappel down the tree on her own terms, rather than gravity's.

Hands shaking, she dug out the rope in her jumpsuit leg pocket. The movement made her swing and her foot hit the trunk of the fat pine she was snarled in. Fresh waves of agony slithered up her leg from her ankle. Amy's heart sank.

For a smoke jumper, an injury to the feet or legs could be career-ending.

"Robinson?" Bear called.

She fought to calm the anxiety and disappointment skittering through her before she answered. "Over here."

"You all right?"

"I'm alive. Hung up, but not French fried thanks to a last-minute reprieve." She began her letdown procedure, one she'd practiced until she could do it in her sleep.

"That was some fancy maneuvering you did to get away from the burn zone. Congratulations."

"Thanks, I—" Another fiery pang ripped up from her ankle. She muffled a hiss of pain as Bear trotted up to her.

"Amy, are you hurt?"

"No. Just winded," she lied. No sense making a big deal of her injury until she knew for sure whether she could stand to walk on it or not. But the instant she reached the ground and tried to stand, gut-churning pain screamed in her ankle. The truth was evident.

Her smoke-jumping season was over.

Chapter 1

David was out of prison.

Amy's gut swooped as if she were in a free fall, and she clutched the edge of her mother's kitchen counter for support. For a moment, she considered hobbling back outside to flag down the cab she'd taken from the airport before it left and heading back to Idaho. Instead, telling herself David couldn't hurt her anymore, now that she was an adult, she growled at her stepfather. "What the hell are you doing here?"

"Is that any way to greet your family?" He furrowed his brow as if wounded by her animosity and spread his arms, inviting her to hug him.

When hell froze.

"How did you get out? *When* did you get out?" As her shock wore off, fury and hatred filled her veins and spiked her blood pressure. She started shaking—from rage, not fear, she told herself. Dear God, she refused to let this man cause her another minute of fear.

David lowered his arms and casually stuck his hands in the pockets of the baggy khakis he wore. His angular face was more sharply cut now, a fact emphasized by the buzz cut of his mud-colored hair and the sunken look of his dark eyes. He may have been moderately hand-some years ago, but time and prison had done him no favors. Getting away from her mother's Southern cooking, dominated by frying and starches, had done that for her, too. That and her squad's intensive fitness regimen.

"I was paroled last week. Got out early for good behavior," he said, smiling.

Amy scoffed and mentally cursed the parole board that had allowed this travesty to happen. She'd sent her annual letter to the prison, arguing for her stepfather to be kept behind bars, but this year, clearly, it hadn't been enough to keep him locked away.

"And Mom let you move back in?" she asked, appalled.

"Shoot, honey. Your mama spoke on my behalf to the parole board. She helped get me released." His term of endearment and crooked grin crawled over her like spiders, and she shuddered.

Amy shook her head, refusing to believe her mother could betray her like that. "You're lying."

He shrugged. "Ask her yourself."

"I will." She narrowed a suspicious glare on him. "Where is she?"

"Work. She should be home any minute, though. She's bringing in Gunther's for dinner. I sure missed Gunther's catfish and hush puppies while I was gone."

Gone. As if he'd been on vacation instead of serving time in the state penitentiary.

His gaze dropped to the walking cast on her foot. "I guess I don't have to ask why you're here. What happened?"

"Broken ankle. I'm out for the rest of jump season."

Again his brow dented as he frowned. "That's a shame." He had the audacity to sound genuinely sympathetic. Like any *good* stepfather would. "Well, despite the reason, it's nice to see you." His smile returned, and her stomach roiled with acid. "I know your mama will be glad to have you home for a while. How long are you staying?"

Her jaw tightened, and she fisted her free hand at her side. "I'm not. Not with you here."

David's shoulders dropped, and he looked crestfallen. "Amy, honey. Can't we bury the hatchet? If I can forgive you for filing trumped-up charges against me, lying about me in court and sending me to prison for ten years, then surely you can—"

Amy nearly choked on her disbelief. "Trumped-up charges? You're both delusional and perverted if you believe that!"

Pressing his lips in a thin line, he gave her a look of dismay. "Do you have any idea how much your actions hurt your mother? What you did to me caused her—"

"What *I* did to *you*?" she shouted over him.

"—more pain that you can imagine. You should be ashamed of yourself for—"

"Me ashamed? You're the one who should be ashamed! You're responsible for what happened to—"

"Hey!" The slam of the door and her mother's voice cut into their argument. "What's going on?" Dropping her purse on the kitchen counter, Bernice Holland, dressed in her nursing scrubs, glanced darkly from her second husband to Amy. Her eyes widened as she recognized her daughter. "Amy! Oh, my goodness, what a surprise!" A smile brightened her mother's face as she stepped close to hug Amy.

"Hi, Mom."

Backing out of the embrace and holding Amy at arm's length, Bernice gave her daughter a comprehensive up-and-down look. "Something's wrong. You never come home during jump season. Why—" Her face fell when she spotted the walking cast. "You're hurt!"

"It's just a broken ankle, Mom. I'll mend." She aimed a thumb at her stepfather. "Why didn't you tell me he was out on parole?"

Guilt flashed in her mother's eyes, and Bernice took a step back before squaring her shoulders. "I was going to the next time we talked. I figured you were busy, out on fire calls and…I didn't want to bother you with—"

Amy scoffed, interrupting her mother. "I guess the bigger question is why is he *here*, in your house?"

Bernice sent an agitated glance to her husband before returning her attention to Amy. "Because it's his home, too. He's my husband, and he belongs here as much as you do."

"After what he did to me?" she volleyed, her voice taut. "How can you let him back under this roof? How can you forgive what he did?"

"David says you misinterpreted what happened. He's just an affectionate man who was trying to express his love for you."

Amy gaped at her mother, shaking from the inside out. "I didn't misinterpret anything, Mom! He *sexually abused* me!"

David grunted and shook his head. Her mother pressed a hand to her throat, and her eyes filled with tears. "Honey, calm down. Let's sit and—"

"No." When her mother reached for her arm, Amy snatched it back. Stiffening, she glared at her mother. "Did you hear me, Mom? Don't sweep this under the rug again."

Bernice huffed and pursed her lips. "I'm not! It's just that term is rather harsh. David's a loving man. He's not abusive."

Amy growled her frustration. How could her mother be so attentive and caring with her patients at the hospital, and so stubbornly in denial about her own daughter's pain? "What term do you prefer? Molestation? Rape?"

"What! That's a horrid thing to accuse me of!" David pointed a finger at her. "I *never* raped you."

"Maybe not in the classic sense of the word," she returned bitterly, "but that's just semantics."

Her mother's jaw tightened, and she wagged a finger in her direction. "Amy, I love you. You know I do. But if you're going to stay here, you need to apologize to David for—"

"I'd rather eat glass!" Hobbling on her walking cast, she stormed back toward the kitchen door.

"Amy, wait! Where are you going?" her mother cried.

"Anywhere but here. It was a mistake coming back, thinking that anything had changed."

She ripped the door open, making the Venetian blinds on the window clatter. "Call me when you're ready to listen to the truth, and you've gotten that scum out of your life."

"Amy!"

She slammed the door, and with hurt and anger burning in her chest, Amy limped to her father's old Mustang in the detached garage. After pulling off the protective car cover, she climbed behind the steering wheel, pulled her key ring from her purse and tried to crank the engine of her father's beloved car. The back bumper still bore a Houston Colt .45s sticker from when her father had first owned the classic model Ford. The Mustang was one of the few things she had left that had belonged to her father, and she treasured it more for its sentimental value than for its historic worth.

She had to try three times to get the engine to start,

allowing enough time for her mother to follow her out to the yard and send her a disappointed look.

"Amy, come back inside and let's talk!" Bernice called over the rumble of the Mustang's motor.

"Sorry, Mom. You made your choice, and you picked him over me," she called back through the open driver's side window, evidence that someone had driven the car while she was gone. "I won't spend even one night under the same roof with him." Amy gave the Mustang gas and peeled out of the driveway, onto the rural road and headed back toward Lagniappe. She could stay at a hotel tonight and either drive back to Idaho in the Mustang or catch a flight out in the morning.

Amy gritted her teeth and choked back the tears that swelled in her throat. She was through with shedding tears over her mother's lack of support, her stepfather's destruction of her innocence and the loss of the home she'd treasured as a little girl. After David's trial, she'd fled Louisiana for the farthest corner of the country, trying to outrun the ugliness of what her stepfather had done to her and her mother's blind denial of the truth. In the Pacific Northwest, she'd discovered an exciting and dangerous career opportunity as a smoke jumper and set her sights on making the elite wildfire-fighting team, a goal she'd reached after two years of hard work and training. She hadn't minded the strenuous workouts and challenging paces the smoke-jumper program had put her through. She'd found the sweat and toil cathartic, freeing. Cheaper than therapy for her broken heart and shattered innocence.

As she sped down the country highway, Amy inhaled deeply the late-spring air, redolent with honeysuckle and pine. She let the fresh scents of the outdoors clear her mind and soothe her ragged nerves. If her mother had told her about David's release, she could have prepared herself, could have been emotionally braced for seeing him again. Or could have stayed in Boise to recuperate and avoided her tormenter altogether.

But staying in Idaho, enduring friends' commiserative platitudes, would have driven her crazy, would have meant constant reminders on the evening news of all she was missing during jump season. As much as she loved her job and the rugged mountain terrain where she fought wildfires, she missed quiet summer evenings by the bayous of her home. She'd looked forward to spending her summer back in the state where she grew up, eating jambalaya and catfish and spending sweltering afternoons at the ballpark practicing her softball swing.

But David had spoiled her plans, just as he'd ruined her high-school years. While she'd known he'd get out of prison eventually, she hadn't been prepared to see him walk free so soon.

Amy had only made it a few miles, her mind distracted by replays of the fight at her mother's house, the shock of finding her stepmonster out of prison, before she noticed the steam billowing out from under the hood of the Mustang.

"Oh, no," she groaned, pulling to the shoulder. Heart sinking, she checked the display on the dash and frowned when she saw the needle of the temperature gauge sitting squarely over the hot-engine indicator. She didn't have to check under the hood to know what had happened. She'd known the radiator was on its last legs. She'd babied it the last time she was home, hoping to delay what was bound to be a pricy repair. Finding replacement parts for her classic Mustang wasn't always easy and was never cheap.

After cutting the motor, she climbed out of the car

and limped up to the hood. Using the edge of her shirt to protect her hand from the heat, she popped the hood and winced as a cloud of steam wafted up to greet her. Leaving the hood open so the radiator could start cooling down, she returned to the front seat to get her phone from her purse. The towing bill into town alone would set her back close to a hundred dollars, she'd bet.

Thumbing the screen of her cell phone, she got her second unpleasant hit in as many minutes. Her battery had died. On the airplane, she'd played word games and read books on her phone all the way from Idaho, including the layovers in Salt Lake City and Dallas. She'd planned to charge it at her mom's house, but...

Tossing the phone back in her purse with a grunt, she accepted the fact that she was stuck. Her best bet was to wait for someone to drive past and hitch a ride to Lagniappe. But patience had never been one of her virtues. Amy preferred action to waiting, so she locked the door of her Mustang and set out down the shoulder of the road toward town.

The doctor in Idaho had advised her to keep her ankle propped up until the swelling receded, but she couldn't stand sitting idle. Not her style. Besides, the confines of the airplane hadn't allow her the luxury of propping her foot higher than a couple of inches off the floor. She gritted her teeth and considered going back to her mother's house. But just the thought of being under the same roof with David soured her stomach.

Hoisting her purse strap high on her shoulder, she hobbled down the side of the highway. She crossed her fingers that someone would come along soon and give her a lift to a repair shop. Her ankle ached as she limped along, but she ignored the pain. She was a smoke jumper, by God. A little pain, a long hike, less than ideal circumstances were all in a day's work for her.

Chapter 2

Grant Mansfield tapped his thumb on the steering wheel, out of time with the music on his truck's radio, as he navigated the country road near his grandparents' old house. *His* house now. The house where he and his high-school sweetheart had moved the day of their wedding. The house where they'd brought two baby girls home from the hospital. The house where he now rattled around, feeling lost and alone, raising two daughters by himself after losing the woman he loved a year earlier to a senseless crime.

He'd had an average day at the family construction office where he managed the accounts and payroll. Nothing particularly trying or exciting. Just…gray, he thought. Like most days since Tracy's death, his life passed in a numbing blur of gray. His girls were bright spots in the plodding parade of days, but he got precious little time with them.

That was about to change, if he didn't find someone to replace his nanny before she left for her new position. Nancy had come to work for him shortly after Tracy's death, but had recently been offered a cushy job more within her area of expertise as a bodyguard.

Yes, he'd hired a trained marksman and bodyguard for his children after Tracy's murder. Was he paranoid and overprotective? Maybe. But the girls had loved Nancy and vice versa, and she'd been willing to put up with his moodiness and hyperconcern for his kids. However, Nancy had turned in her two-week notice three weeks ago, and he couldn't keep asking her to extend her time "just a few more days" indefinitely.

Grant buzzed his lips in frustration. Nannies he trusted to watch his daughters were a rare breed. Though he could ask his parents to watch the kids for a few days, he hated to depend on them long-term. They'd already gone over and above to help out since Tracy died. He had to come up with a plan. Soon. More than once, he'd considered taking an extended leave from Mansfield Construction and escaping with his daughters to the beach, or the mountains, or…anywhere that didn't have reminders of Tracy every time he turned around.

But burying himself in work helped fill the hours and kept the bills paid. He told himself the family business needed him, couldn't survive for a long period without him. Whenever his father encouraged him to take some well-earned time off, Grant brushed him off. He was fine. No need.

Nancy's departure changed things. He might be forced to take time away from work to take care of his girls while he found a new babysitter. If Grant were honest with himself, he was afraid to take a vacation. He dreaded the empty hours with nothing to do but miss his wife. Sure, he could head out to his shed and tinker with the Chevy engine he was rebuilding, but he had no more projects lined up after he finished with the Malibu. He was mulling the idea of starting over again on the Malibu's manifold this weekend to prolong the rebuild, when a dark blue Mustang on the shoulder of the highway caught his eye.

The hood was propped open, and steam wafted up from the engine. He saw no sign of the owner, a repairman, a tow crew. He frowned as he passed the classic convertible and shifted on the seat, a stir of energy spinning through him. What would he give for the chance to get his hands on a car like that? He glanced in the rearview mirror, watching the drool-worthy vehicle disappear behind a copse of trees as he headed around a curve in the road. Nineteen sixty-four, he decided. Maybe sixty-five, but...

He returned his eyes to the road, and his heart slammed into high gear. A woman walked on the side of the road, just in front of him. He jerked the steering wheel hard to the left, swerving just in time to avoid clipping her. *Geez, pay attention to the road, man!*

Heart thumping, Grant pulled to the shoulder of the highway and released a heavy sigh. He raised his gaze to the rearview mirror again, this time looking for the woman. The first thing he noticed was the giant boot cast on her left foot, evidence she had some sort of injury. The second thing he saw was her scowl.

Guilt pricked him as he shifted into Park and climbed from the truck. "Are you all right, ma'am?"

As she hobbled closer, raking caramel-colored hair back from her flushed face, he let his gaze take in her cutoff jean shorts and long, shapely legs. Her sweat-dampened tank top clung to her generous curves. The late-afternoon sun lit her face with a golden glow that highlighted a smattering of freckles on her cheeks and pert nose. Despite her frown, she was an attractive woman, and Grant's libido took notice.

"Do I look all right to you?" she grumbled.

Chastened, he cocked his head and winced. "Sorry

about the near miss. I was distracted by your Mustang. I'm assuming the Mustang around the bend is yours?"

"It is. Apology accepted." She waved him off with a flick of her hand. "You're not the reason I'm peeved." She squinted at him, shielding her eyes from the sun that sank near the tops of the trees. "Hey, I know you. You're—" she snapped her fingers as if trying to recall his name "—Hunter Mansfield's older brother. Greg? No..."

"Grant."

"Right. Grant."

"And you are...?" he prompted when she didn't volunteer the information.

"Oh!" She chuckled and gave her head a little shake. "Amy. Amy Robinson. Sorry. I'm a little distracted by my Mustang, too. And other things. I played football with Hunter."

"Radiator?"

She looked confused for a moment, then her face brightened. "Oh...yeah. I think it's going to have to be replaced. It must be damaged, 'cause it won't hold fluid anymore."

He nodded, digesting that information. "Punter, right?"

Her eyebrows puckered. "Uh...yes. First female punter in the school's history."

He lifted his eyebrows and nodded, impressed. Her slender figure and toned muscle hinted that she was still athletic. Shoving his hands in his back pockets, he cast a glance back down the road. "I'd love to take a look at it, see if I can fix it up."

She hesitated a beat. "You're a mechanic?"

"Shade-tree version. It's a hobby." He nodded toward her cast. "What happened to your foot?"

"Broken ankle." Amy laughed. "Are conversations with you always this zigzag?"

Grant flashed a grin. "Considering some I have with my seven-year-old daughter, I'd say yes. Shall we start over?"

"I have a better idea. Why don't you give me a lift into town? I'm gonna have to get a hotel room until my car is repaired, and my cell-phone battery died."

He grunted and nodded. "How'd it happen?"

"Um…playing Words with Friends on the flight from Dallas earlier today." Her impish grin told him she knew he'd been asking about her ankle and was yanking his chain.

He tugged up the corner of his mouth. "Wow. Word games aren't what they used to be. Was this tackle Words with Friends?"

"No." She glanced down at her walking cast and her scowl was back. "Rough landing during a parachute jump."

He barked a startled laugh and gave her a teasing grin. "Sheesh. I knew the airlines were cutting back services to save money, but now they're not even landing before disembarking passengers?"

She returned a coy smile. "How about that lift, wise guy?"

"How about dinner at my place?" As soon as the words left his mouth and he saw her blink in surprise, he realized how his invitation sounded. He jerked his hands from his pockets and waved them in denial. "That came out wrong. I'm not asking for a date." When she made a wry face, he scrambled for words again. "Not that you're not pretty. You are."

"Thanks—I think."

"Ah, skunk," he mumbled, scrubbing a hand over his face. "I mean…you're very pretty. Hot, even, but—"

She raised a hand. "Down, boy. Don't hurt yourself backing up. I get it. You have a daughter. You're married. I'm not looking for a date. Just a ride to Lagniappe."

"Widowed, actually." Grant grimaced internally. Why had he felt compelled to share that with her? While it was true, telling her made it sound as if he was advertising his availability. Which he wasn't. Advertising… or available. In his heart, he was still and always would be married to Tracy.

Amy gave him the pitying frown of sympathy he'd come to detest in recent months. "Gosh, I'm so sorry. I hadn't heard."

He returned an awkward nod of acknowledgment. "Thanks."

"Was her death recent?"

He shrugged. "Seems that way. But it's been a year."

"That counts as recent. I'm…so sorry."

And that's where the exchange always stalled, because people were usually too polite to ask how Tracy died, even though morbid curiosity was usually plain in their eyes. Before the lull in conversation became even more awkward, Grant rubbed his hands on his jeans and hitched his head down the road toward the Mustang. "Shall we go take a look at your car?"

"Why not?"

He hurried ahead of her to the passenger-side door of his truck and opened it for her. "So you broke your ankle skydiving?"

She limped to the truck and nodded. "Smoke jumping to be precise."

Grant widened his eyes and whistled. "That's dangerous work. How'd you get hooked up with a job like that?"

"Hard work and determination." She slid onto the front seat and dropped her purse on the floorboard. Giving him a squinty-eyed look, she added, "Why? Don't you think a woman can do the same tough jobs a man can?"

He waved a hand of surrender. "I didn't say that. It's just not the kind of work you typically hear about someone having in these parts."

She seemed appeased by his response, so he closed her door and jogged back around to the driver's side. As he settled back in and executed a U-turn on the two-lane highway, she cleared her throat. "Sorry if I came off as defensive. I've gotten a lot of flak from people over my choices through the years, starting with high school and being the football team's kicker. Which wasn't my idea, by the way. Coach Greely saw me at soccer practice and said the team's regular kicker had gotten injured. They needed a replacement pronto, and did I want to try out? I said I would, and then I outkicked the two other guys who tried out for the position."

Grant nodded, impressed. He remembered Coach Greely and the man's high standards. "And smoke jumping?"

"When I graduated high school, I couldn't get far enough from Lagniappe fast enough. I moved out west, not knowing anyone, got a job ringing up groceries to pay the rent. That first summer, some guys at the store were talking about trying out for smoke jumping, and I looked into it. It sounded like my kind of challenge. I was one of three women who tried out that first year. I didn't make it the first time, but I kept trying until I did."

"Hard work and determination," he said, echoing her earlier answer.

"That's right. I made the squad on my third try."

He gave the classic convertible a hard look as he approached, studying the body shape and markings. Once he'd pulled in front of her Mustang and parked on the gravel shoulder, he asked, "Nineteen sixty-five?"

She blinked and sent him a startled grin. "Close. Nineteen sixty-four and a half. You do know your cars. Or was that a lucky guess?"

"I've been a car fanatic since I was old enough to push Hot Wheels around my parents' floor. Started tinkering with engines with my dad by the time I was eight, and had my own shop in our garage by the time I was fifteen."

She chuckled as she popped open the truck door. "Wow. So it's been a lifelong passion? Why not make it a career, then?"

He shrugged. "My family owns a construction company, and I guess I always knew I'd follow my dad into the biz. I studied accounting and business in college and started with the company right after graduating."

She tipped her head in acknowledgment. "As long as you're happy…"

Grant forced a grin. He was content with his job, but happy? He hadn't been truly happy since Tracy died. Some days he wondered if he'd ever feel happy again. Happiness seemed like a betrayal of his wife. How could he be happy when Tracy was dead?

"From what I hear, the '64½ is almost the same as a '65." Amy's comment pulled him from his morose deliberations.

"Yeah, but there are differences. Under the hood primarily." He rubbed his hands together and faked another grin. "Mind if I poke around your engine?"

"Gosh, Grant," she said with a teasingly flustered expression. "We just met. I'm not that kind of girl."

The heat of embarrassment—and lust, if he was honest—prickled his skin, and he rubbed his chin as he floundered for a reply.

She laughed and gave his shoulder a playful shove. "Poke away. The ole girl's not going anywhere without a tow truck or some expert hands-on attention."

Amy slid out of the truck, and the sly smile she slanted at him said she'd intended the sexual overtones of her comment.

Was she flirting with him? He goggled at the notion. Having been a one-woman man since high school, he was inexperienced in dating matters and reading women's cues. That was Hunter's field of expertise. But he couldn't deny the idea of flirting with Amy intrigued him. She was, as he'd so lamely put it earlier, hot. Maybe not beautiful in the traditional sense, but she had a great body and an interesting face and—

He huffed a sigh as a ripple of guilt tripped through him. Tracy had only been gone for a year. What was he doing looking at other women? Flirting with another woman? Especially one with a dangerous job like smoke jumping?

He shuddered, imagining how stressful it would be to date someone, care about someone who risked their life every day that they reported to work. Her broken ankle was a testament to the risk involved in jumping out of a small plane into a wildfire, only to take on raging forest fires with not much more than a chain saw, shovel and backbreaking effort.

He gave the interior of the dark blue Mustang a curious scrutiny as he passed the driver's door and whistled. "You've kept it in excellent condition. Are those the original seat covers?"

"Yep. Haven't changed a thing, right down to her Guardsman Blue paint job. She was my daddy's baby before I came along, and when he died, I inherited her. I've tried to keep her in top form, as best I could. Dad would have expected no less."

"She?" He sent her a knowing look. "Let me guess. You named your car?"

"Hey!" She propped her hands on her hips as if taking umbrage. "Plenty of people name their cars!"

"True." He sat on the ground in front of the 'Stang and flicked a hand to the undercarriage. "Just thought I should at least know her name before I got personal with her engine."

"How gentlemanly of you. Dad named her Stella. Stella, this is Grant. He's going to help you feel better. Say '*ahh.*'"

Chuckling, Grant lay on his back and wiggled his way under the front end of the Mustang. The pavement was hot against his back, and the steam from Stella's overheated radiator billowed around him. He poked around for a moment, then called, "Hey, would you get the flashlight that's in my glove compartment for me?"

"Roger that."

He heard his truck door squeak open then close a moment later, and Amy's face appeared under her car. "Here."

He took the flashlight she held out to him, and she moved from her knees to her back, scooting under the car next to him. "What's the diagnosis, doc?"

Flicking on the flashlight, he aimed the beam at her radiator, searching the undulating ridges for evidence of damage. He paused when he spotted a fine crack and slow drip of yellow liquid. "There's your problem. You were right about the leak."

Sighing with a drama that reminded him of Peyton's antics, she asked, "Can it be repaired or are we talking replacement?"

He turned his head to face her, and his pulse did a two-step, seeing her as up close and personal as she was. Lying beside her in the confines of the undercarriage of her car felt…intimate. He had to clear his throat before speaking. "I don't recommend trying to patch it. I think your dad would want it replaced."

She bit her bottom lip as she wrinkled her nose in frustration. "I was afraid of that. A replacement is going to cost a bundle, isn't it?"

"Well…" He scratched his cheek. "If you—"

"No, don't answer that. Stupid question. Of course, it will cost a bundle. A better question is, can a replacement radiator even be found for a '64½ these days?"

"For a price, I'd think so."

"For a price," she repeated, a groan in her tone.

"But…"

"Uh-oh. What?" She scrunched up her face, clearly bracing for more bad news.

"Not uh-oh. I've made a number of contacts through the years, and I think I can get you a deal. And I won't charge you for labor if you're willing to let me have a go at doing the repair work."

She blinked at him as if she hadn't heard him correctly. "You'd do the repair for free?"

Grant nodded. "Yeah."

Her expression turned suspicious. "Why?"

He gave a casual shrug, even though being this close to a dream project like a classic Mustang—and being this close to *Amy*—had his heart racing and his mind spinning. "Because I love old cars. Because I'm looking for a new project." *Because the work keeps me sane, keeps me from dwelling on Tracy's murder.* He swallowed hard, trying to push down the emotion that rose in his throat.

He didn't want Amy to see his neediness or the desperation in his face.

She chewed her bottom lip some more and stared at the steaming radiator. "Well, that's a generous offer, but I, um…"

She blew out a sigh and fell silent as she considered.

"Amy?" When she angled her head toward him again, her eyes—were they gold or green?—latched on to his. His pulse stumbled again. "It's hot under here. What do you say we continue this negotiation up top?"

She slanted him a wry grin. "Good idea."

Once she'd wiggled out from under the car, he helped her to her feet. As she regained her balance, she wobbled a bit, and Grant caught her elbow. In return, she grabbed his arm to steady herself, her fingers squeezing his biceps.

"Wow." She raised an eyebrow as she glanced up at him then squeezed again, feeling his muscle. "Impressive. How much do you bench?"

He hated to admit how good it felt to have her hands on him. What would Tracy think? "About forty-six pounds. Forty-seven with shoes."

She sputtered a laugh. "Excuse me?"

"I don't usually have time for the gym, but a lot of times, I have to carry my older daughter. I've been known to use her as a barbell when we roughhouse. Occasionally I'll do curls with the baby carrier on the way into the house from the truck."

"Well…" She gave his arm a congenial pat as she moved back. "You're doing something right."

Grant's chest warmed with masculine pleasure over her compliment. Not since high school, when he'd started dating Tracy, had he felt this sophomoric pride and delight over a woman's attention.

"So…" He dragged out the word and took a backward step, as if he could distance himself from the unintended sensations that made him feel unfaithful to his late wife. "Do we have a deal? Will you let me have a go at Stella?"

"Are you good?" She tipped her head and gave him a sultry smile. More sexual overtones. Or at least that's where his sex-starved mind went.

His breath hitched, and he had to swallow before he could answer. "Absolutely. I have years of experience." A gremlin goaded him to raise his palms, wiggle his fingers and add, "I've been told I have magic hands." And, yes, he acknowledged guiltily, he sent her a devilish grin with the quip laced with his own double entendres.

She lifted one eyebrow in intrigue. "You don't say? Well, I guess I'll have to judge for myself."

He hitched his head toward his truck and walked to the passenger's side to open the door for her. "Let's go get some coolant for Stella. She should hold it long enough for you to drive her to my house and save yourself the tow bill."

"Works for me, but…" She paused before climbing on the seat. "You still haven't told me the catch in your deal. What's my end of this bargain, and why do I feel like I'm making a deal with the devil?"

Chapter 3

Grant snapped his chin up. "The devil? Wow. And here I thought I was being an angel offering to fix Stella for the cost of the parts. No strings, no conditions."

"No strings?" She settled in his truck, her tone skeptical.

"I was even going to throw in dinner at my house tonight. But that has more to do with the fact that I'm running late relieving my babysitter." He checked his watch confirming just how late he was. "I won't have time to take you into town until I feed my *ghouls* their dinner. They can be real demons on an empty stomach."

She gave him a wry grin. "We can't loose hungry ghouls on the world."

Pulling out on the road, he whipped a U-turn and headed back toward his house. "After we get Stella a cool drink, give me half an hour to slap hot dogs and chips on the table, and then I'll drive you into town."

"Wow. Free labor, a ride into town and hot dogs with your evil minions?" Her smile brightened, making her green eyes twinkle. "I accept your gracious offer with gratitude. Do I have to sign in blood?"

"Naw. Ketchup will do." He chuckled, realizing how foreign the laughter sounded coming from him…and how good it felt. Just how dour had he been with his daughters lately? That's not how he wanted them to remember him.

"Tell you what," Amy said, breaking into his moody thoughts. "If you have the right ingredients in your pantry, I'll make your *ghouls* my famous spaghetti and meat sauce."

He shook his head. "I can't ask you to cook for us."

"Who's cooking?" she said with a musical laugh that spiraled straight to his core. "I plan on opening a jar of ready-made sauce and adding beef. That's about as near to cooking as I get. But if that sounds good to you, I'm game."

He had to admit, Amy lifted his spirits. He wanted to savor her company awhile before driving her to town. When he stopped at a crossroad, he angled his body to face her. "If you're brave enough to eat spaghetti with my minions, who am I to question?" He offered his hand. "You have a deal."

Amy shook Grant's hand, secretly pleased that she would have a little extra time with him before heading off to sit alone in her motel room. A tingly warmth spread up her arm from his firm grip and into the pit of her stomach. As she met his dark gaze, her breath snagged in her lungs. The rough scrape of the calluses on his palms proved he was no stranger to hard work.

The idea that Grant didn't mind getting his hands dirty appealed to her. Considering how filthy she got fighting wildfires, how backbreaking the work could be, a desk jockey who didn't know the meaning of sweat had little appeal to her. Though why the relative appeal of any man should matter at this point in her life, she didn't know. She wasn't looking for a relationship.

Then why are you still holding his hand? Her heart

bumped when she realized she was still squeezing Grant's fingers. And staring into his brown bedroom eyes. *Hellfire!*

Amy quickly yanked her hand back. Too quickly. Grant almost certainly noticed her odd behavior and read it incorrectly. Or read it correctly, which was worse. Because she didn't want him knowing she'd been gawking, imagining what it might be like to kiss his generous mouth and, well, get sweaty with him.

She cleared her throat and turned toward the side window. "So where do you live?"

"Just a little piece down the road here." Was it her imagination or did his voice sound a bit thicker now, too? "I inherited my grandparents' farmhouse, although the farm animals are long since gone. I use the barn as my garage for tinkering on cars."

Within minutes, he was pulling in the gravel driveway of a two-story clapboard house with a wraparound porch. A little girl with a blond ponytail was in the front yard, and she smiled when she saw Grant's truck pull up.

He cut the engine and sent a side look to Amy as he climbed out. "You can wait here if you want. I'll be back in a flash with the coolant."

"Daddy!" The blonde ran to Grant and raised her arms as she neared, allowing her father to lift her over his head with a playful growl.

His comment about benching "forty-seven pounds with shoes" replayed in Amy's head. She glanced at Grant's arms where his biceps were flexed, and a fresh tickle of appreciation shimmied through her.

"Hey, squirt." Grant lowered his daughter into a firm hug and buzzed her cheek with a raspberry kiss. "How was school?"

"Boring," the girl said, hugging his neck.

"Boring?" he scoffed, "How can school be boring?"

Amy watched the affectionate greeting and felt a tug in her chest.

"Have you finished your homework?" Grant asked.

"Most of it."

"Better finish before dinner. We have company coming for…" Their voices faded as he carried her with him toward the faded red barn Amy could barely see, hidden behind the house.

She smiled watching the father and daughter cross the grassy lawn. She'd had a similar relationship with her dad as a girl, full of hugs and laughter. Was that why she'd trusted David at first? Had she been hoping to fill the void of fatherly affection after her dad's passing?

She closed her eyes, trying to conjure a specific memory of her father, but instead, her argument with David—and her mother's continued refusal to believe her or protect her from David—soured the good mood Grant had given her. She thought of Stella, radiator steaming as she sat on the side of the rural highway, and her mood dipped further.

Her temples gave a throb, and she rubbed her eyes with the heels of her hands. If trouble came in threes, shouldn't she be done now? A broken ankle, David's parole and Stella's busted radiator seemed a trifecta of bad luck.

Hearing the crunch of gravel, she dropped her hands to her lap and blinked. Her gaze darted to Grant as he stalked down the driveway to the driver's side of his truck. His long-legged, confident stride had a certain swagger she was familiar with. She called it the "alpha-male walk." Nearly every guy on her jump team had that same self-assured set to their shoulders and sure purpose in their step. But none of the guys on her jump team made the alpha-male walk look so…*sexy.*

Her breath rushed from her lungs. *Geez Louise!* What was with her? Grant might be good-looking, but she was not in the market for a boyfriend. Especially one that lived two thousand miles from her life, her job in Idaho.

Grant handed her the jug of coolant to hold as he slid behind the steering wheel again.

"Your daughter is cute," she said, as much to remind herself that Grant was a family man, a single father. Another complication that screamed, *Don't go there, girl!*

Not that she didn't like kids. They were okay. Just not for her. She wasn't the motherly sort. She'd rather wield a chain saw than a stroller any day of the week.

Grant shifted into Reverse and curled up a corner of his mouth. "Thanks. I think so, too. Of course." He backed onto the road and headed back toward Stella. "She got her looks from her mother. Thank God."

She almost said something about him being dangerously good-looking himself, but bit her tongue. Hadn't she flirted enough? *Time to dial it down, Robinson.*

Grant pulled up behind Stella and left his engine idling while he refilled her radiator with coolant. When he gave her the thumbs-up, Amy started the Mustang's engine and sent up a quick prayer that she'd make it to Grant's house before the fluid leaked out again.

He followed her as she drove back to his house, and once Stella was safely tucked in Grant's barn, he led her into his house though the back door to his kitchen. A dark-haired woman sat at an oak table with the blonde girl she'd seen earlier and a rosy-cheeked baby in a high chair. The baby had wispy, dark curls, wide brown eyes—and a tray scattered with dry cereal, raisins and banana chunks that she carefully plucked up one at a time with her chubby-fingered grasp.

Grant introduced her to Nancy, the babysitter, as Nancy made a hasty exit, already late for an appointment.

"Skunk! I forgot," Grant said with a grimace. "Sorry. Amy's car broke down. When I stopped to help her, I lost track of the time."

Nancy waved him off. "You're forgiven. But you remember I'm not coming tomorrow, right? I have orientation for the new job."

Pinching the bridge of his nose, Grant sighed. "I remember now."

Nancy ruffled the little girl's hair as she hustled out the back. "See you, kiddo."

Grant saw the babysitter out the door, then turned to Amy to continue the introductions. "Anyway…these are my demons…" He gave Amy a teasing grin. "I mean, *daughters.* Peyton is seven, and Kaylee is fourteen months."

Amy did the math. If Grant had been a widower for a year, Kaylee had only been a couple of months old when his wife died. *Sheesh.*

Grant's older daughter looked up from her wide-ruled notepad and blinked blue eyes. "Your car broke?"

Amy nodded. "The radiator did. It's leaking coolant."

The little girl wrinkled her nose, and Amy kicked herself. Like a kid's gonna know what *that* means. Heck, she had girlfriends who probably didn't know what that meant.

She was *so* out of her league around kids.

"And your car's motor got too hot?" the girl asked, and Amy blinked, stunned.

"Uh…yeah."

Nodding, the girl bent over her work again, satisfied with the answer.

Slack-jawed, Amy looked to Grant, who only grinned like a Cheshire cat. "She knows cars?"

"She helps me sometimes when I tinker and asks questions. She has an incredible memory and a voracious curiosity about most anything. Except her class work."

"No wonder she's bored at school." When he dented his brow in query, she added, "I heard her tell you that earlier, when we picked up the coolant."

"Oh, right." Grant nudged his daughter's shoulder. "Peyton, this is Amy. She's a friend of Uncle Hunter's from high school. Can you say hi?"

Peyton raised her head again. "Hi."

Amy smiled. Kids were so literal. "I thought I'd stay and cook y'all some spaghetti. How does that sound?"

Peyton's eyebrows lifted, and her eyes brightened. "I like spaghetti!"

Grant angled the notepad so he could read the block letters. "How much more homework do you have?"

"I'm done." She tried to scoot away from the table, but Grant stopped her with a hand on the back of the chair.

"Peyton?" His tone was pure doubting parent. "Are you really done?"

The girl gave an exaggerated sigh and shoulder drop. "Yes! I wrote my spelling words three times each."

He angled the pad to check her work. "Okay. Looks good. Put your notebook in your backpack, then you can play until dinner."

Peyton scampered off, but instead of disappearing to the yard to play, she returned to the kitchen. The little girl eyed Amy as Grant searched the freezer and pantry for the spaghetti and meat-sauce ingredients.

"You're a friend of my uncle Hunter's?" Peyton asked, while scratching a scab on her leg.

"Um…well, I was. Sort of." Amy sat down in a kitchen chair and propped up her casted ankle which had started to throb. "We were more like friendly acquaintances, teammates—"

Peyton scrunched her nose in confusion. "Huh?"

Amy chuckled at herself. A seven-year-old didn't care about her shades of gray semantics. "Um, yes. Yes, we were friends. In high school."

Amy startled when a brown tabby jumped into her lap and gave a squeaky meow. "Well, hello." She scratched the cat's head, and the feline responded with a rumbling purr.

"Huh, that's a first. Usually Cinderella hides when new people come in the house. Are you a cat person?"

"You could say that. I always had one growing up. Cinderella, huh? Cute name."

"Her brother is Sebastian." Grant squatted to pick up the raisins the baby was throwing on the floor. "He's the orange-and-white cat around here somewhere. They were my wife's cats before—" He stopped short, leaving the rest unsaid as he glanced at his daughters.

She continued stroking the cat's unusually soft fur as she, too, turned back to Peyton.

Grant's little girl dented her forehead as if ruminating on something. "Why aren't you friends with Hunter now? Did you have a fight?"

She shook her head. "No. I moved away right after high school. I live way across the country in Idaho."

The girl's face lit up, and she chirped, "Way to go, Idaho!"

From the high chair, Kaylee squealed and clapped her hands.

Amy blinked, then cracked a grin. "You're a *Toy Story* fan?"

"Yep!" Peyton looked pleased that Amy knew the source of her quip before her face sobered. "My uncle Connor and aunt Darby and cousin Savannah moved away. But Daddy says even though we can't see them anymore, we will always love them, and they love us."

Amy nodded, glancing to the pantry, where Grant was still shuffling jars and boxes in search of pasta. "That's right."

Peyton gave her a studious look, far too serious for a girl her age. "If you moved away, then how come you're here. Did ya move back?"

"Naw. I hurt my ankle—" Amy waved at her cast as if it weren't obvious "—so I had to take a vacation from work. I came back to Lagniappe, because my mom still lives here. I was going to visit her, but…" The ugly scene at her mother's house flickered in her memory, and Amy worked to keep her frustration and disappointment from her expression. No need going into more detail about that, so she let her sentence trail.

"Is your ankle broke?"

"Broken, Peyton. Not broke," Grant corrected, his head still stuck in the pantry.

"Yes, it's broken," Amy confirmed. "I have to wear this cast for six weeks, so I can't do my job. I'm a smoke jumper." She flashed an isn't-that-interesting? smile at Peyton, anticipating questions about her career. Amy wanted to use the opening to encourage the little girl to set high goals for herself and not let traditional gender roles hamper her. But the questions didn't come.

Instead, Peyton was fascinated with her cast. She stepped closer and tapped on the hard shell around her calf. "Has anybody signed it?"

"Um…no."

"Oh." Peyton considered that as she paused to scratch her leg again. Then sidling closer she added, "When Sophie Blanton broke her arm, everybody in our class wrote on it. I drew a heart with a smiley face." Grant's daughter beamed, clearly proud of her artistic choice.

"Oh, well…that sounds nice." Amy shifted awkwardly in the ladder-back chair.

Whining, Kaylee arched her back and pounded the tray of her high chair. "Down!"

"Just a minute, Kaylee," Grant muttered from the pantry.

Peyton continued to gaze longingly at Amy's cast, and it took a moment for Amy to catch on. "Do you… want to sign my cast?"

Peyton's face brightened. "Can I?"

Amy shrugged. "Why not?"

"I'll go get my pink marker! It smells like bubble gum!" Peyton started out of the kitchen but skidded to a stop near the door. With a gasp, she cried, "Daddy, I'm bleeding!"

"What!" Grant jerked his head from the closet. His eyebrows knitted in concern, as he stepped around the pantry door to look. He visibly relaxed when he saw his daughter dabbing at the seeping scab on her leg. "You were scratching your bug bites again, weren't you?"

Peyton gave him a sheepish frown. "Yeah."

"Manners?" he prompted, arching an eyebrow.

The girl rolled her eyes. "Yes, *sir*." She examined her bleeding leg more closely. "I need a bandage."

He returned to the pantry and pulled a box of elbow macaroni from the back of a shelf. "You do not need a bandage. It's barely bleeding."

Grant's reply had Amy muffling a laugh. His reply reminded her that whenever she had a scrape or cut on the job, her jump partner Bear and the other smoke jumpers liked to tell her to "rub some dirt in it and shake it off."

Judging from Peyton's expression, the request for a bandage had more to do with wanting attention for her boo-boo than medical necessity. But she resisted the urge to point that fact out to Grant.

He turned with an armload of food from his panty and lined the items up on his counter next to the frozen hamburger meat he'd taken out of the freezer. "How's this? I didn't have spaghetti, but we can use macaroni, can't we?"

"Why not?" Amy surveyed the pasta, jar of sauce, canned mushrooms and jar of Parmesan cheese from her seat at the kitchen table. "Looks like we're set. Now I'll need a deep frying pan and a pot to boil the pasta."

Grant squatted to dig a pan from his lower cabinet, and Amy gave the snug fit of his jeans across his butt an appreciative gander.

Peyton returned with her pink marker, and Amy waved at her propped leg. "Go for it." She watched, bemused, as Grant's daughter drew a lopsided heart with a smiley face and printed her name in all caps.

"There." Peyton capped the marker and flashed a grin. "Do you like it?"

"Awesome. Thank you, Peyton." She waited until Grant wasn't looking, then crooked her finger and whispered to the girl, "C'mere."

Peyton sidled closer as Amy dug in her purse for a Band-Aid. After peeling off the wrapper, Amy took the marker from the girl and drew a heart on it. Then patting her thigh, she motioned for Peyton to prop her leg on Amy's lap. Silently she showed Peyton the decorated bandage and applied it to the small red bump on the girl's leg.

Grant was right. The bug bite had already stopped bleeding. But when Peyton saw what Amy had done, a smile blossomed on the child's face, and she whispered loudly, "Now we match!"

With a wink to the girl, Amy held up a bent pinkie, and Peyton hooked her pinkie around Amy's in a sign of solidarity. "Want to help me make dinner?"

"Sure." Peyton tugged a chair close to the stove, as if she'd helped cook before and knew the routine.

"I think we've got this," Amy said, clomping from the table to the stove. "If you have something else you need to do, don't let me keep you from it."

Grant gestured to the stove. "All yours." He lifted Kaylee from her high chair and nodded his head toward the next room. "Kaylee and I will see about ordering your radiator."

He pulled a laptop from a briefcase near the door and set himself up at a table in the next room.

As Peyton washed her hands, preparing to help cook, Amy processed the scene with an odd sense of the surreal. A handsome father at the dining room table, a toddler in his lap and a young girl helping her cook dinner. It was all so...*domestic bliss*. Not that domestic bliss was a bad thing. It just wasn't *her*. Her life was about adventure, danger, hard work in the outdoors and no personal commitments to anyone. So what was she doing here, and why did having dinner with Grant's family feel so comfortable?

After putting Kaylee in her playpen, Grant made himself comfortable at the dining room table and opened his internet browser. He'd bookmarked several web pages where he frequently ordered parts for his car repair projects. He opened his favorite site now, along with one for the local newspaper, his Facebook page and a favorite blog he followed. His younger brother Hunter was on his honeymoon and had posted pictures on Facebook of Hawaii, his infant stepson in sunglasses and a floppy hat, and his new wife, Brianna, mugging with a pineapple. With a click of his wireless mouse, he "liked" all of the photos. He was happy for his brother and Brianna, but seeing their vacation pictures was a bittersweet reminder of the vacations he and Tracy would never take.

"Wait, Peyton. We don't want to add the noodles too soon, or they'll get mushy," Amy told his daughter, and he glanced through the doorway to the kitchen to check on them. For her part, Kaylee seemed content to watch the stranger in her house, gnaw her teething ring and throw blocks out onto the floor.

He closed Facebook and moved on to post a request for the Mustang radiator on the car parts site. The website owner was pretty good about checking requests, and he hoped to have an answer by morning at the latest. Next Grant turned his attention to the online newspaper. He scanned the headlines, more out of habit than real interest. The mayor had given a speech to the garden club, a tax rate hike was up for a vote in the fall, a local student won the state spelling bee, a convicted felon had been granted an appeal hearing for later that week and the zoo—

Grant's heart lurched, and he scrolled back to the previous story.

William Gale, the man his brother Connor had risked his life to help convict of numerous crimes, had won a chance to appeal his life sentence. William Gale, the patriarch of the family responsible for Tracy's murder, was going to court, trying to win his release from prison.

Bile rose in his throat, and he bit out a scathing curse. Which Kaylee immediately repeated. He winced. Great, he'd taught his daughter a bad word.

"What's wrong?" Amy asked, shooting him a concerned look from the kitchen sink, where she was draining fat from the hamburger meat.

Grant rubbed his forehead and flopped back in the chair, glowering at the screen. "Bad news in the paper. A man who definitely does not need to be out of prison is getting a new hearing. He and his expensive lawyers are trying to overturn his conviction on a technicality."

Amy's face grew somber. "I'm familiar with that problem. So much for justice." She fell silent for a moment, then lifted a dark gaze. "What's your interest in this man? Why are you so upset about this particular guy?"

Grant's hands fisted on the table, and his gut churned. "This man destroyed my family. His minions threatened my brother, forcing him into hiding with Witness Security, and—" he swallowed hard, finding the strength to voice the unspeakable truth that had shattered his world "—my wife was a casualty of his vendetta against my brother. Tracy was killed a year ago in car bombing."

Amy sucked in a sharp breath, and her eyes rounded. "Grant, that's… My God! How can they let him out? That's not right!"

His jaw tightened. "No, it's not. And they won't, if I have anything to say about it." He scanned the article again. "The hearing is later this week, and I intend to be there."

Amy noticed Grant's amiable, if low-key, mood, took a turn toward brooding after he found the report about the appeal hearing. Understandably so. She'd been in a foul mood earlier today after her run-in with David. Was the court system totally out of step with justice? She gritted her back teeth in frustration and turned to check on Peyton—just in time to catch the jar of sauce the girl struggled to open before it crashed to the floor.

For the next twenty minutes, Peyton helped brown, boil and stir their pasta and meat sauce into shape. When they sat down to eat, Grant divided a strained smile between Peyton and Amy. "Looks great, ladies. I'm impressed."

Amy returned a wry look. "Don't be too impressed. With this—" she pointed to her plate "—you've seen the extent of my cooking talents."

"I cooked the macaroni!" Peyton added.

"And you did a great job," Grant said, patting his daughter's arm. He blew on a piece of pasta and set it on Kaylee's high-chair tray. Even though the baby had eaten her dinner, she sat with them for the family meal.

"What did you find out about a radiator for Stella?" Amy asked, hoping to distract Grant from the news about his wife's killer.

"I found one in North Carolina for a reasonable price. I emailed the seller for more information, but thought I'd show you the other search results before I ordered one."

She shrugged and tucked into her dinner. "You're the mechanic. I trust your judgment."

Grant seemed pleased by her faith in him, but he angled his head and arched an eyebrow. "I'd still like you to sign off on the one we order. I don't feel right spending your money without at least showing you the options."

She nodded. "In that case, I'll take a look after we eat."

"Will you play Hearts with me after supper?" Peyton asked.

"Well…" Amy sent Grant a questioning glance. She didn't want to promise something that would interfere with his plan for Peyton's evening.

"After we eat and clean Kaylee up, we're driving Amy into town to a hotel." Grant spooned another noodle onto Kaylee's tray. She grabbed the noodle in her chubby fist and popped it greedily into her mouth.

"A hotel?" Peyton did the scrunched-up nose thing again. "Why?"

Amy grinned at Peyton, warming to her inquisitive nature. "Because I need someplace to sleep while your daddy fixes my car."

Her cell phone buzzed in her pocket, and Amy sent Grant an apologetic grimace as she pulled it out to silence it. "Sorry."

Grant waved her off. "Take the call if it's important."

She read the caller ID and groaned. "No. It's my mother. That call will keep."

Silencing the phone, she slid the device back in her pocket.

"Why aren't you sleeping at your mommy's house?" Peyton asked.

And just like that, the child's queries weren't so cute. Amy's stomach bunched, and she set her fork down. When she glanced at Grant, his expression said, *Good question. Why didn't I think of that?*

"Because…" Amy floundered for a second but decided to go with a highly filtered version of the truth. "I had a fight with my stepfather and my mother took his side."

Peyton's eyes grew. "So you ran away from home?"

Grant grunted and scowled at his daughter but didn't comment.

"Uh…" Amy's heartbeat tripped. The child was more

right than she knew. She'd run away today, just as she'd run away seven years ago. "Yeah. Sort of." She pushed her pasta around her plate, suddenly not nearly as hungry as she'd been earlier. "I, uh…was mad at them and didn't feel comfortable staying there."

"What was your fight about?"

Amy shifted on her chair. The honest answer to that question was not appropriate material for a little girl, even if Amy was willing to divulge the dark secret she carried about her past. Which she wasn't.

Grant sent his daughter another scolding look and aimed his fork at her plate. "None of your beeswax, squirt. Eat your dinner."

"Sometimes I run away when I'm mad, too. But Daddy says I have to be home by dark."

Amy forced a smile. "He's right. You wouldn't want to miss dinner or sleeping in your warm bed."

"Does your mom know where you are?" Peyton pressed.

"Well…no."

"Won't she be worried?"

Not in the way that matters, she thought glumly.

Suddenly Peyton jerked straight in her chair, her face brightening. "Hey! You can sleep at our house!"

Chapter 4

Grant's head came up. "Peyton—"

Amy covered a startled chuckle and shook her head. "Thanks, sweetie, but I can't."

"Why not?" she pressed, ignoring her father's hushing glare. "We have another room. Uncle Hunter and Aunt Brianna stayed there before."

Amy sent Grant a sympathetic glance for the awkward position his daughter's offer put him in. "Thank you, but no. I'd be an imposition."

"What's a *impolition*?"

Grant rubbed a hand down his cheek and seemed to be considering ways to muzzle his daughter.

"An imposition," Amy repeated, exaggerating the *s* to gently correct the girl, "means I'd be in the way. I'd be too much trouble to you and your dad."

"You wouldn't be an imposition," Grant said quietly, without any conviction.

Amy faced him, lifting an eyebrow. "You don't need to do the polite routine. I'll be fine at a hotel. Really."

"You wouldn't be an imposition," he repeated, more emphatically. He set his fork down and leaned back in his chair. Leveling a steady, assessing gaze on her, he cocked his head and studied her through slightly narrowed eyes. "I should have thought of it myself. Like she said, we have a guest room that's not being used, and—"

"Grant, no." Amy raised a hand to cut him off. "Thank you, but…please don't ask because she put you on the spot. I'll be fine."

"I'm asking," he said calmly, the corner of his mouth twitching in an alluring grin that caused a tickle in her belly, "because I like the idea. There's no point in you wasting your money on a hotel when I've got a perfectly good room upstairs."

His point about the money struck a nerve. She had limited paid medical leave and would miss the rest of jump season thanks to her broken ankle. Money was going to be tight for the foreseeable future.

"You'd have to share the room with Sorsha for a little while, though," he amended.

"Sorsha?"

"My sister-in-law's cat. I'm cat-sitting while she and my youngest brother are on their honeymoon. Sorsha doesn't get along with our cats, so she's staying in the guest room."

"Oh. Well…"

"You did say you liked cats, didn't you? Do you mind bunking with Sorsha?"

"Uh, no, I don't mind." In fact, she loved cats but couldn't own one thanks to her crazy schedule during jump season, when she would frequently be working fires or living at the fire call center for days at a time. "But I haven't said I'd stay."

She shifted her gaze to the lopsided pink heart and scrawled letters of Peyton's name on her cast, and a flutter of unease tangled with a stirring of warmth.

"Please?" Peyton begged, and—darn it all—the girl's eyes were round and heart-tugging like a stray puppy's.

Amy'd have to have been made of stone to deny that sweet face what she wanted. But...

"I can't let you fix my car for nothing *and* live in your house for free. That's asking too much. If I stay, and that's an *if*, I have to reimburse you somehow. Let me pay rent or help out somehow."

Grant scowled. "I won't take your money."

"Then I have to decline. I'd feel...*weird* accepting so much charity from you."

He squared his shoulders, and his frown deepened. "It's not charity. At least I don't mean for it to be. I just thought..." He turned up a palm. "I just wanted to help, to make things easier on you."

She gave him a lopsided smile. "Thanks. That's really sweet."

He flinched a little at the *s* word, and her grin spread. Alpha guys like Grant hated that word.

"Please?" Peyton repeated.

"That's enough, squirt. Don't pester her. Finish your supper." Grant scooped another bite of pasta onto his fork and drew his eyebrows together. "All right, ten dollars a night to save your pride."

Amy blinked. Was he serious? When he met her gaze, his bedroom eyes held no humor, only a silent plea, a loneliness and hope that shook her to the core. He must have sensed that she saw his vulnerability, because he shrugged and added a hitch of his head toward Peyton. "She really wants you to stay."

"Fifty a day, half the groceries, and half the housework." When he arched an eyebrow, she quickly added, "But not cooking, and I don't know anything about child care, so don't ask me to do that."

"A quarter of the groceries, since there are four of us."

She shook her head. "But the kids don't eat as much as an adult."

"Yeah, but have you priced baby food lately?"

Peyton's head swiveled back and forth, following the ensuing negotiation until they reached a compromise on her rent, her share of the groceries and what household duties she'd take over. A list that excluded babysitting, but rooked her into cooking one night a week.

"I can live with that," she said after he summed up the final terms.

She offered her hand, and they shook on the deal. As before in his truck, the warmth of his grip and slight scrape of calluses on his palms sent heady swirling sensations skittering through her. His crooked grin, the dimple in his cheek and the sparkle that replaced the forlorn look in his eyes were a potent combination. She was in big trouble here.

Are you crazy, agreeing to live with this drool-worthy single father? Her electric attraction to him was understandable. He was sinfully good-looking and sexy in his own soft-spoken way. But for her to be so fascinated with him was—well, unusual for her. She didn't *do* relationships. Sure, she had the occasional date and took note of an attractive man here and there, but this kind of sweaty palm, rapid-heartbeat interest was new. She wasn't sure how to handle her attraction to Grant. She didn't want to act like some foolish smitten kitten or give him the wrong impression about her intentions toward him. She'd have to watch herself, school her expression, which she'd been told was an open book of her emotions.

She disengaged her hand from his, squelching the urge to rub the lingering tingle on her palm with her thumb.

"So," she said, facing Peyton, "Looks like I can play Hearts with you after all."

Peyton cheered, and Grant quirked an eyebrow. "You don't have to. Remember, babysitting is not part of the agreement."

She lifted a dismissive shoulder. "Who's babysitting? I'm playing cards. I like Hearts." She pushed back her chair and hobbled to the sink with her plate. She flashed Grant a lopsided grin. "I cooked, so you have to do the dishes."

"Fair is fair." Grant surveyed the pile of pots and plates and grunted. He sent his youngest daughter a wry glance. "Kaylee, I think I've been swindled."

Peyton dumped her dishes in the sink with a clatter and sped off. "I'll get the cards!"

"Don't let her cheat," he said aiming a thumb toward the room where Peyton had disappeared.

Amy chuckled. "She cheats?"

"She tries. She thinks it's funny. I'm trying to teach her it's dishonest and unfair. Back me up, okay?"

"Roger that, boss." Amy headed into the living room, musing over Grant's request. A flutter of panic tickled her gut when she thought about the implications of his instructions. Peyton would see her as a role model. She had a responsibility to the girl and to Grant to be a positive influence. She might not be Grant's babysitter or a fill-in parent, but she could have an impact on shaping Peyton's life. And she, more than most folks, knew how one person could change the direction of a life.

David had only lived with her and her mother a couple of months before she learned that hard lesson. He was still influencing her choices, her reactions to people and her ability to give herself. David was the reason she buried herself in her work, why she didn't see herself as part of a cozy home or ever becoming a mother. She couldn't imagine bringing a child into the world, loving them with all her heart and knowing they'd be vulnerable to the same kind of pain, caused by predators like David. She'd go ape worrying for her own daughter's safety. She'd overwhelm her own child trying to protect them from the evils of the world.

But just because she never planned to have children of her own, she still had to honor the position she was in as a guest in Grant's home. She blew out a deep breath and wiped her hand on her shorts as she joined Peyton on the living room floor. *Don't screw this up.*

The next morning, Grant woke to the sound of Kaylee crying from her crib, even before his alarm went off. He rolled to his back and rubbed his eyes with the heels of his hands, struggling to shake off the cobwebs of sleep. Angling his head toward the empty pillow beside him, a sharp pang of grief and loneliness speared his heart as it had every morning for the past almost year. The grief was followed by an irrational anger. How could Tracy die and leave him to raise their girls alone? How could she leave *him* alone? They were supposed to grow old together.

And like every morning for the past eleven months and twenty-three days, he shoved down the grief and anger, chastising himself for blaming Tracy. It wasn't her fault she was gone. That blame lay squarely with the Gales, the crime-connected family Connor had testified against. Their thugs had set the car bomb that killed Tracy. And while he had a righteous hatred for the Gales, he also still carried the less rational hurt and anger toward Tracy. Friends and family told him the anger was natural, part of the grieving process, but he still felt guilty blaming the woman he loved for leaving him. *Damn, he was screwed up.*

He draped an arm over his eyes and gritted his teeth against the pain that swelled in his chest. He had to get his emotions back in the little box where he shoved them in order to face each day and not scar his girls with the blackness he lived with. He renewed his daily promise to Tracy to protect their daughters from harm and give the girls the best life he could. He'd made the same promises to Tracy on their wedding day. And failed her…

Kaylee's wails went up in volume, and he dragged the covers back with a groan. He needed to get her before she woke Peyton. Shuffling out to the hall, his pulse jumped when he found a woman standing just outside Kaylee's door. A shot of adrenaline jolted through him, spiking his heart rate. Now wide-awake, he snapped on the hall light and squinted in the bright glare.

The woman winced and with a grunt, shielded her eyes. "Oh. G'morning."

Amy.

Skunk! How could he have forgotten she was staying here?

"Morning." He exhaled as his pulse slowed back to a normal pace. "Sorry if Kaylee woke you. She usually sleeps a little later than this."

"No problem. I'm an early riser." She finger-combed tousled hair back from her face, and her gaze lowered, taking in his dishabille.

His gut swooped. *Double skunk!* He was standing there in his boxer-briefs sporting a morning stiffy. Rubbing a hand on his bare chest, he winced. "Sorry about… I wasn't expecting to run into you."

She bit her bottom lip and averted her eyes. "Mmm-hmm."

"I'll, uh…be sure to put on my jeans…next time," he fumbled, noticing Amy's shapely legs and the old football jersey she wore as a nightshirt. She wasn't exactly dressed for a hallway meet-up, either.

She nodded but wouldn't meet his eyes.

Folding her arms over her chest, she hitched her head toward Kaylee's door. "She's getting louder. Maybe you should check on her?"

"Right." He edged past her and backed into the nursery, closing the door behind him. What the hell had he been thinking when he agreed to have a woman stay with them? A beautiful, intriguing, tempting woman. Obviously he hadn't thought through all the ramifications when he'd made the offer to Amy last night. That was unlike him. He was usually much more deliberate and practical about decisions.

"Da-dee!" Kaylee whined, bringing him out of his self-recriminations.

He turned toward his daughter's crib. Her arms were outstretched, her curls tousled, and Grant's heart melted. He lifted Kaylee from the crib and tucked her under his chin for a hug. "Morning, kitten."

Plenty of times he grumbled about raising his girls alone. The inconveniences, the messes, the frustrations and fatigue of trying to juggle supporting the family and parenting alone. He wasn't the world's first single parent, so he really had no room to gripe. Yet even with the help of his parents and brothers, sometimes he felt overwhelmed.

But in moments like this, when his baby girl reached for him, called his name and cuddled her cheek against his shoulder, he knew the struggle was worth it. His daughters were the world to him, and he'd fight giants, if needed, to provide for them, comfort them, teach them and protect them. He could do it all. He had to. Even if that meant doing it all alone.

For a minute, he just stood by Kaylee's crib, holding her, savoring her, letting his brain wake up to the new day. He often took a moment like this with Kaylee in the morning, easing into the day with a hug and time for reflection. Today, instead of thinking about Tracy and how much he missed her, his mind conjured an image of Amy standing in the hall wearing a Drew Brees jersey and not much else. Of course, the fact that he could hear her in the bathroom across the hall, water running, the towel hoop rattling, made it easy to keep her front and center in his thoughts.

Another prickle of self-censure crept down his back. What would Tracy think of him having another woman in their house, around their girls, leading his thoughts astray this way? He couldn't imagine she'd be happy about it.

But now that he'd promised the room to Amy, shaken on the terms, he couldn't back out. He'd have to deal with the situation and keep any lecherous thoughts in check. Amy might be the only woman to turn his head since he'd married Tracy, but he wasn't ready for a new relationship—especially not one with a woman in such a high-risk career. He'd already lost one woman he loved, and one tragic death was one too many.

Amy finished in the bathroom and tiptoed back to the guest room. As she passed the nursery, she could hear Grant's deep voice talking softly with his daughter.

"There you go, kitten. All clean and ready for the day." Kaylee babbled, and Grant answered with, "That's right. Good girl."

The pride and love in his tone washed through her,

reminding her of days past with her father. Days that had ended far too soon. When her mother had remarried, she'd had hopes of a healthy father-daughter sort of relationship with David. Instead she'd got a nightmare. Manipulation. Hurt. Shame. Conflict and betrayal. Gritting her teeth, she shoved aside the anger those memories caused. She refused to let David steal another moment of her joy.

Once back in the guest room, she crawled back into bed. Sorsha, the fuzzy black cat that was her roommate, stood up from her place at the foot of the double bed and waltzed up to greet Amy.

"Morning, fluff." She gave the cat a scratch behind the ears then snuggled into the covers, hoping for another couple of hours sleep.

Sorsha had other ideas. The cat walked around Amy's pillow, head-butting her and mewing. Amy patted the cat, then gently pushed her away. But Sorsha returned, more determined and purring loudly.

"What do you want?" Amy asked, seeing her chance to go back to sleep in jeopardy.

The cat meowed loudly. Amy didn't speak cat, but she thought maybe she could bribe the cat to leave her alone. Crawling back out of bed, she poured a large bowl of dry food in the cat's bowl, and Sorsha pranced over with a chirp and commenced chowing. Score one for Amy.

Going back to the bed, she pulled the covers up to her chin and sighed contentedly. But sleep was still elusive. Images of Grant as he'd looked minutes ago when she'd encountered him in the dim hallway paraded through her brain. The sexily rumpled bed head, the sprinkle of dark hair on his wide, taut chest and the impressive evidence of what was hidden inside his boxer-briefs—whew!

Heat stung her face, and her heart beat faster. She

was no stranger to seeing men first thing in the morning. When she worked a wildfire, she often had to camp out at the fire scene until the job was done, and her fellow smoke jumpers were all men. But she didn't feel the same crackling attraction to any of those men.

Maybe accepting Grant's generous offer of lodging was a mistake. She had no objections to a consenting-adults fling, but Grant didn't seem the type. He was obviously still not over his late wife. Even if he was up for exploring the smoldering chemistry she sensed between them, she guessed he was looking for someone to build a future with, someone to mother his children and grow old with. Amy wasn't that girl. She had no experience with kids, no domestic skills and no particular interest in settling down, either. She wasn't looking for anything long-term, especially not with a family man from the town she'd worked so hard to escape. Live down the road from David and her mother? No, thank you! She would be on her way back to Idaho as soon as Stella was road ready.

So pursuing the sparks she felt with Grant was not an option. She knew better than most women about the dangers of playing with fire. Grant was dry kindling, so she needed to cool the smoldering heat she felt around him before one of them got burned.

Chapter 5

Bright and early on Thursday morning, Grant's cell phone trilled as he was climbing out of the shower. He considered ignoring it, but when he saw the caller ID was his mother, who was supposed to be watching the baby while he went to the appeals hearing for William Gale, he answered the call with a sense of dread. "Please don't tell me you're backing out of babysitting," he said without preamble. "Nancy is still at orientation for her new job and I haven't found a replacement yet."

A deep cough was his mother's reply. "Okay, I won't tell you. But I am. Your father and I seem to have caught the crud that's going around at church. Walter Perriman is even—" *cough* "—in the hospital. I don't want Kaylee around these germs."

He suppressed a groan. His mother hadn't got sick on purpose, and she was right not to expose Kaylee. Thumbing the speakerphone setting, Grant set the phone on the bathroom counter and wrapped a towel around his waist. "You're right about that. A sick kid is the last thing I need."

"I'm sorry, honey." *Cough, cough.* "But maybe this is a sign that you shouldn't go to the hearing. I really think our family should give that man and his family a wide berth. No point poking a hornet's nest."

He pinched the bridge of his nose, feeling a tension headache building—and it wasn't even 7:00 a.m. yet. He opened his medicine cabinet and took out the bottle of aspirin along with his deodorant. "I need to be there, Mom. I can't sit back and risk them letting him go free without considering the gravity of his actions. I'm hoping they'll let me make a statement as a victim of his crimes and criminal connections."

His mother said nothing but coughed again.

Grant popped a couple of aspirins in his mouth and scooped a sip of water from the faucet with his hand. "Hey, you and Dad take care of yourselves. See a doctor. And thanks for calling. I'd better get busy finding a sitter."

"Oh, Grant. You know I worry about you. I just think—"

He swiped on his deodorant and recapped it. "Feel better, Mom. Love you."

She sighed her resignation, which gave Grant an indication of just how sick she felt. "I love you, too."

After replacing the aspirin and deodorant in the medicine cabinet, he thumbed his cell phone to end the call and began scrolling his contacts for possible babysitters. Most of his go-to sitters from when he and Tracy used to go out at night were high school girls who'd be in class this morning.

The obvious answer was to ask Amy to watch Kaylee, but he'd promised her that wouldn't be part of their arrangement. As he continued scrolling his contacts with fading hope, he recalled the way Amy had humored Peyton about signing her cast, how she'd patiently showed her how to cook spaghetti, how they'd played cards together and giggled over silly things. For all her talk, Amy *was* good with kids.

Hearing Kaylee in her crib, he stashed his phone,

dressed quickly and hurried to get his baby girl out of bed. On the way downstairs, he checked that Peyton was getting ready for school and gave her his usual warning not to dawdle.

Once Kaylee was buckled in her high chair and the coffee was brewing, he pulled Tracy's address book out of the kitchen junk drawer and paged through it. Seeing her handwriting, her personal notes scribbled in the margins and her trademark smiley faces in hearts shot a sharp pain of longing and grief to his heart. He braced a hand on the counter and fought for a breath. Damn it! The kamikaze reminders of his loss were the worst. He didn't have a chance to steel himself, to rein in the heartache.

"Dink!" Kaylee squawked, pounding her tray.

"Right." He took a deep breath. No time for feeling maudlin. "Hang on, kitten." He located the number he was looking for and dialed the elderly lady who'd watched Peyton a time or two when Peyton was a baby. Holding the phone tucked between his ear and his shoulder, he grabbed a clean sippy cup for Kaylee.

"Mrs. Greenbaugh, hi. This is Grant Mansfield," he said when a croaking voice answered.

Peyton strolled in and took her place at the table with a sleepy yawn.

Grant reminded Mrs. Greenbaugh who he was, explained that Tracy had died, apologized for the short notice and inquired about the chances the woman could babysit that morning, all while pouring Peyton a bowl of raisin bran, cutting up half of a banana for Kaylee and fixing himself a much-needed mug of coffee.

After learning that, no, Mrs. Greenbaugh couldn't watch Kaylee because she had doctor appointments today, Grant wished the older woman well and turned his attention to his own breakfast. He was out of frozen waffles, eggs and his favorite cereal. A trip to the grocery store was long overdue, but going shopping with two small girls in tow was high on the list of things he dreaded, and he was procrastinating. In the back of the freezer, he found an ancient bagel and brushed frost off it and popped it in the toaster. At least the coffee was fresh.

"How long until Christmas?" Peyton asked while playing with her cereal.

"Months."

"How long is that?"

"A month has about thirty days. It's still a long way off." Grant stopped Kaylee from squishing the banana in her fingers and wiping it on her face. Both of his daughters believed breakfast was an opportunity to be creative with their food, he thought with a frustrated sigh.

"Can I write a letter to Santa anyway? I know what I want for Christmas. A dog!"

Grant suppressed a groan. A dog was just what he needed to add to the general chaos of his house.

"We'll see," he said, deploying his mom's favorite response when he'd been a kid. Great, he'd become his mother!

Once the toaster popped his bagel back up, Grant settled at the kitchen table with Tracy's address book and his food. While thumbing through names he didn't recognize and entries he ruled out for various reasons, he sipped from his favorite Mansfield Construction mug and glanced across the table at Peyton. His daughter was picking the raisins out of her cereal and making a milky pile on the table by her bowl. "Squirt, you need to stop playing and finish your breakfast. The school bus will be here soon."

"I'm not playing. I'm saving the raisins for last."

"Well, less saving, more eating. You need to hurry, or you'll miss the bus."

"Do I have to go to school today? Can't I stay home and play with Amy?"

"Amy's not here to play with you. She's here because her car broke down, and I'm fixing it for her." And because you have an inappropriate attraction to her, his conscience added. He needed to face the truth that had Stella's owner been an old man with a comb-over, he'd not have been quite so willing to have a houseguest during the repair.

"My ears are burning. What did I miss?" Amy thumped into the kitchen with her walking cast and gave Peyton a wink.

Peyton scrunched her nose in confusion. "Your ears are burning?"

"It's an expression that means she knows we were talking about her," Grant explained, then waved a finger at his daughter's breakfast. "Eat."

"Amy, will you play with me today? I can show you my fort in the woods."

"Don't you have school?"

Peyton pouted. "Yes."

"How about you show me the fort after school?" Amy asked, her gaze drifting from Peyton's face to the coffeepot like a heat-seeking missile. "Mind if I pour myself some joe?"

"Help yourself. Sugar's in the dish by the cookie jar." He pointed to the Cookie Monster jar on the counter.

"Stupid school," Peyton grumbled. "How come Kaylee doesn't have to go to school?"

Amy muffled a laugh, and Grant gave his daughter a did-you-really-just-ask-that? look. "Why do you think?"

"Because she's still a baby?"

Grant touched his nose. "Now, stop stalling and finish your breakfast."

Kaylee squawked and reached for Grant's plate. He tore off a small bite of bagel and handed it to her, and the toddler started nibbling on it happily.

"It's not fair." Peyton grumbled, poking at the soggy cereal with her spoon. "I wish I was a baby. I want to stay home, too."

"Peyton," Grant started, but the honk of the school bus horn interrupted. He shoved back his chair and rushed for the front door. "That's your ride, squirt. Hustle!"

Peyton grabbed her pile of raisins and shoved them all in her mouth at once. Grant grimaced as he scooped up her Hello Kitty backpack and lunch box from beside the umbrella stand. Once again his daughter would be going to school without brushing her teeth. Tracy would be horrified.

When he returned to the kitchen, he found that Kaylee had rejected the bagel bite, thrown it on the floor and was giggling as Cinderella sniffed the gummy bread. Amy appeared from behind the refrigerator door with the jug of milk which she poured liberally in her coffee. Spotting the bagel on the floor, she pulled a lopsided grin and squatted to pick it up and give Cinderella an affectionate pat. "Are all mornings like this?"

"No," he said, sitting at the table and opening the internet browser on his laptop. "Some are worse."

"Why not hire help?"

"I had help for a while, but she resigned for a better job. You remember the lady who ran screaming from the house the other day when we first brought Stella here for repairs?" He used the touch pad to open the web page for the local newspaper want ads.

"I don't recall any screaming, but now that you mention it, I remember your sitter said something about other obligations."

"Yeah. She quit a few weeks ago. Finding a replacement nanny is on my to-do list, but the few leads I had didn't pan out."

Amy bit her bottom lip and squinted one eye. "I know this is where I'm supposed to offer to help, at least for a while, as return payment for the room, but…I've never been that good with kids. To be honest, they're completely alien territory for me."

Grant tore his gaze from his scan of the local want ads to send her a startled look. "Gosh, no! I didn't mean to sound like I was hinting… I told you the other night— no strings attached to staying here. I'm glad to let you use the guest room."

She sipped her coffee, a knit in her brow. "I mean, I don't mind helping out where I can. I just…being in charge of two little people is kinda…well, scary to me."

Grant grinned and glanced at Kaylee, whose face and hair were painted with banana mush. "Yeah, they're pretty intimidating."

Amy's coffee mug plunked onto the table, and she chuckled. "I mean the responsibility for them is scary. Anything could happen. I'm totally ignorant when it comes to what to do with a baby."

"No worries. I promised not to foist them on you, and I won't." He checked his watch, then glanced at Kaylee. He couldn't drag his daughter to the courthouse, even if the visual of the motherless little girl would be a poignant reminder for the judge of what Gale had done and why he needed to stay in jail. He gnawed the inside of his cheek. "Amy…"

"Yes, I will." She flashed a saucy grin when he raised a startled look.

"I didn't ask anything."

"You were going to, though. You were going to ask me to watch the baby while you went to court. Am I right?"

He sighed. "I just finished promising you I wouldn't."

"And I just finished telling you I'd help out when I could, scary or not." She eyed Kaylee. "You'll be good for me today, right? No sticking things in a wall socket or tumbling down the stairs when my back is turned, right?"

Kaylee gave Amy a grin that showed off her two bottom teeth and the nubs of the new teeth coming in on top. Grant's heart flip-flopped. Tracy shouldn't be missing these precious moments, her daughter's heart-tugging smiles. And William Gale shouldn't be on the verge of getting his conviction set aside. A fresh stir of anger churned in his gut, and he worked not to let the frustration and fury show in his expression or voice. He tried so hard to hide his grief from the girls. They needed him to be strong, be positive.

He closed his laptop and chugged the rest of his coffee. As he carried his mug to the sink, he cut a side glance to Amy. She was studying Kaylee as if trying to solve a puzzle. He appreciated her willingness to step outside her comfort zone to help him out. "I don't know how long I'll be. Are you sure you don't mind?"

"I'm up for it. I'm not Mary Poppins, but I won't let her starve or sit in a wet diaper."

"Thanks." He managed a maudlin smile, the weight of the hearing and the reminder of Tracy's horrific death pressing hard on his chest. As he turned to go upstairs and dress for court, Amy caught his hand. He met her gaze, expecting her to ask a question about Kaylee's care or tell him she'd changed her mind. Instead, she squeezed his fingers and gave him a confident nod. "You've got this. Go fight for justice."

Her support, the simple words of encouragement burrowed deep inside him. Warmth surrounded his heart and chased out the chill of dread for what the day held. Amy's faith inspired him in a way no one else had been able to in the year since Tracy's death. At some point, he should probably consider why that was. Right now, though, he had to get ready for court and brace for the battle to keep William Gale behind bars.

"All rise. The Honorable Judge Thomas Fitzpatrick presiding."

Grant rose stiffly to his feet, glaring at the back of William Gale's balding head. The old man stood at the defendant's table and conferred in a whisper with his lawyer. The perfectly cut Italian suit Gale wore probably cost more than the entire contents of Grant's closet. Grant gritted his teeth, not caring about the expensive attire of the convict, but hating that his wealth bought him lawyers who could waste the court's time with endless motions and appeals.

Judge Fitzpatrick took his place and motioned for everyone to sit. As the proceedings started and Gale's lawyers presented their case for overturning the old man's conviction on technicalities, Grant's gut twisted tighter. The lawyer went so far as to claim his colleague in the firm had not given Gale competent representation, offering his partner as a sacrificial lamb for his wealthy client. And how much had Gale and his family paid the attorney to take the fall this way?

The law partner was present and testified to the several legal technicalities he felt were grounds for overturning the conviction, including his own lapses in representation. Much of the trial law quoted and legalese used meant little to Grant, but the lawyer's self-admitted claim of incompetence clearly struck a chord with the judge. His expression changed, and he leaned forward, listening more intently. Grant shifted nervously on the hard bench seat. Did this mean Judge Fitzpatrick was actually buying these desperate attempts to free Gale? The prosecuting attorneys looked uneasy, as if they, too, were reading meaning into the judge's reaction.

Grant listened with growing dismay as William Gale's new attorney presented motions for overturning the old man's conviction, a move that would free Gale permanently on the fraud and money laundering charges due to double-jeopardy laws. All the sacrifices his brother Connor had made to see justice served were slipping away, and Grant felt helpless to stop it. Worse, the man he held responsible for Tracy's murder would have his life, his family, his freedom back, while Tracy had nothing. He, Peyton and Kaylee had no wife and mother. The injustice curdled in his gut, and he trembled with frustration and rage.

Because Gale's attorneys had presented such lengthy arguments for each motion, the hearing was still far from over when the judge took his lunch break. As Grant stood and shook the tension and stiffness from his muscles, he glanced toward William Gale in time to see him embrace a man about Grant's age. Grant hesitated, flashing back to Tracy's funeral when one of William Gale's sons had shown up at the cemetery, supposedly to offer his condolences. But the tension and bitter animosity between this son, James, and Grant's brother Connor, had been palpable. Grant had even taken a swing at the eldest Gale son, unmoved by the false-sounding condolences and enraged by the man's audacity showing his face at a private family interment.

As the hug ended, William was led away by guards, and James started down the center aisle of the gallery with his father's lawyers flanking him. When James spotted Grant, he slowed his steps, schooled his face and gave a stiffly formal nod of acknowledgment. Grant fisted his hands at his side and shoved down the hot ball of fury that gnawed at him. Nothing would be accomplished by getting in James Gale's face and lashing out about the farce his father was playing out today.

William's lead attorney put a hand on James's shoulder and nudged him forward. William's son exited the courtroom, and Grant sucked in a cleansing breath. His appetite gone—not that he'd had one, thanks to the disturbing progress of the hearing—Grant opted to walk the streets and city parks of downtown Lagniappe during the recess to burn off the restless energy pulsing in him.

He turned his cell phone back on and checked in with Amy.

"Oh, hi, Grant. I'm glad you called. The funniest thing just happened!"

The chipper sound of Amy's voice and the background noises of Kaylee's gurgles and children's programming on the TV worked wonders soothing his knotted neck muscles.

"Tell me." He rubbed his cheeks, realizing he'd been clenching his teeth most of the morning and his jaw ached. He worked his lower jaw as he crossed the freshly mown grass of the city park. "I could use a laugh."

"Kaylee was eating her lunch—I gave her the leftover pasta from the fridge and cut up a hot dog really small like you said to do—anyway, she started throwing the hot dog on the floor, and suddenly there were cats all around her high chair scavenging her offering."

Grant grinned and nodded, picturing this common occurrence. He didn't have the heart to tell Amy, for whom this trick was a novelty, that he was well aware of his daughter's penchant for feeding the cats and that he discouraged it.

"Cinderella even jumped up on the seat beside her and started eating off the chair tray," Amy continued, chuckling. "Well, Kaylee thought this was hilarious. Oh, my God!—her laughter is contagious! I could barely shoo the cats away, I was laughing so hard."

Grant's heart warmed, and he nodded, even knowing that Amy couldn't see the gesture. "There is no better sound in the world than a baby's laugh."

"Other than the lunch antics, things are going pretty well here. She's been cranky at times, but I'm managing. How are things at court?"

Just like that his mood dimmed again. "Awful. I think the judge is buying the dog-and-pony show. That rat bastard could actually get out."

Amy huffed her dismay. "Not again. What ever happened to keeping the bad guys behind bars?"

He puzzled briefly over her "not again," wondering what other instance of injustice she meant, but she asked, "So when do you expect to be home?"

"Later than I told you this morning. I still have errands after court wraps up. It could be supper time."

"Should I make dinner for us?" She sounded reluctant to take on the task, and he remembered her saying what a terrible cook she was.

"I can bring something in. You've helped enough just watching the girls for me. But make sure Peyton starts her homework if she has any. She'll tell you she doesn't, but the teacher sends home a check sheet every night for parents to sign. Her assignments are listed on that sheet."

"Got it."

"Thanks, Amy." He cleared his throat before adding, "I appreciate your help more than you could know."

"Forget it. I'm glad I could help."

He thought about telling her it was more than the babysitting he was grateful for. That her laughter, her presence at this juncture in his life, her positive outlook were buoys when the world seemed to be drowning him. But such a strong sentiment might be too much, too soon for Amy. She wasn't staying after Stella was repaired, no matter how much the idea appealed to him.

Grant pictured Amy at his house, feeding Kaylee, helping Peyton with her homework, and his heart gave a little tug. *Don't go there,* his head warned him. *Amy has no interest in becoming a mother.*

And you have no right to replace Tracy so soon, guilt added. Assuming he were willing to start something with a woman in such a high-risk career. Which he wasn't. He was no glutton for punishment and heartache.

"Oops. Gotta go. Kaylee found the bowl of potpourri and is trying to eat it," Amy said.

"Right. Bye—"

She was gone before he could finish. Kaylee had tried to eat the potpourri before. He should throw the stuff out, he thought with a soft grunt. It didn't have any scent anymore, and the collection of dyed wood shavings and perfumed sprigs wasn't the kind of decor any man chose for his home.

But Tracy *had* chosen the potpourri. They'd teased about her choice to set out bowls of the purely feminine stuff, and even now, despite the fact the scented garnish was dusty and without any smell, he hadn't the heart to change anything about the house that Tracy had done. Tossing out her touches of feminine decor felt like ridding himself of her memory, erasing her from his life, stealing his children's mother from them. He clung to every scrap of Tracy that he could.

He turned the phone off again, per court rules, and stashed the cell in his pocket.

The clock in the courthouse tower struck the top of the hour, and Grant made his way back to the courtroom. Almost instantly the tension he'd worked off on his walk corded his neck and shoulders again. The proceedings after lunch went much the same as that morning and by 3:00 p.m. Grant could see the writing on the wall. William Gale was going to win his appeal if Grant didn't do something.

When the judge left the courtroom to deliberate, Grant hurried up to the assistant district attorneys and introduced himself. "My brother is Connor Mansfield, your key witness in bringing the original conviction against Gale. I'm also the widower of Tracy Mansfield." He explained how Tracy had died in the car bombing that had been targeting Connor and his belief that William Gale had ordered the bombing. "I want to make a statement against releasing him. Surely as the family of a victim of his crimes, I have a right to my say in court."

The ADAs exchanged glances, and a woman in a dark brown skirt and matching blazer said quietly, "Mr. Gale has never been charged with any crimes connected to your wife's death, Mr. Mansfield. We never had substantial proof that he had any connection with the car bombing."

"I'm perfectly aware that he's never been charged. But we all know he's connected."

"Without proof, our hands are tied." The neatly

groomed woman sighed and furrowed her brow. "The fact of the matter is, the only crimes William Gale has been convicted of are fraud and money laundering charges your brother testified to. That's what this hearing is about. You have no connection to those crimes, and so you have no right to make a statement."

Grant gripped the railing that separated the well of the courtroom from the gallery. "My brother is in WitSec because of threats to his life, because of his testimony against Gale. Doesn't that count for anything?" he argued, his voice tight.

"It means a great deal," the ADA assured him in placating tones, "and we'll always be grateful to your brother for his help winning that conviction, but it has no bearing on the issues being heard today."

"No bearing? That monster cannot go free!" Grant countered, his volume loud enough to attract the attention of the bailiff.

The ADA motioned to the police officer that all was well, and Grant took a deep breath to gather his composure. "There has to be something we can do to fight this."

"Believe me, Mr. Mansfield. Our office is doing everything we can to prevent having the judgment set aside, but ultimately the decision belongs to Judge Fitzpatrick."

Twenty minutes later, Judge Fitzpatrick returned, his expression grim, and Grant's gut knotted. It was as he feared.

He sat with his jaw tight and his hands fisted as William Gale's conviction was set aside, and the man he blamed for Tracy's death was released to rejoin his family. A luxury Tracy didn't have.

Chapter 6

"That was your dad," Amy told Kaylee, who sat in her toddler swing, watching the squirrels and birds while chewing the sleeve of her jacket. She'd been whiny that afternoon, and Amy thought the change of scenery might help the baby's mood. She'd been partially right. Kaylee had perked up for a while but had continued to whimper and act restless. "He's finished at the courthouse but has to stop at the grocery on the way home."

No, she didn't expect Kaylee to answer or understand, but after a full day alone with the baby, Amy was missing adult conversation.

"He wanted to know if things were all right here. I told him you tried to sneak out your bedroom window to meet your friends at a keg party, so I grounded you and took away your cell phone."

Kaylee blinked at her drowsily. She'd refused to nap for Amy, and that had to be contributing to her cranky mood.

"Dry wit is wasted on you, eh? More of a slapstick girl?" She buzzed her lips and made a crazy face for the baby.

Now Kaylee chuckled and kicked her dangling legs.

Amy shook her head. "That's what I thought." She turned her face toward the warm spring breeze, enjoying the sun and peaceful beauty of Grant's backyard. "Your dad sounded stressed. I got the impression things didn't go well, but I didn't ask. I'm sure he'll tell us all about it when he gets home later."

She glanced back at the dark-haired baby, and Kaylee gave her a sleepy pout. "Feel free to nap. I'm running out of conversation topics, seeing as I'm doing all the talking." Hearing the rumble of the school bus, Amy glanced toward the front of the house. "Sounds like your sister is home from school."

Perking up, Kaylee shifted her attention toward the road and the sound of squeaky brakes, too. "Pey?" She clapped her chubby hands, clearly excited that her big sister was home.

"Oh, you know the sound of the bus, do you?" Amy leaned over to lift Kaylee from the swing. "I had a dog in high school that would come running when he heard the school bus." She propped the wiggly baby on her hip and started toward the front yard to greet Peyton. "Not that I'm comparing you to a dog."

"Doggie? Woof!"

She grinned. "Yes, a dog says *woof.* You're pretty smart for a toddler."

Kaylee was craning her head, looking around the yard. "Doggie?"

"No, there's no dog here. But look! There's a sister. There's Peyton." She pointed toward the school bus, where Peyton was struggling down the steps with her too-big pink backpack. Amy waved, then lifted Kaylee's hand to wave. "Hi, Peyton!"

Peyton returned a wave, but what caught Amy's attention was the sedan behind the school bus. As the bus chugged away, the silvery-blue sedan turned up Grant's driveway, following Peyton.

Amy squinted to see the driver through the reflection of the sun and dappled shade of Grant's tree-lined drive.

"Hi, Amy!" Peyton greeted enthusiastically, dropping her backpack in the yard and scurrying up to hug her legs. "Are you going to play with me?"

"Um, sure. In a minute, sweetie," she said, distracted by the car. "Let me see who this—"

The driver rolled down the window and gave her a smile. Her blood went cold. *David.*

"Well, hello! So is this where you're staying?" he asked, propping his elbow in the open car window.

Amy groaned internally. She hadn't wanted David to know where she was, damn it!

"Who are these cuties?" he asked, flicking a finger toward Peyton, his gaze taking on a predatory gleam.

"No one you need to worry about. Stay away from them, David. I'm warning you."

"Warning me? Geez, Amy, what are you afraid I'll do?" He gave a chuckle that was almost certainly intended to sound baffled and harmless, but Amy heard scheming in every note.

She gritted her teeth. "What are you doing here? How did you find me?"

He turned up his hand, feigning innocence. "I wasn't looking for you. Although I'm sure your mother would want to know that you are still in town, just down the road."

"Amy, Amy! Look! I found an inchworm!" Peyton raised a leaf with a small green caterpillar on it.

Amy gave the caterpillar a cursory glance and ruffled Peyton's hair. "That's nice, sweetie."

"You should stop in and see your mom," David said.

Amy dismissed his suggestion with a grunt. "Why are you here?"

"Just sayin' hi. Lucky timing that I was driving by and saw ya, so—"

"Right. You want me to believe you just *happened* to be driving by when—" Amy stopped, an oily feeling settling in her gut. Anger filled her, making her limbs tingle and her head pound. She stalked closer to David's sedan, pitching her voice lower so Peyton wouldn't hear. "You smarmy son of a bitch. You were following that school bus! What, were you trolling for new victims?"

He blinked and had the audacity to look affronted. "Hell no! It was just coincidence that I got behind the bus. I've been at the dentist this afternoon and—"

"Bull crap!" She leaned closer to the driver's window, snarling. "Tell me something, David. Have you registered with the sheriff yet as a sex offender? Do the neighbors know that you're a convicted pervert, so they can watch their little girls?"

Kaylee seemed alert to the grave tone of her voice, and she whimpered as she tucked her head against Amy's shoulder.

David's face darkened. "Listen here, Amy. I've about had enough of your accusations and slander."

She stiffened and cut a quick glance to Peyton. The little girl seemed absorbed in playing with the inchworm, but she still stepped closer to David's sedan and lowered her volume another notch. "I don't care what you're tired of. I know who you are, *what* you are. I know what you did to me. I know you need professional help, and I know I will not back down from speaking my mind or protecting other children from you. My mother may be blind to who you really are, but I will never forget or forgive you for what you did to me."

A muscle in David's jaw flexed as he gritted his teeth. "Clearly we are at an impasse over the past. We'll never agree on what really happened, and I've already paid the price of your accusations."

Amy's gut churned every time he called his abuse "her accusations," belittling what happened as nothing more than the hysterical allegations of a teenage girl.

"But the past is behind me, and I want to make a fresh start with your mother, with my life and, yes—" he raised his chin, giving her a patronizingly patient look, as if she were a child and he was dutifully waiting out a temper tantrum "—with you, if you're willing. What I will *not* do is sit by and let you ruin my chances of rebuilding my life."

He wagged a finger at her, and she swallowed the urge to smack the condescending look off his face.

She struggled to keep her composure for the sake of Grant's daughters. She didn't want to scare them by yelling or giving David the piece of her mind she really wanted to give him. "I don't give a damn what you do with the rest of your life, so long as you don't hurt any more children. Or my mother."

He shook his head, his expression wounded again. "I have no intention of hurting your mother. I love her. And if *you* loved her, you'd see how *your* actions are causing her pain and worry." He furrowed his brow and turned up a palm. "What am I supposed to tell her about you staying here?"

Amy shifted Kaylee from one hip to the other. "Nothing. It's not your business to tell her."

"How long are you staying here? How do you know this family?" His gaze wandered to Peyton, and Amy took an awkward sidestep with her cast so that she blocked his view of the little girl.

"Again, none of your business."

"So are you a nanny now? That hardly seems your style."

Why was she still talking to him? Amy turned away from David and called to Grant's daughter, "Peyton, grab your backpack, sweetie, and let's go inside."

"Peyton, huh? That's an unusual name," David said.

Amy bristled and marched a few hobbling steps closer to David's car. "For the last time, David, stay the hell away from these girls. Stay out of my life and mind your own business. I'm through with you, and if my mother chooses to believe you and stay with you, then I'm through with her, too. I can't make it any simpler."

David huffed a sigh and glanced away as if her warning grieved him. "Amy, Amy, Amy…"

"If I see you or this car anywhere near this house or Peyton's school bus again, I will call the sheriff, David. I swear, I will." She shook to her core, filled with loathing, anger and, yes, fear. For Grant's daughters and for herself. She hated that David still caused the deep-down chill and sickening dread he'd instilled in her the first time he came into her bedroom in the middle of the night. She'd tried to outrun the feelings of vulnerability and hatred, but just five minutes in his presence dredged up the old sense of anxiety, the sickening panic. She infused her tone with as much steel as she could muster, "Now get off Grant's property, and stay away from me."

Turning, she headed back toward the house as fast as her cast and the weight of her small passenger would allow. Drawing a slow breath, she forced down the sour taste in the back of her throat. "Peyton, come on in. We'll get a snack."

"I'll tell your mother you said hello!" David called cheerfully, as if they'd just had a friendly chat. "Nice to meet you, Peyton."

Amy stumbled to a stop, whirling to glare at David.

"Bye, mister!" Peyton called back innocently, giving a big wave.

Ice sluiced through Amy, and she called again to Grant's daughter. "Peyton, inside! Now!" Her shout held more starch and frost than she'd intended. For that she blamed David. She could, in fact, trace every bad thing in her life back to David. Okay, maybe that was an exaggeration. But she knew he was the cause of most of her hardships, and she knew she would do everything in her power to protect Grant's girls from David's evil influence.

The next morning, because he still hadn't found a suitable replacement for Nancy, Grant stayed home from the office. He was able to do a little work from his home computer, but he also used the time to put another ad for a babysitter in the local newspaper and on Craigslist. He also sent a request for recommendations and referrals from his friends on Facebook. Surely somewhere in Lagniappe, Louisiana, or a nearby town, a reliable babysitter had to be looking for a position. After placing his new ads, he checked a few more sources for the parts he'd need to fix Amy's radiator. For good measure, he also printed out and read an article specific to repairs for the '64½ Mustang.

Amy hobbled into the living room, where he had his laptop set up, and cast him a curious look as she settled on the couch with a book. "Whatcha got there?"

"Instructions on replacing your radiator."

Amy gave a mock cough. "Instructions? You told me you knew what you were doing. Is Stella safe with you?"

He lifted a corner of his mouth. "Perfectly safe. I'm

just doing my due diligence, checking on specifics for Stella's make and model."

"Whew!" She flashed a teasing grin. "You had me worried for a moment."

He lowered his gaze to the page he'd printed again, but with Amy nearby, even just sitting across the room, he found he read the same paragraph three times without absorbing it. Finally, he gave up and focused on her. "What are you reading?"

"Something I found in the guest room. A historical romance. I usually read mysteries or something with suspense, but it was this or a book about viral microbes or some such."

Grant nodded. "Those would be Brianna's. My new sister-in-law has a broad range of interests, to say the least. She's stayed in that room a few times in the past several months."

"Sorsha's owner?"

"Yeah."

"Hmm." She raised an eyebrow. "Next time you talk to her, ask her if her cat has an off button. That fluff ball was all up in my face in the wee hours this morning and wouldn't take no for an answer. Nice cat, but not what I wanted at o-dark-thirty."

He grunted. "Sorry about that. I can move her into my room."

"No, no. Not necessary." She raised a hand and grinned. "Sorsha and I will work it out. Perhaps a play session before bed to wear her out. A full food bowl before lights out. We have options." She set the book aside. "So…do you have plans today? Working from home? I don't want to get in your way."

"Actually, you maybe could help."

She tipped her head, her face lighting with intrigue. "Oh? How's that?"

"I've got a new radiator ordered, but I thought that as long as I was home today, I'd take the old one out. Do a general checkup on Stella. Oil, plugs, belts. If you plan to drive her cross-country, she needs to be in tip-top shape."

Amy's brow puckered. "True. But…how much will all that cost? Being out of work this summer, I'm already going to have to stretch my finances like a rubber band."

"Oh. Well…" Grant scratched his chin and twisted his mouth as he made mental calculations. He'd been so enthused about working on the Mustang, he'd forgotten about the expense. "How about this? Tinkering on cars has always been my hobby. I've always taken on the cost of that hobby, same as a golfer pays his green fees or a hunter buys his guns and ammo."

Already she was shaking her head. "Grant…"

"If you want, we can share the cost of the parts and you can pay me back in installments when you're able."

She grimaced and shifted on the couch. "I don't want to be a charity case."

"It's not charity. I love cars. Especially the classics. Getting under the hood of ole Stella would be fun for me. A distraction from the stresses of my life. I *want* to do this."

She gave him a measured look. "Far be it from me to deny you a distracting hobby."

"Then you'll let me cover the cost?"

She gave him a reluctant sigh. "Okay. As long as you let me return the favor when the opportunity arises." She smiled at him, and his chest filled with a warmth unrelated to the promise of his new project. Her smile was full of sunshine, and her good mood helped dispel a few of the clouds hanging over him.

He slapped his hands on his thighs as he stood. "Well, no time like the present. Want to help? You can be like my surgical nurse, handing me tools and maybe learning something about Stella that will help you in a mechanical emergency down the road."

"Ha, very *punny*!" she said with a lopsided grin as she struggled to her feet.

He thought about what he'd said and groaned. "Unintentional. But…" He waved a hand as he led her toward the back door. "Let me just get Kaylee and move her to the portable playpen in the barn."

Kaylee, having woken up early that morning, had easily gone down for a midmorning nap. While on one hand, he hated to wake her now, he also wanted her to stay on as close to a regular schedule as possible. Fortunately, his youngest daughter, like Peyton, loved the outdoors, loved being in the barn while he worked.

After rousing her and grabbing a sippy cup of juice from the refrigerator, he met up with Amy in the barn. Amy already had Stella's hood up and was leaning over to inspect the engine. Grant's step faltered when he spotted her.

Her position—hip cocked to the side to favor her injured ankle, shorts pulled taut across her fanny as she bent over the front fender, shirt gaping open a bit and providing an enticing peek at her cleavage—was the stuff of car magazine pinups. Heck, she was the stuff of nudie magazine pinups, minus the nude, which was all the more enticing to him. He preferred a little left to the imagination—and his imagination was firing on all cylinders at that moment.

She angled her head and sent him a smile as he approached, and something in his chest stumbled like a clogged carburetor. *Steady, boy!*

Kaylee kicked her legs happily and pointed toward the sunny sky. "Bird!"

He dragged his attention from the comely woman waiting by the Mustang and found the hawk that circled overhead. "That's right, kitten. That's a big bird, isn't it?"

"Bee Bird?" Kaylee's little brow wrinkled in confusion, and he recognized his mistake.

"Not Big Bird from *Sesame Street.* Just…a large—" He shook his head. "Never mind." He carried Kaylee to her outdoor playpen and kissed the top of her head before leaving her to amuse herself with her bounty of toys.

"So…" Amy propped her hands on her hips and tilted her head. "Where do we start? What do I need to do?"

"First thing you can do is drive Stella up onto these wheel ramps." He pulled two large steel ramps from the rack where he stored them and lined them up with the front tires of her Mustang.

"It's okay to crank the engine? What about the coolant?" She hop-stepped to the driver's side door and scooted onto the front seat.

"No, we won't crank the engine. I'll push and you steer. Take off the emergency brake and put her in Neutral." He lowered the hood of the Mustang again so she could see where she was going.

"Roger that, boss."

He draped a protective blanket over her rear bumper to prevent scratches and pulled his truck behind her. Nudging Stella gently, he gave his truck a tiny amount of gas and Stella rolled forward. Carefully, Amy eased Stella into position and hit the brakes when the Mustang rolled into place atop the tire ramps.

Grant retrieved his toolbox and both of his creepers, and he rolled the dollies toward Stella with his foot. He'd bought the extra one for Peyton or one of his brothers to use if they happened to be helping him. "So this could get a bit messy. You don't have a problem with getting greasy and dirty do you?"

She laughed, and he arched an eyebrow in query.

"Did I say something funny?"

"Oh yeah! If you'd seen me at the end of most fire jumps, you wouldn't have asked about my problems with getting dirty."

The reminder of the dangerous work she did for a living backed the breath up in his lungs, and he quickly redirected his thoughts. Just the idea of waiting for her to call in safe at the end of each fire raised a fine sweat on his brow.

"I'm usually caked with dirt, soot, sweat and general grime from head to toe," she was saying when he refocused his attention. "By the time we put out a wildfire, mud wrestlers have nothing on me."

That redirected his worry! Grant's breath caught, and his groin tightened picturing her in a pit of goo wrestling another woman. *Skunk.* He certainly didn't need that erotic image in his head before squeezing himself under an engine with her.

He wasn't sure which was worse—worrying about the danger she routinely faced or lusting after a woman he had no right wanting. He cleared his throat and shoved aside the tantalizing fantasy. He forced a grin he didn't feel and rubbed his hands together. "All righty, then. Let's get at it."

Selecting his first wrench and a snake light, he lay down on his creeper and rolled under the Mustang. Amy joined him in the confines of the undercarriage, and the faint scent of fruit greeted him over the smell of oil and exhaust. He gritted his back teeth to suppress a groan of frustration. How was he supposed to keep his mind on removing the radiator with the enticing scent of peach and provocative images tickling his libido? A man had his limits.

Grant forced himself to concentrate on the job at hand, tuning an ear to the sound of Kaylee babbling and playing nearby and reminding himself of the reasons why getting involved with a smoke jumper from Idaho was all kinds of bad idea.

Before he knew it, he'd passed the morning working beside Amy with only the occasional randy distraction. They managed to remove the cracked radiator and change her oil before they took a short break for lunch. While Amy made sandwiches for them, Grant fed Kaylee and put her down for her afternoon nap. When they returned to the barn to replace her spark plugs and check her belts and hoses, Grant brought the baby monitor out from the kitchen and set it on a shelf near his tools.

Immersed in the job and enjoying friendly banter and amusing stories with Amy, time flew. Midafternoon, the rumble of the school bus dropping Peyton off roused him from under Stella's hood, and he flipped his wrist to check his watch. "It's three o'clock already?"

"Is it?" Amy asked, stretching her back. "I haven't kept track."

"Hi, squirt," he called to Peyton, "We're over here, working on Amy's car."

Peyton spotted them and changed direction, dropping her pink Hello Kitty backpack on the driveway and skipping toward the barn.

"C'mere," Amy said, stepping close to him.

"Hmm?"

She reached up and cupped his face with her hand, using her thumb to wipe grease from his face. "You've got oil all over you," she said with a chuckle.

Her touch sent a jolt through him. He met her gaze and couldn't help smiling in return. She, too, wore engine grease on her cheeks, her chin and her nose. Without analyzing his actions, he reached for her and swiped at a smudge near her chin. "You're one to talk. How the heck did you get grease in your ear?"

When he tucked her hair behind her ear and rubbed her earlobe between his fingers, Amy's breath caught and her lips parted.

Grant's attention shifted to her mouth, and the urge to kiss her slammed him like a full body blow. He swallowed hard, his pulse kicking as she wet her lips.

"I don't—" she started, her voice suddenly breathless.

"Hey!" Peyton shouted, clearly disgruntled.

Grant jerked taut and took a quick, guilty step back from Amy.

"I'm supposed to help you fix cars!" his daughter fussed as she stomped into the barn. She divided a suspicious look between him and Amy, a deep scowl contorting her face.

Grant rubbed his hands on the seat of his jeans. "Um…you were at school," he replied stupidly, as if the obvious explained why he'd thrown over his junior helper mechanic for Amy's assistance.

"But *I* wanted to help you!" Peyton whined.

Guilt kicked him in the shin. Not only had he disappointed his daughter, she'd caught him ogling their houseguest. "Sorry, squirt. You can help next time."

His offer met with an icy glare.

"We're almost done, but you can take my place if you want." Amy tipped her head toward the open hood and plucked a shop rag from the tool shelf to clean her hands.

Peyton gave a dramatic huff of fury and ran from the barn in the direction of her playhouse.

"Peyton!" he called after her, but his daughter ignored him. *Great, Mansfield. Way to let your daughter down.* Why the hell weren't there instructions for raising an emotional daughter alone? *Skunk.* At this rate, Peyton will be wearing Goth makeup and piercing her body parts in rebellion by the time she's ten.

"I'll go talk to her if you want me to." Amy handed him the shop towel, and he wiped his hands.

"Thanks, but no. I'm the one who messed up. I'll give her a few minutes to calm down, then talk to her myself."

A muffled whine crackled over the baby monitor, letting him know Kaylee was waking up, right on schedule. He'd need to tend to her before he made his apologies to Peyton.

Grunting, he tossed the shop rag down with more force than necessary, frustrated with himself. Wasn't his life a big enough mess without alienating his daughter and testing himself by getting too close to his sexy houseguest?

Amy would be leaving in a few days, so no matter how tempting it was to kiss her, or work off a year's worth of pent-up sexual tension in recreational, no-strings-attached sex, he had to put his family's needs first.

Chapter 7

After Peyton stomped out of the barn, she headed straight to her playhouse in the backyard. Seeing Daddy smile at Ms. Amy and touch her the way he used to touch Mommy made her stomach hurt. She liked Ms. Amy. Mostly. But the way Daddy acted around her bothered Peyton. He paid so much attention to Amy it was as if he forgot Peyton existed. As if he'd forgotten about Mommy.

He'd let her be his special assistant. That was her job! It wasn't fair!

Once inside her playhouse, she went straight to her secret box. She opened it and pulled out Mommy's shirt. Mommy's picture.

Tears filled Peyton's eyes as she slid to the floor of the playhouse Daddy, Grandpa and Uncle Hunter had built her. She held Mommy's shirt to her nose and sniffed. It still had a little of Mommy's sweet smell on it, but it was fading. It made Peyton even sadder to think that the shirt might lose all of Mommy's smell. She should save some sniffs for later, but right now she needed a few more to make her feel better.

She curled up with the shirt and her old blankie that she'd got out of the attic. If the kids at school knew she still snuggled with her blankie in secret, they'd tease her about being a baby. So she had to be sure no one ever found her hiding place.

The sound of Amy laughing drifted across the yard and into her playhouse. She'd bet Daddy hadn't even noticed she left. He was so busy talking to Ms. Amy that he ignored her.

When he was around Amy, Daddy smiled sometimes. That was good. He hadn't smiled too much since Mommy died. She wanted Daddy to be happy, but why couldn't he be happy about spending time with *her*? She was his family. His squirt. They used to do lots of things together. Working on cars used to be *her* special time with Daddy. Then Amy came and nosed in.

Her stomach hurt worse, and her teardrops rolled down her cheeks. She wanted Mommy. Mommy could always make things better. She curled in a tighter ball, and her hands squeezed into fists. Her sad became mad. Mad at Daddy for ignoring her. Mad at Amy for butting in on her special time. Mad at Mommy for leaving her. Mad at herself for being such a baby about it all.

Peyton kicked at the chair next to her and growled. Sometimes she got so mad, even screaming didn't help. Someday she was going to just run away and never come back. That'd show them. If she did run away, would Daddy even notice? Would he even care?

Before Mommy died, she was sure he would have. Now she didn't know anymore. And that made her cry even harder.

That evening, hoping to cheer Peyton up and make amends for what the girl perceived as a slight because he'd worked on the Mustang without her, Grant allowed Peyton to pick a place to eat dinner out. Eating out suited Amy fine, since it meant she didn't have to cook.

When her father made the offer, Peyton's face instantly lit with anticipation. "Can we go to Mr. Gator's?"

An almost imperceptible wince twitched Grant's brow before he gave his daughter a forced grin. "Sure, squirt. If that's where you want to go. Go put your shoes on. I'll meet you at the truck."

Peyton scampered away, and Grant's shoulders sagged. He gave a muffled groan and mumbled, "Lord help us."

"What am I missing?" Amy shoved her hands in the back pockets of her shorts. "Is there something wrong with Mr. Gator's?"

She followed Grant into the kitchen, where he poured Cinderella and Sebastian a bowl of kibble and locked the back door. The look he gave her as he swung Kaylee's diaper bag over his shoulder could only be characterized as apologetic. "No, not if you like subpar pizza, hyper kids, noisy video games, and college students wearing grungy alligator costumes."

Now it was her turn to groan. "Seriously?"

Moving to the living room, he lifted Kaylee from the floor where she played with her toys on a pink quilt. "It's Peyton's favorite place, but a parent's worst nightmare. If you're prone to migraines, take your meds now."

Amy gave a wry snort. "Oh, goody."

"You don't have to go. In fact, I wouldn't blame you for bowing out." With one arm, he propped Kaylee on his hip and used his free hand to dig his keys out of his pocket. "Train's leaving the station, squirt. Let's go!"

"I can't find my other shoe!"

Amy scooped her purse off the washstand by the front door. "No college student in a gator suit is going to intimidate me." The hyper kids were another matter. She put on her game face and headed for the door. "Count me in."

Mr. Gator's Pizza and Prizes was everything Grant warned her and more. The shrill of sirens and clang of bells from the games combined with children's shrieks and shouts to form a cacophony the likes of which Amy had never heard. The scent of oregano and tomato sauce only barely covered the smell of stale grease and sweaty children that permeated the restaurant. Despite her best intentions, Amy balked when she stepped into the brightly lit play place. She paused to take in the zoo-like atmosphere, sweeping her gaze around the room full of clamoring kids playing skee ball and whack-a-mole as machines with flashing lights disgorged prize tickets. "Wow."

Grant slowed, waiting for her, and lifted a cheek in amusement as she gaped at the chaos. "Told you."

Peyton tugged her father's hand and bounced on her toes. "Come on, Daddy! The skee ball is open."

Amy reached for Kaylee. "I'll take her if you want."

He passed the baby and the diaper bag over to her. "Thank you. Try to get a table to the back away from the stage. Last time we were here, the animatronic swamp band scared Kaylee."

Amy glanced toward the currently quiet creatures on the stage and pulled a face. "I can see why. I'm a little scared by them myself. That possum looks possessed."

As he left to supervise Peyton, Grant gave her their drink orders and told her to surprise them with the pizza toppings. Amy took a fortifying breath and headed into the dining room. As she scanned the area farthest from the stage for an open table, she spotted a familiar face that stopped her in her tracks.

David sat at a booth by himself, a half-eaten pizza on his table.

A chill slithered up her spine as she gaped at him. The

implications of her stepfather sitting alone in a restaurant crawling with children made her gut swoop and sour.

Drawing Kaylee closer to her, she cast a glance to Grant, wishing she could tell him they needed to leave. But Peyton was so obviously thrilled to be there, and Grant wouldn't want to disappoint his daughter without a good explanation for Amy's concerns—an explanation she wasn't ready to give him.

Steeling herself, she stalked over to David's table, and let the diaper bag land next to the leftover pizza with a thunk. "What are you doing here?" she snapped.

His attention shifted to her from the ball pit where two little girls were engaged in a squealfest. Amy's skin crawled imagining where David's thoughts might be concerning those innocents.

"Well, well. Evening, Amy. Nice to see you." He gave her the congenial smile she'd learned to see through.

"What are you doing here?" she repeated through gritted teeth.

"Your mom had a dinner meeting at the church, so I was on my own for supper. I had a hankering for pizza, so…" He waved a hand as if the rest was obvious.

"So you came *here*?" Her tone made plain her skepticism. Grant had called the pizza subpar. She gave the congealed grease and cardboard-thin crust on his pan a meaningful look. "Out of all the pizza places that deliver, you came to the one place in town that serves the worst excuse for pizza with the most annoying ambience."

He gave a negligent shrug. "I like the food here. Beats prison food any day of the week." He angled his head and aimed a finger toward an empty basket in front of him. "Be sure to get the cinnamon bread sticks. They're a real treat."

She shook her head, and the muscles in her neck

bunched in painful knots. "I don't buy it, David. You're here because of the children."

He gave her a dismissive sigh and leaned back on the bench seat. "Believe what you want. Clearly you don't want to hear the truth."

She weighed the situation, her heart firing a rapid beat, and she narrowed her eyes. "Does your parole officer know you're here?"

"If you mean did I invite him to join me, then no. We really don't have that kind of relationship. But I guess I could ask him next time. It would be polite."

She felt her cheeks flush as her blood heated. "Don't be deliberately obtuse. You know what I mean. I bet the terms of your parole forbid you to be here, around these kids."

He twisted his mouth in a dismissive moue. "Nope. I'm free to eat pizza in any restaurant I choose."

Kaylee wiggled and turned looking for Grant. "Daddee?"

Amy cut a look toward the skee ball games to make sure Grant wasn't watching her conversation with David. She should walk away before her interest in David raised any questions, but she didn't feel right letting David's presence in the child-focused pizza pub drop. "Maybe I should call the police and tell them where you are."

His expression sobered, his jaw growing rigid and his eyes cold. "Maybe you should mind your own business, Amy. I'm here eating pizza. Period. I have a right to dine in any restaurant I choose. So if you're through indulging your paranoia and disturbing my evening—" he threw his napkin down on his plate "—then I'm going to pay my check and go rent a DVD." He slid to the end of the booth and stood, crowding her. "Unless you have a problem with me renting *Captain Phillips*, too?"

"Nobody rents DVDs anymore," she muttered peevishly. "They stream from the internet."

He raised an eyebrow as he scowled. "Excuse me for being behind on the latest tech trends. I've been away from such conveniences the last few years…thanks to you."

An angry retort sprang to her lips, but she choked it back. She swallowed hard, the bitterness leaving a sour taste in her mouth and a tremor of fury in her veins. She would not rehash this argument in public. Or ever. In fact, why was she still talking to the cretin?

She glanced toward the skee-ball game and found Grant staring at her, a curious knit in his brow. When she turned back to David, his eyes had shifted toward Peyton and Grant.

"Still playing house with the neighbors?"

When Kaylee babbled and kicked her legs again, he reached for the baby's cheek.

Amy took a step back from her stepmonster, pulling Grant's daughter away from his touch. "Stay away from me and Grant's children. In fact, stay away from *all* children, David. Because I *will* call the cops if I get even a hint that you're up to no good."

She made a mental note to call the Department of Corrections and speak to his parole officer first thing in the morning. Despite David's claim he had the legal right to be at Mr. Gator's, she knew in her gut he was trolling for his next victim.

"Go ahead," he said, challenge glinting in his eyes. "If what you want is to hurt your mother even more. The cops won't find anything, and once again you'll look like the vindictive bitch that you are."

Amy's pulse pounded so hard in her temple, she thought she might burst a vessel. But David stalked past her and tossed his bill and some money at the teenager manning the register before storming out the front door.

"Everything all right?"

She startled at the sound of Grant's voice next to her. She'd been so focused on David's exit that she hadn't seen Grant and Peyton approach. "Oh, uh…yeah."

"Who was that?" he asked while Peyton tugged on his arm, begging for more quarters to play something called "Razzle Jackpot."

She inhaled a cleansing breath and blew it out through her pursed lips. "My stepfather."

"Oh," he said in a tone that implied he understood her upset. When in fact he only had a tiny piece of the picture. Grant cut a side glance toward the door, concern denting the bridge of his nose. "Anything I can do?"

"You can change the subject. I don't want to talk about him."

Grant's eyebrow twitched up briefly, and she saw a flash of hurt in his eyes.

"Skunk," she grumbled. "I'm sorry. That came out all wrong. I just don't want to waste any more energy on him tonight. We're here to have fun. Right, Peyton?"

"Yeah!" Peyton cheered and pointed to the ball pit. "Can I go in there, Daddy?"

And just like that, the subject of David was shoved aside, at least on the surface. Amy did her best to keep the mood light and enjoy herself, but David had cast a shadow over the evening. Every now and then she caught Grant looking at her in a way that said he knew where her thoughts were, but he refused to pry where he wasn't wanted.

Amy held David responsible for that extra wall between her and Grant. While she knew her eminent departure for Idaho meant she couldn't let herself become too deeply entwined in Grant's and his children's lives, she didn't want the distance between them to be rooted in painful secrets. She considered telling Grant about David's abuse, but what was the point? She wasn't looking for his sympathy and in a couple of weeks she'd be out of his life.

Before she left town, she would talk to Peyton about stranger danger and give Grant a general warning about predators in his neck of the woods. That and Grant's already-protective nature should be enough to keep Grant's daughters safe.

"Amy, look! I won!" Peyton's excited cry pulled her out of her troubled musings and drew her attention to the string of tickets pouring out of the latest game machine Peyton played. Dozens of tickets. Maybe hundreds.

"Holy cow, Peyton. You hit the motherload," she said with a chuckle as prize tickets continued to puddle on the floor. She knelt awkwardly with her casted foot behind her to help the little girl collect her booty.

"Now I can get the stuffed alligator!" Peyton squealed.

"Just what you need. Another stuffed animal," Grant said dryly.

When Amy chastised him with a frown, he hitched his head toward the prize counter. She scanned the shelves of toys and candy for several seconds before her gaze shifted upward to the colossal alligator suspended from the ceiling. They'd be lucky if the thing fit in the backseat and didn't have to ride home in the truck bed. Amy covered a laugh. "Oh. Wow. That's quite the prize."

As it happened, Peyton just missed having enough tickets for the giant alligator and spent the tickets on a cache of smaller toys, candy and three helium-filled balloons. "Here, Daddy. This one is for Kaylee," Peyton said, handing Grant the string of a red balloon as they left the restaurant. "Can you tie it to her arm?"

"Thank you, squirt. It's nice of you to share." He paused on the sidewalk and set the diaper bag down to free a hand.

While he loosely looped the string around Kaylee's wrist, Amy said, "Peyton, want me to tie the other ones on your arm?"

"Okay. But just one," Peyton said, offering Amy the string to a purple balloon. "I got the yellow one for Mommy."

Amy's heart lurched. For Mommy? Had something about the evening led Peyton to believe Amy was her new mother?

"Um, honey, I'm...not your mommy." She glanced at Grant, who looked as dumbstruck as she felt.

"I know. My mommy's in heaven," she said quietly. Then, whispering to the yellow balloon, she stepped off the sidewalk and let the balloon float out of her hand. "I'm letting it fly up to heaven for Mommy."

Grant's chest heaved as he drew a sharp breath, his wide-eyed gaze latched on his daughter.

Amy's heart somersaulted, and she tipped her head back to track the balloon as it ascended in the purple-hued dusk sky. A hush fell over them as they watched the balloon float higher. Even Kaylee seemed awed by Peyton's gesture.

"Yellow was Mommy's favorite color, right, Daddy?" Peyton asked as the last sight of the balloon disappeared.

"Yeah, it was," Grant said, his voice noticeably husky.

Peyton seemed pleased with this confirmation and started across the parking lot toward the truck.

"Look for cars! Hold Amy's hand!" Grant shouted, and Amy hobbled quickly to catch up with Peyton.

When Peyton took Amy's hand, she asked, "Do you think Mommy will get my message?"

"What message is that, sweetie?" She opened the truck door, and Peyton hopped up and settled in her booster seat.

"The one I whispered to the balloon. I told her I love her and miss her."

Amy's heart wrenched a notch tighter, and she blinked back the moisture in her eyes. "I know she'll get your message." Her answer clearly pleased the little girl. "And know what else?"

Peyton wrinkled her nose. "What?"

"I know she loves you and misses you, too."

Grant's daughter tipped her head. "How do you know?"

"Because when I was young, my dad went to heaven, and I know that he still loves me. And even though I miss him, I know that love is stronger than death. I can feel his love around me, like a hug."

Grant opened the door on the opposite side of the truck and put Kaylee in the baby seat. "Everything okay here?"

Amy consulted Peyton with a look. "Are you good?"

Peyton gave a nod, then wrapped her arms around Amy's neck. "I'm extra good."

Heart lurching, Amy hugged the girl back and raised her gaze to Grant. Was Grant aware of how much Peyton missed her mother? If Amy could tell how hard the girl was looking for a mother figure to fill the void in her life, how could Grant not know?

Not that she was volunteering for the role. She didn't need to be another broken bond for the girl, losing her mother and then her nanny. She'd need to watch her step in the next few days, until Stella was road ready, and not give the child false hope.

"Guess we're set, then." Grant put the diaper bag and a sackful of Peyton's loot onto the floor of the backseat and climbed in the driver's seat. As Amy buckled in, he sent her a smile that made her toes curl and her pulse stutter like a schoolgirl. *Thank you,* he mouthed, and she saw a flicker of something in his eyes—Affection? Expectation? Yearning?—that stopped her.

She'd seen his attraction to her, felt the crackling physical chemistry between them before, but this glimmer of naked emotion was new. And a bit upsetting. Maybe *Grant* was the one she needed to avoid giving false hope.

Or, judging from the way her heart wrenched at the thought of leaving for Idaho soon, maybe she needed to guard her own expectations. Falling in love with Grant and his daughters would be a complication her life didn't need.

Chapter 8

The next morning, Grant was prepared to stay home from work again, still lacking any replacement for Nancy. When the school year ended next week, he might have to settle for a teenager looking for summer employment, but he was uneasy about the idea of stepping down from Nancy, a trained bodyguard, to a teenager with limited life skills. He set his cell phone on speaker as he talked to his father and fixed Kaylee her breakfast. "I know the contracts are backing up, Dad. Maybe I can bring Kaylee with me to the office long enough to clear out my inbox later this morning, but she'll need a nap by about ten-thirty."

"It's okay, son. I can cover for you. And I'm sure when your mom gets over her virus, she'll be happy to fill in until you hire a new nanny."

"I know she would. I just…" Grant pulled a frown as he sliced a banana and put the bites on Kaylee's highchair tray. He knew his parents had his back. They'd gone above and beyond helping him in the past year. But depending on his parents so heavily made him feel like a failure. *A thirty-three-year-old child experiencing failure to launch.* He hated imposing on them, hated letting his father down when so much needed to be done at the office, hated seeing the pity in their eyes when they answered the call to help their poor widowed son.

Amy walked into the kitchen, bringing with her the floral fresh scent of her morning shower.

Grant's libido responded with a kick of lust that licked his veins and shook him to the core. The past year of celibacy weighed heavily on him as he watched her cross the floor in her tank top and cutoff shorts. With her shapely limbs and ample breasts, she made the simple street clothes as sexy as French lingerie.

She stretched to take a mug down from the cabinet, and her shirt rode up, giving him a peek of taut midriff. "Boy, will I be glad when I don't have to wear a plastic bag on my foot in order to wash my hair."

"Who's that?" his dad asked.

Amy sent a startled glance to his cell phone then cringed guiltily, mouthing, *Oops.*

He waved dismissively. He had enough guilt on his plate without feeling like a teenager caught making out on the family couch. Bad enough that he'd been ogling his houseguest.

"It's Amy Robinson. She's staying with us until her car is repaired. I did mention last week that I was replacing the radiator in her Mustang, didn't I?"

"You did. But you didn't say she was staying with you." His father paused. "Why doesn't Amy watch the—"

"No," he said before his dad could finish. "I promised her I wouldn't dump my kids on her. She's not here to be my sitter."

Amy cut a side glance from the coffeepot where she poured herself a mugful. "I've been thinking about that deal, and it seems a bit selfish of me. You're helping me out in so many ways. I can handle a little babysitting to help you out in a pinch. Go to work. I'll cover things here."

"There you have it," his dad said. "Problem solved."

"No. Not solved, just postponed." Grant added a small handful of Cheerios to Kaylee's tray, then settled at the table to eat his own breakfast. "I still need a replacement for Nancy ASAP. School will be out soon, and watching two kids all day is a bigger deal than one typically agreeable toddler."

"But Amy can handle things for you today, right? And I'll see you at the office in a little while?" his dad pressed. "We need to discuss the Hanaford deal before we sign off on it."

Amy nodded at him.

Resigned to once again depending on others for help, he sighed. "Yeah, okay. I'll come in for a few hours. But we're also gonna discuss me taking leave until this nanny business is settled. Maybe you can hire a temp at the office and suspend my salary for a few weeks to pay them."

His dad scoffed at the idea but agreed to discuss the matter when Grant got into the office.

Grant ended up working half the day and going home at lunch so that he was at the house when Peyton got home from school. For the next week, he did the same, spending the afternoons working on the Mustang, tuning up the engine, detailing Stella inside and out and rotating the tires. As much as his tinkering with Stella relaxed him, the extra time around Amy filled him with a growing sense of peace—and, at the same time, an increasing restlessness. Having her around made him think more and more about what his life was missing, what his home lacked, what his kids needed.

He wanted to remarry. He wanted a second chance at growing old with someone special at his side, but was

Amy that woman? As good as she was with his girls, she still denied she had any mothering skills. As pleasant as it was coming home to her warm smiles, he knew she still intended to return to Idaho, to smoke jumping. Her risky career still filled him with a chill of dread. And the guilt of picturing himself with someone other than Tracy in his twilight years still stung.

But he couldn't deny he was becoming more attached to the spitfire smoke jumper—her sass, her sense of humor, their easy camaraderie in the evenings. So much so that when the mailman delivered the radiator he'd ordered for Stella, Grant felt a pang of disappointment. He had no excuses left not to fix Amy's Mustang and send her on her way. He just wasn't ready to have her leave.

Peyton sat at the kitchen table writing out her addition tables and wishing she was outside in her playhouse instead. Math was stupid. School was stupid. She already knew her addition tables. She scribbled her answer and cut a glance to the backyard. She wanted to climb the big tree by her playhouse before it got dark!

The phone rang, and Amy called from upstairs, "Peyton, can you answer that please? I'm up to my elbows in your sister's poopy diaper."

"Okay!" she yelled back and ran for the phone in the living room. She couldn't reach the phone in the kitchen.

"Mansfield residence. Peyton speaking," she said as she'd been taught.

"Hello, Peyton. Is your father there?" a man said.

"No, just Amy. She's changing a poopy diaper, though." Peyton covered her mouth as she giggled.

"I see. How old are you Peyton?" the man asked.

"Seven. Who is this?"

He was quiet for a second, then said, "Someone your

father and uncle know. Our families have unsettled business."

"Oh." She didn't know what that meant, but…whatever. She remembered what else she was supposed to say. "Can I take a message?"

"Tell me, Peyton. Where is your uncle Connor living these days? Do you or your father ever talk to him?"

"Huh-uh. I mean, *no, sir*." Oops! She hoped this guy didn't tell Daddy she forgot her manners. "Uncle Connor and Aunt Darby and Savannah all moved away somewhere secret."

"I can keep a secret. Where did they go?"

"I don't know 'cause it's a secret." Silly man. Didn't he know what a secret was?

"I bet your father knows. Why don't you ask him?"

Peyton wrinkled her nose. The guy was sure stupid. A secret was secret. "Daddy doesn't know. He told me nobody's supposed to know. That's why it's a secret."

"Mmm. In that case, you can give your father a message for me."

She sighed and looked around for a pencil. "Wait a minute. Let me write it down." She hated when there was a message. She didn't know how to spell names, and when she forgot to give Daddy his messages, he got mad. She found a pen clipped to Amy's crossword puzzle and turned the puzzle sheet over to take the message. "Okay. Ready."

"Tell your father that William Gale saw him at court last week. Tell him there is still unsettled business between our families. Victor will be avenged."

Peyton twisted her mouth in thought. She wrote *Wilum* and was trying to remember the last name. The man was still talking.

"Tell him I hold Connor responsible for my youngest son's death, and I will have my own form of justice."

Peyton tried to write Uncle Connor's name, she knew how to spell that, but her pen ran out of ink. She shook it and tried again. *C-O-N...*

"You'll give that message to your father? Right, Peyton?"

"Um…" Her shoulders drooped, and she chewed her bottom lip. She hadn't got even half of what he said. Daddy would be frustrated with her and roll his eyes. She hated letting Daddy down. "Can you say the last part again?"

But a click from the phone told her the guy had hung up. *Oh, well.*

She looked at what she'd written and decided it was better to not tell Daddy anything instead of half a message so that he made that growling sound under his breath and shook his head at her. She balled up the sheet of paper and shoved it to the bottom of the kitchen trash can. Before going back to the table to finish her math, she looked out at the backyard through the window in the door. Maybe if she just played for five minutes…

She could finish her homework later.

"Hey there, kitten. Were you a good girl today?" Grant dropped his keys and a grocery bag on the counter and bent to give Kaylee a kiss on her cheek. She rewarded him with a four-tooth smile that shot straight to his heart. He raised his gaze to Amy, who stood with the freezer door open staring at the contents with a furrowed brow. "How'd it go this afternoon?"

She hummed distractedly. "Okay."

He walked to her and tipped his head to glance in the

freezer with her. "Are you defrosting the ice box or wait-ing for divine inspiration from the frozen vegetables?"

She jerked her gaze toward him as if startled to see him beside her. "Huh? Oh!" She closed the freezer door and gave a self-deprecating laugh. "Sorry, my mind was somewhere else."

"Clearly." He walked back to the bag of groceries and started unpacking his purchases. "Did the kids behave for you today?"

"Well…" She glanced at Kaylee with a frown, hesi-tating.

"Well?" He paused with a can of coffee raised halfway to the shelf and angled his head, waiting. "If something happened with my kids, I need to know."

"It's just that Kaylee was real fussy this afternoon. Nothing made her happy. Maybe it's just that I'm no good with kids, but…she spent most of the afternoon whimpering."

He glanced at his youngest, who seemed quite con-tent at the moment. "You checked her diaper? Tried a sippy cup?"

"Yes and yes. I tried rocking her and reading to her and feeding her and putting her down for naps, which she refused to take, by the way, other than five minutes in her high chair right before you got home."

He strolled back to Kaylee's high chair and felt her forehead. Her skin was a tad warm but nothing alarm-ing. "Nancy said she thought she might be about to cut a new tooth. Maybe that's the problem."

"A tooth?" she asked, sounding baffled.

He ruffled Kaylee's curls and faced Amy again. "Her gums hurt when she's teething. Was she chewing on her fingers and blankie a lot?"

Her eyes widened. "Her fingers, her sleeve, her toys,

the cat's tail, anything in reach." Her shoulders dropped, and she shook her head. "Well, duh, Amy." Meeting his gaze she said, "Teething, huh? I thought the girl had a strange mouth fetish. Some Freud-esque fixation."

He snorted a laugh. "Freud? Well, maybe one day. But for now I think a little gum-numbing gel will do the trick."

"Right." She rubbed her hands on the seat of her shorts and opened the freezer door again. When she'd stared blankly for a few seconds, he crossed to her again and cleared his throat. "Maybe if you tell me what you're looking for I can help you find it before the ice cream melts."

"What?" She glanced up and him, then winced. "Cra—uh, *skunk*!"

He winked his thanks to her when she caught herself and used the family's G-rated curse. Somehow, knowing she was making an effort to change and meet his family's needs gave him an odd warmth in his chest. Curbing her language was such a little effort in the scheme of things, but it meant a lot to him.

He reached around her and closed the freezer door. "You seem distracted. Anything you want to talk about?"

She took a breath, as if to explain herself, but caught her bottom lip with her teeth instead, clearly shoving down whatever she was about to say. When Cinderella rubbed against her leg, she bent down to lift the cat into her arms and scratch her behind the ears. "No, I'm... just trying to decide what we should have for dinner."

He knew there was more going on, but he didn't want to push her. If she didn't feel as if she could confide in him, who was he to force the issue? He had plenty on his mind that he hadn't shared with her. She wasn't his wife, wasn't even his nanny. Her private concerns were none of his business.

He retrieved the teething gel from the windowsill over the kitchen sink, uncapped it and squeezed a blob on his finger. "I told you earlier not to worry about supper. We can fix something simple. Hot dogs. Mac and cheese from a box. Or we can order a pizza."

"I warned you that I didn't cook." She hobbled to the pantry with Cinderella still snuggled close to her chest and stared at the shelves now.

"You did." He rubbed the gel on Kaylee's gums and felt the nubby bump where a new tooth was coming in. "That's what's hurting my girl. Does that feel better, kitten?"

Kaylee bit down on his finger, gumming him like a teething ring. "Gaa."

With a loud meow, Sebastian trotted into the kitchen as well and joined Amy in the pantry. Seeing her brother, Cinderella jumped to the floor and paced over to the food bowl, where she sat down to await her supper.

Grant rolled his eyes. His cats had an infallible internal clock. Kissing Kaylee on the head, he nudged Amy aside and retrieved the bag of cat food from the pantry. "Okay, critters. Here you go."

Sebastian and Cinderella dived into their food with happy feline chirps.

As he returned the cat food to the shelf, he noticed that Amy still gnawed her lip and fidgeted with her fingers as she perused the cupboard. Something more than Kaylee's teething had upset her, he was sure of it. Her distraction and brooding were unlike her.

"Where's Peyton? Did she do her homework?"

Amy hesitated and frowned. "No." She shifted her weight uneasily. "When I insisted she had to do her homework before playing, she got sassy, and I sent her to her room."

Grant groaned, earning another wince from Amy. "I hope that's okay. I don't want to step on any toes with her discipline, but—"

Raising a palm, he stopped her. "No. If she needs discipline, mete out what she deserves."

He moved closer to her. "Is Peyton's sassing what's got you upset?"

She blinked. "Wha—? No. I mean…sure it was frustrating, and I felt bad punishing her, but—"

"Peyton!" Grant shouted, using his best stern-father voice.

Amy jolted, and her eyes widened in alarm. "Grant, don't yell at her. I didn't mean to get her in trouble."

He put a hand on each of her shoulders. "Don't blame yourself. You did the right thing telling me."

"Maybe, but—"

"Peyton Marie! Get down here!"

She stuck a finger in her ear. "Wow. I bet the neighbors heard that."

He gave a dismissive shrug. "Nah. The nearest neighbor is almost half a mile. We can yell to our heart's content around here." Twisting his mouth in a quick wry grin, he added, "Ain't country living great?"

"Um…" Amy's brow puckered again. "Speaking of neighbors…"

"Yeah?"

"Did you know there is a website where you can look up where registered child predators live in your area?"

He arched an eyebrow. "Really?"

"Yeah. So…I checked it today and…well, there are a couple that live within a three-mile radius."

He pinched the bridge of his nose. "Great. Like I need another thing to worry about with my kids."

"I'm sorry. I don't mean to add to your worries. I just thought…you should be aware."

"You're right. Thanks. I'll check the site tonight." He sighed then glanced toward the entryway where Peyton had yet to appear. Cupping his hands around his mouth and leaning away from her ear, he shouted, "Peyton! Now."

Upstairs, he heard the stomping of feet, and a grumpy voice hollered back. "All right!"

"Along those same lines…I had a conversation today with Peyton about stranger danger. Not to talk to men she doesn't know. Not to take candy from strangers or help them look for lost puppies. I hope I didn't cross a line by—"

"No! That's… I'm glad you did!" Grant blinked his surprise, and an odd warmth twined with the chill that wound around his heart at the thought of a predator coming after Peyton or Kaylee. Knowing that Amy cared enough about his girls to be proactive with Peyton, that she shared his concern for their safety, impressed him. He respected her all the more for her efforts. In fact, he felt—

A loud thud from the steps derailed his train of thought. He leaned back enough to peer into the entryway. Peyton's backpack lay at the foot of the stairs, clearly the victim of a little girl tantrum.

"Peyton! Get down here, now!"

"Grant, maybe this could wait until we are all in better moods? I mean, there are worse things than procrastinating on homework and talking back to a babysitter. Can't we let her slide tonight?" Amy put a hand on his arm, and the pleading in her eyes echoed her voiced appeal for leniency.

He shook his head. "Tracy always insisted that consistency is the key to parenting. If I let her off this time, it sets a bad precedent."

To his dismay, Amy's eyes filled with moisture. "But I feel responsible. I don't want to be the cause of any tension between you. I—"

"You're not." Grant didn't think about his next move, he simply acted.

One second Amy was looking at him with teary eyes, her voice cracking with emotion, and the next he'd pulled her close and kissed her forehead. Her arms wrapped around him, and he returned the gesture as she buried her face against his chest. He felt the shudder that raced through her, and he tightened his hold on her. If he were honest, he needed that hug as much as she did. He'd had a rotten day, and clearly Amy had, as well. Seeing as how she'd been watching his kids, he accepted responsibility for her distress.

Closing his eyes, he stroked her back and savored the embrace. He'd missed having someone to hold, having a woman's arms to lose himself in, a mutually safe place to take and provide refuge from life's worries. The peach scent of her shampoo teased his nose, and the soft press of her body against his nudged his libido. What he wouldn't give for some hot sex to work off the day's frustration and help him forget—

"She's not Mommy!" an angry voice said.

Chapter 9

Grant's heart contracted guiltily, and he snapped his head up.

Amy jerked free of his embrace and stumbled back awkwardly on her cast.

He reached for her, grabbing her elbows to steady her, but Amy waved him off. "I'm okay."

Bracing himself, he turned toward Peyton and met his daughter's hostile gaze. "No, she's not Mommy. I was hugging her because…she was worried about something. I wanted her to feel better."

Peyton crossed her arms over her chest, pouting. "She's *not* the boss of me."

Grant arched an eyebrow. Did this mean his daughter's anger was over Amy's punishment and not the hug? Relief loosened the knot in his chest, but he still harbored a twinge of guilt having been caught holding Amy. And for liking the embrace so much.

He swiped a hand over his face and sent Peyton a level glare. "I hear you didn't do your homework when Amy asked you to and that you were rude to her."

Peyton snarled at Amy. "Tattletale!"

Amy flinched. "Peyton, I'm sorry, but your dad—"

"I hate you! I thought you were my friend."

"Peyton Marie!" Grant stepped over to his daughter

and took her firmly by the arm. "That's enough. Apologize to Amy. Right now."

The tone of the voices in the room—or perhaps just her sore gums—started Kaylee whimpering. *Please, Lord, just one cranky child at a time.*

"No!" Peyton stomped her foot. "She *is* a tattletale, and I hate her! She can't tell me what to do 'cause she's not my mommy!"

He struggled to keep his voice calm and reasonable. "But she was the adult in charge while I was gone, and that gives her the authority to tell you what to do."

Peyton continued pouting.

"I'm waiting for that apology, young lady," he said.

"Grant, maybe——"

"No," he interrupted, before Amy cut his daughter any slack and an excuse to not obey. "She needs to learn manners and respect for adults." He squatted down to eye level with his stubborn daughter. "Peyton, apologize to Amy for being rude."

"No!"

Kaylee's whines grew louder, and Amy limped over to stroke his youngest's head in sympathy.

He ground his back teeth together and fought for patience. "No dinner, no TV and no computer games until you tell Amy you're sorry and also do your homework."

"What? That's not fair!" Peyton whined.

"It's up to you."

"Grant…" By Kaylee's high chair, Amy shifted her weight again, her tone uneasy.

He glanced back at her with a trust-me nod, even though his own gut was knotted. He hated playing the bad guy, the disciplinarian, but his mother assured him Peyton would love and respect him all the more for being firm with her. That kids needed boundaries to feel safe, blah, blah, blah…

All he really knew was that most days he felt as if he was groping blindly in the dark in regard to parenting, praying he was getting it right.

Peyton remained silent, glaring at him.

He huffed a sigh. "Fine. Go to your room, and don't come out until you are ready to say you're sorry and do your homework."

"I hate you, too! You're mean! I want Mommy!" Peyton ran from the room and pounded up the stairs to her room in tears.

I want Mommy, too. Grant dropped his chin to his chest, deflated, feeling like the worst father in Louisiana. A warm hand squeezed his shoulder, and he sobered quickly. He didn't want Amy seeing just how big of a mess he was. He drew a cleansing breath as he pushed to his feet and pasted on a fake smile for his houseguest. "Well, that was fun."

Amy had given Kaylee a toy to gnaw on, and the baby gummed it for all she was worth.

With a sheepish look, Amy stroked a hand down his arm in sympathy. "I feel like this is my fault. I started it by sending her to her room this after—"

He pressed a finger to her mouth. "Stop beating yourself up. Peyton has always been headstrong and ornery. She'll come around."

When she nodded, causing her lips to caress his finger, a bolt of electricity shot through him. A jolt of sexual awareness. His pulse jumping, he pulled his hand back and swallowed hard. He had no right to be attracted to Amy only a year after losing Tracy. He'd pledged Tracy his heart until death do us part.

But Tracy is dead, a renegade voice in his head taunted, *and you're not.*

"Let me go talk to her," Amy said softly, pulling him back to the moment.

He shook his head and stepped back, wiping suddenly damp palms on the seat of his khakis. "No. Not yet anyway. She, uh…" He cleared the thickness from his throat. "She needs time to think about her actions and calm down."

Amy twisted her mouth, and Grant had to drag his gaze away to avoid further lustful ideas regarding Amy's lips.

"Yeah, but she's also a little girl who's lost her mother and probably thinks I'm trying to take Tracy's place. I feel like I should reassure her that I'm not trying to replace her mother, that no one ever will."

Grant's chest contracted. Hadn't he just been close to imagining Amy taking Tracy's place in his bed? Fresh compunction and recriminations shot through him with a sobering coldness. When he didn't answer her, Amy added, "Remember, I lost my dad when I was young, and I know how lost you can feel, how betrayed you can feel when the other parent moves on with their life."

"You think Peyton feels I've betrayed her or her mom?" The notion horrified him. "I never want her to feel that I'm not 100 percent behind her and that she has all my love and—"

"I didn't say you *had* betrayed her." Amy put a hand on his forearm and squeezed. "And I don't know that that is even how she feels. I just think that since I've been there, since I lost a parent, too, that maybe if I talk to her, I can help her with anything she's going through."

"Thanks, but…it is possible that my daughter is just being the drama queen, cantankerous mule she's always been. Five dollars says, tomorrow this will all be for-gotten."

Amy tipped her head. "You really think so?"

Before he could answer, the stomp of feet on the stairs echoed through the house. Peyton stormed back into the kitchen wearing her Hello Kitty backpack and a scowl.

"I'm running away."

"Peyton…" Amy started, a plea in her tone.

Grant held up a hand to stop Amy. "You're sure about this? Wouldn't you rather just tell Amy you're sorry?"

"No! I'm running away. Forever!" His daughter nar-rowed a challenging glare on him, daring him to try to stop her.

Instead, familiar with the routine, he spread his hands and shrugged. "Okay. We'll miss you. You're welcome to come home whenever you're ready."

"Wh—? Grant?" Amy whispered, stunned.

He waved subtly to her, silently saying, *I've got this. Don't worry.*

"I'm not coming back!" Peyton stomped over to the pantry and pulled out a box of cookies.

"Hold on, missy," Grant said, taking the box from her as she tried to shove the treats in her backpack. "Cook-ies will spoil your dinner."

Thwarting her snack only heightened Peyton's ire. She growled, fists clenched as she tramped to the back door. "I hate you! Goodbye *forever*!"

Slam.

His daughter's melodrama wounded and frustrated Grant…but also caused a wry chuckle. Especially when Kaylee waved her chubby fingers toward the back door and chirped, "Buh bye."

In the past, he and Tracy had shared private chuckles over Peyton's theatrics. The child was the queen of hyperbole and emotionalism.

"Grant!" Amy fussed under her breath, hobbling to the back door window. "It's not funny. Stop her!"

"She's fine. She's 'run away'—" he made quotation marks in the air with his fingers "—dozens of time. She generally hides out in her playhouse for a couple of hours, until she either gets hungry or it starts getting dark. It gives her time to cool off. Her bedroom, her playhouse…all the same to me."

Amy shot him a worried look. "Are you sure?"

He nodded and plucked Kaylee from her high chair. "She'll be back by dinner."

But dinner came and went, and Peyton hadn't returned. When the sun started to sink below the tree line and cast long shadows on the yard, Grant caved. He headed out to Peyton's playhouse to fetch his daughter.

But the playhouse was empty.

Daddy was *so mean*. Amy was stupid and was *not* her mother! Peyton was still mad, even after sitting in the playhouse for a while. When she started getting hungry, she thought about going back inside, but she wasn't done being mad at Daddy and Amy.

Once Uncle Hunter had told her she could come to his house anytime she wanted. But Uncle Hunter was gone with his new wife on his honeymoon. She frowned and crossed her arms over her chest, feeling betrayed by Uncle Hunter, too. Everything was changing. Aunt Darby and Savannah had gone away with Uncle Connor. Mommy was dead. Daddy was sad all the time.

Her stomach growled, and she thought about all the good food Grandma always cooked when she was there. And Grandpa always took her for ice cream for dessert, even when Grandma made cake or cookies. He said grandkids were allowed to have both.

But Grandma and Grandpa lived in town. Too far to walk. Peyton thought hard. Maybe if she walked to her friend Olivia's house, she could use Olivia's cell phone to call Grandma to pick her up. Olivia was so lucky to have a cell phone.

She'd asked Daddy for one a couple of weeks ago, and he said seven-year-old girls didn't need cell phones. Meanie.

Peyton traipsed down their long driveway toward the road. She knew the way the bus went to get to Olivia's house, and she was sure she could walk there. It was a pretty long way, but she could do it. Daddy thought it was too far for her to walk alone, but she'd show him.

When she got to the end of her driveway, she saw a car she didn't recognize parked on the road. When she started walking along the side of the road, the car's headlights flicked on and the engine started. The car rolled up close to her, and the man inside called to her. She ignored him just as Amy had told her to and walked faster.

The man drove past her, parked on the side of the road in front of her and climbed out of the car.

Peyton stopped, her heart beating fast. Maybe she should turn around and go home.

The man looked all around as if he was looking for something, then walked toward her, fast.

She gasped and tried to run back toward the house, but the man caught her and clamped a hand over her mouth when she tried to scream. He had a smelly rag in his hand that he held over her nose. She wiggled and kicked, fighting to get away, but the man was so strong, and the funny smell made her head feel fuzzy. Sleepy...

Her head grew too heavy to hold up, and she closed her eyes. This was wrong. Bad. Scary...

Daddy, help!

Chapter 10

Grant spent the next hour searching the yard and the woods surrounding the house while simultaneously using his mobile phone to call his parents, the parents of Peyton's friends and his closest neighbors. No Peyton. She'd just…disappeared. He fought to keep the frantic beat of panic from crushing him. He had to stay in control, had to think clearly, despite the frenzied clawing of self-recrimination and worry inside him.

Within minutes of calling his parents to ask if Peyton had called them or shown up at their house, his mother and father were at his house joining his agitated pacing and offering advice.

Through it all, Amy was right beside him, keeping a level head and helping him in innumerable ways, even though her own concern was evident in her expression and the way she repeatedly finger-combed her hair. She offered reassuring hugs, took care of Kaylee's needs while he handled the crisis and traipsed on her broken ankle through the night-darkened woods with a flashlight, calling for his daughter. Even when it started raining, Amy stuck by him, searching the property surrounding his house. Even when they'd covered each inch of his home and Peyton's playhouse twice, she helped him hunt for his daughter. Even when he didn't realize it was what he needed, she volunteered exactly the right thing at the right moment.

Amy and his parents were a blessing, because all he could think about was Peyton and how he'd messed up, letting an upset little girl run away from home. Amy only left his side for a moment to make a private phone call. Grant watched her step into the next room to dial her cell, a dark look in her eyes, then immediately hang up without speaking when the phone was answered. Momentary relief filled her face before she rejoined him and his parents.

"Who was that?" he asked as she sat next to him.

She shook her head and gave him a half smile. "Just a crazy theory. But I was wrong."

When, having searched the woods, the house and the barn and calling everyone he could think of turned up nothing, Grant dug his truck keys out of his pocket. "I'm going to drive the roads, check the nearest businesses, show her picture around."

His father stood from the couch. "I'll do the same and cover the businesses to the south."

"Wait, Stan." His mother sent his father a silent message through a look that she'd no doubt perfected through forty-one years of marriage. Turning then to Grant, she said, "Don't you think it's time to call the police, honey? It has been more than ninety minutes since you realized she was gone. Time is crucial in these cases."

These cases. Grant's knees buckled, and he slumped into the recliner. A tremor rolled through him. Calling the police was the wise thing to do, but seeking help from the authorities meant admitting Peyton was…*missing*. Officially, gut-wrenchingly, back-of-milk-carton missing.

Nausea swamped him, and it was all he could do to

keep his supper down. Amy sat on the arm of the recliner and scooped his hand between hers. He turned a desperate look to her, praying she'd have an alternate suggestion that would make more sense, that would be the answer to finding his daughter and setting things right.

But her eyes held the same bleak resignation that his parents' did. "She's right. It's time. Past time."

His gut roiled, guilt and despair hammering him. *Oh, Tracy, I'm so sorry. I lost our little girl. It's my fault. I failed you. Failed to keep her safe like I promised. Failed to protect her like I failed to protect you.*

He swallowed hard, tasting the bile that inched up his throat, and gave a weak nod.

Numb with the ramifications of the evening, certain he had to be caught up in a nightmare he couldn't wake from, Grant stared blankly as his father dialed the phone.

"Yes, we need to report a missing child…"

Officer Smith of the Lagniappe PD responded to the initial call. Officer Smith took the missing person report and drank several cups of the coffee Amy brewed to keep them going through the night. When he realized the gravity of the situation, he called in backup, and additional officers reported to Grant's house to take statements and organize the release of alerts to state agencies. The officers questioned each of the adults separately, their questions clearly looking for family involvement. While Grant understood eliminating the family as suspects was routine police procedure, stemming from the sad truth that most cases of missing children turned out to involve immediate family members, he hated the delay. His baby was out there, somewhere, alone. Scared. Possibly injured…or worse. His brain shied away from darker scenarios. He simply couldn't entertain the possibility of losing Peyton without going insane.

His parents were equally worried, and by midnight, his mother had called Hunter in Hawaii to break the bad news. His brother had promised to be on the first flight they could get home, cutting his honeymoon short by a couple of days. Not for the first time, Grant wished Connor and Darby were still around. His family had pulled him through the early days of Tracy's death, and he knew that until Peyton was home safely, his family would be his lifeline.

What he hadn't expected, but didn't really find all that surprising in hindsight, was how much he leaned on Amy through the wee hours of the night. She lifted his morale when she sensed his spirits flagging. With her gentle touch and uncanny anticipation of his needs, whether more coffee or a pen at the ready when he had to sign papers or a word of encouragement, she proved a rock that he depended on again and again throughout the night. But more than her assistance with mundane tasks or attempts to bolster his mood, he treasured her simple presence. Knowing she was *there*, being able to reach for her hand or exchange a look or share his thoughts, made him feel less *alone*. Sure, his parents and the police were there. His living room was full of people, but he felt a connection to Amy that was different. That was special. A connection that scared him with its depth and its value. Because too soon she would be gone.

The first watery rays of daylight were filtering through the curtains in his kitchen before Officer Smith and his cohorts had all the information they needed to start a search for Peyton. Missing child alerts had been issued, the media contacted and the proper agencies put on notice. Plans were in the works for a formal search party, including scent-tracking dogs, to return to Grant's house by early afternoon. With promises to keep Grant posted on their progress, warnings not to take rash actions and instructions to keep phone lines open in case of a ransom, the police left Grant's house, and a chilling silence overtook him and his family. Outside, the patter of rain added an ambience of gloom.

Grant faced the room with a silent question echoing in his head. *Now what?*

"Why don't you try to get some rest, sweetheart?" his mother asked. "We'll manage things down here."

He scrubbed hands over his face and groaned. He couldn't possibly sleep knowing Peyton was still missing. He had to *do* something.

"No, I want to search the woods again. Now that it's daylight again, maybe we'll see something we missed last night."

His mother glanced out the window. "It's still raining. Why don't you wait until—"

"Wait?" he barked, letting his fatigue and anxiety sharpen his tone. "I don't care if it's pouring boiling acid from the sky. My baby is out there, and I have to do something! I have to find her!"

"Son…" His father stepped close and put a hand on his shoulder. Stan Mansfield's expression both scolded him for the tone Grant took with his mother and empathized with his pain and panic.

Grant cursed under his breath. "Sorry, Mom."

She shot him an understanding smile.

"I know the police will be back to search this afternoon. But I *am* going out in the woods now. I can't sit still. I have to…" He let his sentence trail off and shook his head when he heard the first peeps from his youngest, waking upstairs. "I have to do something with Kaylee. I can't drag her out in the woods in this weather."

"Let us watch her," his mother volunteered quickly. "We'll take her back to our house where she can nap and have her lunch on schedule and you can focus on finding Peyton. Dad's gotta pick up Hunter and Brianna at the airport in about an hour, and he can come back with them after that to help you look."

A combination of guilt and relief tangled in Grant's gut. He hated that his crisis meant his brother had cut his honeymoon short, but Hunter had military training that might serve them well in their search for Peyton.

His mother went upstairs to retrieve Kaylee from her crib and kissed the girl's cheek as she carried her into the living room. "Come on, little bit. Want to go to Granny's?"

"Nanny?"

His mother's eyes watered as she smiled at Kaylee. "That's right, sweetie. Nanny's house."

"Thanks, Mom."

His dad pulled out his keys and gave Grant a supportive squeeze on the shoulder. "I'll be back as soon as I can get your brother from the airport. Hang in there. We'll find her." Stan nodded to Amy as he led Julia out to their minivan.

"Well," Amy said, casting a wary eye to the sky. "Maybe we should get going while there is a break in the rain? The radar shows bigger storms headed this way."

Grant heaved himself up from the sofa. His limbs felt like lead, weighted down with worry and grief and dread of what he might find in the woods. Or not find. He hesitated as he made his way to the back door, remembering something that sent a chill to his bones.

"Tracy's last words to me were a warning to keep

a close eye on Peyton," he said under his breath. He closed his eyes as a sense of failure and disappointment washed over him. "She was worried about Peyton getting hurt because she'd already started showing her fearless, adventurous nature." His throat tightened. "I promised Tracy I would keep Peyton safe. It was the last promise I made to her and now—"

He stopped as his voice cracked. Damn it, the last thing he wanted was to have a breakdown in front of Amy. He didn't have time to indulge in self-pity, but the pain of having let Tracy down, having let Peyton down, scraped through him and left him raw.

Amy said nothing at first, but she stepped close to him and gave him a bear hug from behind, wrapping her arms around his chest and resting her chin on his shoulder. She squeezed him tight and held on. In the silence of the following moments, Grant covered her hand with his and took a few restorative breaths. Amy's embrace said more than anything she could verbalize.

When everyone else seemed delayed, distracted or preoccupied, Amy was there for him. Her friendship had come to mean so much to him in just a few days. Sure, he recognized his physical attraction to her for what it was, but he'd also grown close to Amy on a personal level that went far deeper than sexual chemistry. That connection scared him. He only had this sort of connection with one other person in his life. Tracy.

He hated to think of losing Amy, losing this connection in a couple of weeks when she returned to her home in the Northwest. But at this moment, one of the lowest in his life, having her support, her companionship, her assistance meant the world to him.

"Let's go bring your little girl home," Amy whispered, her breath tickling his ear.

"Right." He gave her hand a final squeeze before heading out to the backyard and bracing against the cold wind that whipped in from the approaching storms.

The sky was a mass of roiling gray clouds, and Grant's gut tightened. If they didn't find Peyton soon, his baby girl would be out in the elements when the worst of the storms hit.

"Peyton!" he called as he marched toward the line of trees that bordered the lawn. "Peyton Marie!"

Amy hobbled beside him, cupping her hands around her mouth and adding her voice to the calls for Peyton. The late spring had painted the woods in every imaginable shade of green. Every scrub bush and tree sprouted new leaves, and tiny wildflowers dotted the landscape with yellow, violet and white. If he weren't sick with worry about his daughter, Grant might have enjoyed the beauty of the scene. Instead, the new lush foliage and touches of bright color made the search more difficult. Had it been winter, the bare tree branches would not have encumbered his view, and Peyton's brightly colored clothes would have stood out among the dull browns and grays of the dormant woods.

"Peyton!" he shouted so loudly his throat started to hurt. After two hours of combing the forest, his voice had started to sound raspy, but an achy throat and scratchy voice wouldn't stop him. He'd stay out here yelling Peyton's name until his vocal cords bled if it would bring his daughter home safely.

They'd hiked about two miles into the woods in a somewhat zigzag fashion, when Amy stopped and leaned against a tree, taking her weight off her injured foot. She waved at him to keep going. "Don't mind me. My cast has rubbed a blister, and I just need a moment to rest. I'll catch up."

He shook his head. "We can stop for a minute." He scanned the area and huffed a sigh. "In fact, I think it'd be smart to loop around that way—" he waved his hand to the south "—and start making our way back toward the house. I just can't imagine she'd make it this far. She's stubborn, but she's smart enough not to go this far from our yard."

Amy's look said, *Evidence would suggest otherwise.*

He gritted his teeth and squared his shoulders. "I know my daughter. I know how it looks, but the fact that she's not answering, that we can't find her near the house tells me something happened. She's hurt or lost or…" *Kidnapped.* He swallowed hard, unable to vocalize the dread building in his gut. The anxious look on Amy's face said she was thinking the same thing.

He recalled the leering smile of William Gale when he walked out of the courtroom, and a chill swept over him. Grant simply couldn't write off Peyton going missing days after Gale's release as coincidence. Grant closed his eyes and said a prayer. Because if William Gale was to blame for Peyton's disappearance, his daughter was in more danger than he'd originally feared.

Even though she'd called her mother's house last night and David had answered, Amy began doubting her original belief that his being home when Peyton first disappeared cleared him of suspicion. Who knew how long Peyton had been gone before she called the house. Could he have abducted her, stashed her somewhere and returned home before Amy had called?

Yes, she decided with a knot in her chest. Easily. If David took Peyton, Amy thought as they made their way back toward the house, the little girl was in more danger than Grant knew. Not that she thought David would physically hurt Peyton, but if he molested her, the scars of that abuse would haunt the child for years to come.

And if that scenario were true, Amy would never forgive herself for not having told Grant sooner about the monster living down the highway from him. The lump that sat in Amy's chest made it hard to breathe. She needed to call her mother's house again, follow up on her suspicion, if only to ease her own doubts and worry so she could concentrate more fully on the search.

When the house came into view again through the boughs of late-spring leaves, she cast a side glance at Grant. "What do you say before we search the woods to the south, we take a bathroom break? Maybe grab a snack to refuel?" And steal a moment alone to call her mother and check up on David's whereabouts and activities for the past twenty-four hours.

A muscle in Grant's jaw twitched. In his expression she could read the battle between his reluctance to stop searching and his sense of the practical. He looked up at the clouds, which grew steadily thicker and darker. A light rain had begun to spit at them, and the air was already a good ten degrees cooler. The storm front was almost upon them.

"All right. But just for a minute. I want to check the radar, see where the worst weather is now, and call my parents to check in. Maybe Peyton's called them."

Amy doubted that was the case. If his parents had heard from Peyton they'd have called Grant's cell, which he'd been checking for calls or texts every two minutes as they hiked.

When they reached the house, Amy availed herself of the restroom, found a Band-Aid for her blister and grabbed a granola bar for herself and one for Grant out of the pantry. She peeked into the living room, where

Grant had the television turned to the weather station and the phone pressed to his ear while he paced the floor. "We searched the woods to the northeast and didn't find anything. Now we're headed out to the south side…No." Pause. "We will. Yeah, it's closing in fast, but I think we have maybe thirty minutes…"

Amy backed toward the kitchen door. She only had a moment before Grant would finish his call and would want to start searching again. But a minute was all she needed to confirm or allay her fears.

As Amy limped back out onto the back deck, the wind whipped her hair into her face and roared through the leaves of the surrounding trees. The rumble of distant thunder struck an ominous chord as she settled on the deck steps and pulled out her cell phone. Saying a silent prayer that she was wrong about her stepfather's involvement, Amy called her mother's house and waited anxiously for someone to pick up.

Grant disconnected the call to his mother and went into the kitchen looking for Amy. He'd heard her milling about in here moments earlier, but the kitchen was empty. He filled a glass with water from the sink and took a long drink to soothe his throat and stared out the kitchen window at the backyard. *Where are you, Peyton? Why haven't you come home?*

Acid churned in his gut, and he sent a silent plea heavenward. *Watch over our girl, Trace. I'm sorry I let you down. I promise I'll do better, if you'll just help me get her back safe and sound. Please, God, bring Peyton home safely. I'll do any—*

The shrill of the house phone interrupted his petition, and he hurried back into the living room to grab the cordless extension there, praying for good news about his daughter.

"Hello?"

"Grant Mansfield?" a male voice asked.

"Yes." A prickle of foreboding crawled down his spine. "Who is this?"

"William Gale."

Chapter 11

Amy released the anxious breath she'd been holding when her mother answered instead of David. "Mom, it's Amy."

"Amy, honey." Her mother sounded relieved to hear from her. "I'm so sorry about the fight we had. Are you back in Idaho?" Amy blinked, surprised. "David didn't tell you?"

"Tell me what?"

"I'm still in Lagniappe. I'm staying with a friend. Just down the road, in fact. David saw me the other day. You mean he didn't tell you?"

"Well, no. I guess he just forgot."

Yeah, right. That's the reason he didn't say anything.

"Listen, Mom, is David there?"

Her mother hesitated. "Why do you want to speak to him?"

"I *don't* want to talk to him. I just need to know if he's there at the house."

Another pause. "Why? What's going on?"

"A little girl is missing—the daughter of the guy I'm staying with, in fact."

"Oh no! How terrible," her mother said, then, "Wait a minute. What does this have to do with David? Are you accusing him of something?"

"I'm not accusing him of anything." *Yet.* "I just need to know if he's there. I'm trying to rule out all the possibilities. I'm trying to find Peyton."

"Well, I can assure you David has nothing to do with it," her mother replied, her tone reflecting the insult she took.

Frustration and a familiar sense of betrayal—how could her mother side with that jerk?—filled her. She pushed the twist of emotion aside. What mattered now was Peyton, getting her back home safely. "Answer the question, Mom. Is David there? Has he left the house today, even for a little while?" Her mother hesitated again, and Amy's skin prickled. Her mother was covering for him. She could sense it.

"No, he's not here. He went to run some errands for me. We wanted to get a few things before the storm hit."

Her gut tightening, Amy asked, "How long has he been gone? When did he leave? Was he gone last night around supper time?"

"Amy, he doesn't have anything to do with that girl going missing," her mother said, her voice cold and angry.

"Are you sure, Mom?" Amy's temper flared as well, rooted in a protective love for Peyton. She could understand the mama-bear instinct to defend her young when she thought of Grant's girls being in danger. "Are you sure enough to stake that little girl's life, her innocence on it?"

"That's insane! David's not a kidnapper! Don't you dare start making false accusations again, trying to cause trouble."

Amy opened her mouth to deny the accusations were false, that she had cause for her assumptions, that the "trouble" in the past had started with David. But she'd sung that song before and repeating the same refrain didn't change her mother's mind, it seemed. "Whatever. Just ask David about Peyton Mansfield when he gets home." She struggled to keep her tone even, when what she wanted to do was scream. Or cry. Or shatter from the frustration and tension that had built up inside her over the years. Gritting her teeth, she said, "She's seven years old. Long blond hair. Red jacket and blue tennis shoes. Please keep your eyes open for her or anything that can help us locate her."

Her mother huffed a sigh. "Of course we will. Let us know if we can help any other way. Putting up posters, making calls, anything."

She knew her mom was sincere in her offer. Her mother genuinely cared about people, loved animals, had a compassionate heart. But her blind spot regarding David, her inability to accept the truth about her own daughter's pain…

Stop it. That's the past. Peyton is what matters now. "Thank you," she said with a formal coolness. "Good-bye." She disconnected the call, her hand shaking, and closed her eyes.

David was out "running errands." Which meant he could be anywhere. He *could* have Peyton. Maybe she was being paranoid, but—how could she *not* suspect him? And if even the remotest chance existed that Peyton was with David, that the girl was in danger, didn't she have to pursue the possibility?

Which meant she had to come clean with Grant. She had to tell him about her past, about David's sexual abuse. Just the idea of talking about that stain on her teen years made her palms sweat. She'd never talked with anyone outside of her mother, court-appointed counselors and law enforcement about what happened.

She didn't want her friends' image of her tarnished with the truth of her abuse. She didn't want the pitying looks, the whispers and speculation about her "asking for it," the crude innuendos, the awkward distance, the unspoken stigma. And most of all she didn't want to risk having her friends call her a liar. Her own mother hadn't believed her.

Law enforcement officials had kept a professional detachment when she finally reported David. The psychologist assigned by the state had been sympathetic and had testified on her behalf, but she'd never confided in anyone close to her. She'd kept her secret to herself throughout high school and had never mentioned it to any of her new friends in Idaho. David's trial had even been moved to a different city to protect her identity. No one in Lagniappe knew what she'd been through, and that was how she wanted it.

But for Peyton's sake, she would bare her soul, her private hell and darkest secret to Grant. Before she lost her courage, she pushed awkwardly to her feet and clumped with her bulky cast back into the house.

A chill slithered through Grant. *William Gale?* "What the hell do you want?"

"A better question might be what do *you* want?" William said. "For example, do you want your daughter back in one piece?"

Grant's gut gave a violent lurch. "Wh-what?"

"She's here with me, and I'd like to discuss a trade."

Shuddering, Grant gripped the phone tighter. "She's with you? You mean you kidnapped her!" Icy fear and simmering rage surged simultaneously, leaving him shaking and sweating at the same time. "If you hurt her," he grated through clenched teeth, barely able to keep the bile from rising in his throat to choke him, "I will kill you myself and dance on your grave, you bastard."

"You're in no position to make threats, Grant."

His skin crawled hearing William address him as if they were best friends. "Let me talk to her."

"Aren't you interested in hearing the terms of her return?"

"Let me talk to her!" Grant shouted, quivering. "I need to know you really have her and that she's not hurt before I make any deal."

William was silent for a moment, then said, "Fine."

Grant held his breath, waiting, listening. Through the phone, he heard shuffling sounds, footsteps, creaking doors. His heart pounded so hard he thought it might burst through his chest. He heard a low male mumble, then, "Daddy?"

Tears rushed to his eyes. "Peyton! Baby, are you all right?"

"I'm scared, Daddy. I wanna come home," she cried.

"I'm gonna get you home, sweetie. I promise."

"Hurry, Daddy." Peyton's tears broke his heart.

"I love you, Peyton. Be brave for me. I—"

"That's enough." William was back on the line, and in the background, he heard Peyton wail, "Daddy!"

"Put her back on! I'm not through talking to her!"

"Yes, you are."

"Listen here, you monster…" Grant would have reached through the phone and strangled Gale if he could have, simply for terrorizing his little girl. "If you hurt her, I'll—"

"Yes. You'll kill me. So you've said," William interrupted. "Enough threats. It's time to talk about my terms."

* * *

Amy nibbled her bottom lip as she crossed the deck and paused briefly at the kitchen door.

Would the truth change Grant's opinion of her? Would knowledge of her past douse whatever chemistry they had? If so, maybe telling him was for the best. She couldn't start a fling with him, however short-lived, if his attraction to her was based on a lie.

When Stella was repaired, she had no excuse to stay in Lagniappe any longer. She would stay until Peyton was found, of course. She couldn't walk out on Grant in the middle of a crisis. And if David *was* behind the little girl's disappearance, then she needed to stay and do everything in her power to see her stepfather put back behind bars. Peyton would need counseling, a friend to confide in. Grant would need her support—assuming he was even speaking to her, since she was the reason David had hurt Peyton.

Okay, you're getting ahead of yourself. She lumbered up the back-porch steps and calmed her racing mind as she pulled open the kitchen door. She didn't *know* that David had Peyton. That was just a theory. A possibility.

Please, God, don't let David have her.

Grant wasn't in the kitchen, and the house was eerily quiet. "Grant?"

"In here."

She followed the sound of his voice toward the front rooms, checking his study and the dining room. The hardwood floors creaked, a hollow, lonely sound that echoed in the still house as she plodded from one room to the next.

When she found Grant sitting in the living room, she could tell right away something had changed. Grant's skin had a ghastly pallor, and he wore a stricken expression as he stared into near space.

Her stomach pitched. "Grant? What is it? What's happened?"

He didn't look at her, only let the cordless phone in his hand tumble onto the coffee table. "I had a call."

A chill shimmied through her, as she imagined the worst. She moved on wobbly knees to the nearest chair. "The police? Did they…find her?"

He shook his head slowly, his eyes sliding closed. "No. A ransom call."

Nausea churned inside her. Ransom. Did that mean David *had* taken her? If so, then Peyton's kidnapping was on Amy's head. She'd led David here. She was to blame if—

Grant looked up at her at last, his eyes bleak. "It's just as I feared. Gale has her. William Gale took Peyton as leverage."

A shiver of relief chased through her. Not David! It wasn't her fault! That was quickly followed by the gut-wrenching truth of what Grant had said. *Oh, God. Peyton was with crime boss William Gale!*

"You said he asked for ransom." She swallowed hard, trying to remember how much she had in her savings account. She'd give it all to Grant if it would help bring Peyton back. "How much money does he want?"

Grant heaved a burdened sigh. "Not money. He wants revenge."

"What?" She shook her head, confused.

"He said if we want Peyton back, that I have to get him a private face-to-face meeting with Connor."

"Your brother that's in WitSec?"

He nodded stiffly.

She flopped back in the chair digesting the information. "Do you think Connor will agree to a meeting?"

Grant nodded, his face dented with certainty. "Absolutely. Connor would do anything for his family. He loves Peyton."

When Grant's expression remained grim, she followed the situation to the next step, and her pulse slowed, seeing the problem. "But he's in WitSec. So...how do you reach him? How do you arrange something like that?"

Grant's Adam's apple worked up and down as he swallowed. "I can't."

Chapter 12

Amy said nothing for long moments.

"You wanted me for something?" Grant said, refocusing his attention, with effort. As frightening as it was to know Peyton was with William Gale, at least he had answers. And he had information he could take to the police.

"Um…" She looked away, rubbing her hands on the legs of her pants. She seemed nervous.

Grant pivoted on the couch to face her. "Amy, is something wrong?"

She laughed stiffly. "You mean besides Peyton being kidnapped?"

"I mean, you were looking for me. Was there something you want to say? A reason you need me?"

She wet her lips and took a deep breath. Then shook her head. "Never mind. It will keep."

He eyed her, concerned. She looked really agitated over something. "You sure?"

"Yeah. Forget it." She blew out a big breath, forced a stiff smile and shoved back to her feet. "Have you reported the ransom call to the cops?"

"Um…" He blinked hard and pinched the bridge of his nose. "Not yet. I just got off the phone with Gale."

"Oh. Well…" She backed toward the kitchen. "I'll

start a pot of coffee while you call the police. That Officer Smith really likes his java, huh?"

He grunted, his mind already going back to the few precious seconds he'd had to talk to Peyton. She was scared. His heart ached knowing that, knowing he couldn't hold her and soothe her.

But she was alive. At least he could stop worrying that she'd been hit by a car or killed in some other freak accident. But mother of God…William Gale? The man had no compunction about taking lives to further his cause or exact his revenge. Tracy was proof of that.

He pulled out his cell phone to call Officer Smith and got the man's voice mail. He left a message, summarizing the call and asking the officer to call him back—as if the man wouldn't respond to this dramatic lead in Peyton's disappearance. Blowing out an anxious breath, he dropped his cell on the coffee table and stood to pace.

Was there any chance in hell that the US Marshals who'd hidden Connor and Darby would get a message to him? Connor had come out of hiding once to save his own daughter's life. Would he come back to Lagniappe again to save Peyton?

Of course he would. As he'd told Amy, Connor loved Peyton and would do anything for his family. Even risk his own life. But how did he find his brother? And was there another option he was missing?

He rambled into the kitchen where Amy was starting a pot of coffee and dragged both hands through his hair as he staggered to the kitchen door. Staring out the door's window to the sprawling backyard, he mumbled, "Guess we don't need to go back out and search to the south now."

She hummed her agreement, adding, "Probably a good thing. The sky looks really nasty."

Grant's gaze locked on Peyton's playhouse at the far back corner of his property. He thought about the other times Peyton had "run away" and how he'd find her playing in her playhouse a couple of hours later, her indignation over whatever had upset her already forgotten.

His heart wrenched. Would Peyton ever play in her house again? She was in the hands of William Freaking Gale! If he touched one hair on her h—

He slammed his eyes shut and stopped the negative thought in its tracks. Tracy had always believed in the power of positive thinking, in sending out the vibes and energy you wanted to surround yourself with. *Negative only feeds negative,* she'd say.

"What did Officer Smith say?" Amy asked.

He sucked in a few deep breaths, trying to calm his racing heart. *Positive. Think positive.*

What would Tracy say, do, focus on at a time like this? *Help me, Tracy.*

"Grant? Are you all right?"

He startled when Amy touched his shoulder. "I…yeah. I just…"

Without really thinking about where he was going or why, he yanked open the back door and stalked out. He hurried down the deck steps and strode across the backyard. He made a beeline for the playhouse, needing to feel Peyton close to him, wanting to surround himself with the sweet memories associated with his daughter's happy place.

He barely noticed the fat raindrops pelting him or the wind kicking up. He just needed an escape. Time to pull himself together.

Twisting the knob on the playhouse door, he ducked his head to enter the miniature building, and stooped over, he walked to the center of the playroom. Still unable to stand up straight, he crouched and took in the small chairs and table littered with coloring books, the shelf where Peyton had put her soccer trophy, a plastic storage bin full of toys and a contraband box of chocolate chip cookies. The walls had been painted yellow and blue, Peyton's choice, and a true reflection of both sides of her nature. One minute a girlie girl and the next a tomboy.

Turning, he spotted a new addition to the walls, a One Direction poster with a red heart drawn by one member of the boy band. Since when did Peyton care about boy bands? Or boys? Geez, she was only seven.

Rain had soaked his hair, and now dripped on his face as he took in the other additions to the playhouse, including a box under the wooden table. The corner of a familiar blanket hung over the side of the cardboard box, and Grant sat on the floor and dragged the box to him. Peyton's old blanket, her "binky," was on top, and he pulled it out and held it to his nose. Hadn't they moved her binky to a box in the attic when she outgrew it? The scent of baby shampoo clung to the blanket in addition to a new fruity scent that smelled a lot like Peyton's favorite flavor of Kool-Aid. Under the blanket he found another item that should have been in the attic storage, an old doll Tracy had given Peyton as a baby. Beneath the doll was a T-shirt. One of Tracy's T-shirts, he realized, and a jolt kicked his heart.

At the bottom of the box was a framed picture of Tracy holding Peyton when she was a baby, a photo that had been in Peyton's room for years. How could he have not noticed the picture was missing from her nightstand?

His shoulders dropped as he realized what this odd collection was. Peyton's comfort box. Memories of her mother, her old snuggly binky, the soft little doll she used to sleep with. His daughter was a little girl who missed her mother, who needed familiar things and comfort from her babyhood to help her cope with her loss.

Why had he not known she'd brought all these things out to her playhouse? That she was still hurting, confused and needing something to cling to? Had he been so wrapped up in his own busy life, his own grief, his loss that he'd missed the signs of how much his daughter needed him? Apparently. Fresh waves of guilt and frustration poured over him, and he clutched the binky and the picture of Tracy to his chest. And let the tears he'd held at bay for the past year fill his eyes.

Amy stared out the back window, watching the storm worsen and debating whether to go after Grant. She understood his need to be alone. Maybe to cuss a while. Or pray. Or just pull himself together in the wake of such worrisome, frightening news.

He never said whether the police were on their way out to take a statement or if they had any advice or instructions. He hadn't said much of anything before he stormed out into the rain and disappeared into Peyton's little house at the far corner of the yard.

Amy sipped a mug of the coffee she'd made as she mulled her next move. Cinderella wove around her legs and mewed softly asking for her lunch.

"Good girl, Cinderella. I'll get your food in a second." As Amy stooped to give the cat a pat, lightning flashed outside, followed immediately by an earsplitting clap of thunder. Cinderella bolted from the kitchen to hide under the coffee table in the living room. Amy, too, felt a bit jumpy, especially when her cell phone began screeching the emergency services warning tone. She silenced the phone and read the weather warning her service carrier had sent. Severe thunderstorm warning for their parish. She snorted. No kidding? Then she stilled as she continued reading. The parish just to the south had a tornado warning. The super cell containing tornadic activity was headed their way.

What was Grant's word? *Skunk.*

She set the phone down on the kitchen table and hobbled to the back door. Surely, having heard the thunder, Grant would head back to the house now? But he still didn't come, and Amy began to worry. Not just because of the weather, but because of the turmoil Grant had to be going through. She'd given him time alone, but now, with the weather growing dire, she decided she needed to check on him, to warn him about the weather alerts if nothing else.

Ignoring the fact that she'd get her cast wet, Amy grabbed an umbrella from beside the front door and headed out to the backyard. The wind whipped around her and tugged on the umbrella as she plodded through the pouring rain and rumbling thunder toward the playhouse.

"Grant?" she called, even though the driving rain and wind almost certainly drowned her out. A powerful gust hit her just as she neared the playhouse and inverted the umbrella, even as the force of the wind ripped it from her hands. Amy gasped and chose to abandon the umbrella, instead hurrying to the shelter of the playhouse. She gave only a brief warning knock before she trundled inside the miniature structure and fought the door shut behind her.

She swiped rain from her face as she turned, hunched over in deference to the low ceiling, and spotted Grant sitting on the floor, his back leaning against a wall.

"Hey," she said, raking her wet hair back from her eyes. "I got worried when you didn't come back."

He nodded. "I was gonna wait out the rain."

"Oh…right." She gave him a sheepish grin. "Good thinking." She raised her hands to indicate her soaked clothes and chuckled. "I started with an umbrella but… it's somewhere in the woods now. Sorry. I'll buy you a new one."

He lowered his gaze to the floor again and shook his head. "Forget it."

"No. I broke it, so I'll—" She stopped as she glanced around the playhouse. "Holy cow! She has carpeting in here? And crown molding?" Amy gaped as she stepped farther into the room and cast her gaze around. "It's like a little house!"

"Yeah. Exactly like a little house," Grant said without looking up. "The best Mansfield Construction has to offer. From the concrete slab and treated hardwood studs to the asphalt shingles on the roof, Peyton's house is everything we'd do for a customer but scaled to three hundred square feet."

Amy gave a marveling laugh. "Wow. Lucky girl. Having a construction company in the family has perks, huh?"

"I wouldn't call her lucky." Grant's voice was dark and quiet. "She lost her mother when she was six. She's been kidnapped by a convicted felon with a grudge against her family. And she has a father who's so blind to her pain she has to turn to her dead mother's T-shirt for comfort." He held up a blue T-shirt before letting his hand drop to his side again.

Oo-kay. Grant was in a worse way than she'd imagined.

Amy cleared her throat and shuffled over to him.

Bracing a hand on his shoulder for support, she lowered herself to the floor beside him and stuck her cast out in front of her. "Want to talk about it?"

He drew and released a heavy breath.

"Grant?" She wrapped her hand around his and laced their fingers. "Clearly, this is about more than Peyton's kidnapping. What's going on? What's with the shirt?"

"It's Tracy's. Peyton brought it out here, along with other stuff we'd stored in the attic from when she was a baby."

Lightning flickered again, and when the accompanying thunder quieted, Amy said, "Maybe we should discuss this back in the house? I came out here to tell you the worst weather is about to hit. I just got a warning about tornadoes southwest of here."

"Tornadoes?" Grant raised his head finally, and she met his gaze.

The whites of his eyes were bloodshot, and his lashes were damp. Had he been crying? The notion shook her. Grant always seemed so...strong. So stoic, despite the weight of worries he carried.

Before she could answer, the sound of the rain changed. Grew louder.

She rolled to her knees to look out the window. Tiny pebbles of hail bounced in the grass and clattered on the roof.

"Uh-oh." She glanced back at Grant. "Hail. Shall we make a run for it?"

He furrowed his brow and crawled up next to her. "If not for your cast, I might say yes, but..." He grunted. "Even pea-size hail like that hurts like the dickens when it hits."

Larger balls of ice, some as big as nickels, struck just

outside the window and the racket from the roof became deafening.

"Okay, that'd be a no," Amy said, chuffing a humorless laugh. "I vote we stay put until the hail clears out at least. You did say the playhouse was quality construction, right. Solid? Secure?"

He rocked back onto his butt again and rested his head against the wall. "Yeah. We'll be fine here until the hail blows over."

Amy continued watching the pounding hail, mesmerized by the force of nature. "Thank goodness Stella is in your barn. This is brutal. I hope your truck is insured."

Grant hummed distractedly. Hail damage was clearly not his biggest concern. At that moment, the storm was merely an ill-timed delay in finding his daughter and getting her back from her captor.

Amy knew finding some of Tracy's possessions here in the playhouse had played a part in Grant's dark mood, layering on more heartache when he least needed it. She was weighing what, if anything, she could say to support him and ease his worry, when a loud thump on the outside wall drew her attention back to the scene out the window. A large branch from one of the tall hardwoods bordering Grant's lawn had fallen and smacked the playhouse.

"Yikes. That was close." She cast a glance back at Grant. "A branch fell and almost hit the window."

He nodded but didn't look up.

Concerned about Grant but equally bothered by the powerful storm, Amy turned back to the window. The sky had an eerie greenish cast that sent a prickle down her spine, but of greater concern was the tumble of odd-looking debris. Someone's trash maybe? Or...*insulation*.

A chill sliced to her marrow. "Grant, you should come take a look at this."

Her frightened tone must have resonated with him, because he scrambled over to kneel beside her.

She squinted at the yard, double-checking her suspicion, and her heart sank. Scraps of wood, pink insulation, and roofing materials swirled in a macabre dance. *Swirled...*

The truth clicked at the same moment Grant yanked her back from the window and shoved her to the floor. "Tornado!"

Heart pounding, she scuttled with Grant toward the tiny wood table where Peyton's drawings sat. The table was too small to cover more than their heads and chests, but she was grateful for even that much protection. The roar of wind and crash of debris escalated to a deafening level.

Grant rolled her beneath him, just as the glass window shattered. With a startled gasp, Amy buried her face in his chest.

"Hold on to me! Don't let go!" he shouted in her ear.

As if she needed his instruction. Her fingers were curled in a death grip on the front of Grant's shirt, but as the suction and swirl of the funnel cloud neared, she locked her arms around him clutching his back. She squeezed her eyes shut, protecting them from the flying glass, twigs and scraps of building material caught in the raging wind. A loud crack sounded near them, above the din of the wind, spiking Amy's pulse. Within seconds, she heard another crash. The playhouse shook, then something hard struck her legs as the world seemed to collapse around her.

Grant jerked as he cried out, clearly in pain.

"Grant!"

"Hang on!" he shouted, his grip tightening on her. "I've got you."

Cold rain splattered her, and strong gusts carrying shrapnel-like shards of glass and splintered wood pelted her. Even without opening her eyes, she knew the playhouse roof had been ripped off or caved in. Their protection from the wrath of the tornado was gone.

Chapter 13

Adrenaline coursed through Amy, shaking her as hard from the inside as the storm lashed her on the outside. The terror of howling wind and the chaos of storm-tossed debris ravaged them for what seemed, impossibly, both a mind-numbing eternity and a devastating instant at the same time. When the thunderous cacophony subsided and the clamor around them calmed, Amy dared to crack open her eyes. She peeked up at what used to be the ceiling and found they were lying beneath a cage of branches and leaves. She swiped water off her face and craned her neck for a better look.

Yes. They were surrounded by a broken tangle of fat limbs and broken two-by-four studs. A tree had fallen on the playhouse, and only the small wooden table and a couple of well-positioned branches had kept the trunk of the oak tree from crushing them. Amy drew a shuddering breath. "Grant? Are you okay?"

He groaned, and his hand flexed against her back.

She remembered his cry of pain, and her chest tightened. "Grant?" She tried to scoot back from him, and her head and shoulders bumped a wall of bark. Trying again, she tipped her head at an angle and met the pained expression in his eyes. "Are you hurt?"

His cheeks and forehead bore a few tiny cuts from the

shards of glass and splintered wood. Raising her hands into her line of vision and touching her cheeks, she discovered she had similar minor injuries.

"I'm still trying to decide," he murmured.

She understood. Shock still had her numb and trembling. When the adrenaline wore off, she would likely feel the brunt of the lashing they'd taken. Amy took a minute to calm her frayed nerves and slow her breathing. She took a mental assessment of her condition. The hard thwack on her legs, she realized, had been a branch of the tree as it crashed onto them. With effort, she moved her leg. No sharp pain indicating a break. She could slide her foot side to side a few inches, so she at least wasn't pinned by the tree, even if the branches caged them. She managed to raise her head a few inches and gaze down the length of their bodies, checking for blood, for a gap where they could wiggle free. She saw neither.

"Grant…" She twisted as best she could in the confined space beneath the table and the cave of limbs. "I think we're trapped. Can you see a way out on your side?"

He didn't respond, and she cut her gaze toward him again. His eyes were closed, his face contorted and his breathing shallow. "Grant? You *are* hurt. Where?"

"I took a rabbit punch to the kidney. I'm sore, but…I doubt there's internal damage." Keeping his eyes shut, he drew a slow breath through his nose and blew it through his lips.

Her gut twisted. Clearly he was in pain. The sooner they found a way out and got him to a hospital, the better. "Are you hurt anywhere else? Are your legs trapped?"

He shifted his body then grunted in pain. "No. And can you stop saying *trapped*?"

She frowned, puzzling over his strange request. "What?"

He drew another slow breath and opened his eyes to find her gaze. "When I was eight, I was playing along the river's edge with my best friend, and we found an old refrigerator someone had dumped. We didn't know not to play in it, and…we got trapped."

Amy stilled, her stomach swooping. "Oh, my God."

She'd heard of the danger improperly discarded freezers and refrigerators posed. The appliances were airtight and impossible to open from inside. If locked inside, a person could suffocate if not freed quickly. "Obviously you got out all right, so—"

"I did. But…Joseph didn't."

A shudder raced through him, and she pressed her fingers to his cheek. "Oh, Grant. I'm sorry."

He closed his eyes again as his breathing grew rapid. "I only survived, because…someone found us after about…three hours. They revived me, but Joseph never came to again."

"How frightening for you!" she murmured, a sympathetic ache filling her chest. And then she got it. His closed eyes, his ragged breathing. She gasped. "You're claustrophobic now, aren't you?"

He groaned. "I know it's stupid, but—"

"It's not stupid. It's perfectly understandable. You suffered a trauma as a kid. You lost your best friend. I get it." She stroked her hand from his cheek to his hair, brushing away tiny bits of debris from his face.

"It's not small places. Like the playhouse…as long as I know I can get out, I'm okay. It's just when I know I'm… trapped," he said, clearly embarrassed by his phobia.

She took stock of their situation, hemmed in by the heavy old oak. Peyton's small table had saved them, but now created a low ceiling over them. The effect was rather daunting, and tomb-like even to her. The rumble of departing thunder and eerie stillness of the woods and wind in the wake of the twister added to the ominous atmosphere.

Grant drew another deep, slow breath, battling to stay calm. She needed to do *something*. She patted her pocket for her cell phone, praying it hadn't got damaged in the storm. But the phone wasn't there. "Crud. I left my phone in the house."

He sighed. "Same here."

"Well…" She examined the fat limbs around them again, looking for a weak spot, a gap. "Surely we can push away one of these branches or squeeze out somehow." She picked the branch she considered the best candidate and pointed it out to him. "Help me push right here."

He aimed a skeptical look at her but gave a tight nod and put his shoulder into shoving the impeding branch beside him. They went exactly nowhere.

Although he didn't say it, his expression said, *I told you so.*

"Okay, so help me find another spot to try."

Grant's jaw tightened, and a muscle in his cheek twitched as his gaze darted around them. "I don't see anything promising, Amy."

Neither did she, but she kept that to herself.

"Damn it, I have to get out of here! My daughter needs me!" Grant growled, slamming a palm against the thick branch over their heads.

She could feel his frustration, his anxiety and fear for Peyton roll through him.

"A murderer has kidnapped her, and I'm stuck here, doing nothing to find her!"

Already Grant's respirations were speeding up and sounding panicked again. If they weren't going to get out, she needed to do something to keep him calm. She ran through—and discarded—several ideas in rapid-fire succession. Singing to him. Slapping him. Redirecting his thoughts from Peyton.

Finally, when she thought he might be about to hyperventilate, she kissed him.

If lightning had struck him, Grant couldn't have been more jolted, more charged. Stunned though he was by her move, pounding desire shot through him in an instant. His body caught fire, and only this sexy firefighter could put out the blaze.

Sinking his hands into her rain-dampened hair, he curled his fingers against her scalp, holding her head close as he returned her kiss. His past year's abstinence had left him starving, and he was especially hungry for Amy. He'd been battling his appetite for his houseguest for days, and given this taste of her, he caved in to his craving.

A thick groan rumbled from his throat as he angled his head to fit his mouth more fully over hers. Her lips were tender and sweet, just as he'd imagined they'd be, and he easily lost himself in her. Which was her intention, he was sure. He forgot the refrigerator and Joseph. He forgot the old oak caging them. He forgot all the reasons he had never kissed Amy before. All he wanted at that moment, and for the immediate moments to come, was to sink deeper into this woman, this kiss, this…

Crack!

Amy jerked away with a gasp as a clap of thunder shook everything around them. "Whoa! That was close."

The loud boom shot sobering adrenaline through

Grant, and he blinked away the haze of lust muddling his brain. The harsh interruption to their kiss was as effective as Tracy reaching down from heaven to slap him for his betrayal.

"Yeah, too close," he muttered, closing his eyes and moving his hand from Amy's hair to her back. So close he'd almost forgotten his vows to his wife. He'd almost forgotten the urgency of finding Peyton. Almost. For just a few seconds. But now both Tracy and Peyton flooded his mind, along with a heavy dose of compunction.

If he could have put a few yards distance between himself and the source of his temptation, he would have. But thanks to the storm, his body and Amy's were tangled up beneath the limbs of the old oak he used to climb as a kid. They were tra—

He took a quick breath. They were…not going anywhere anytime soon. Skunk! If ever he needed a distraction, this was it. Not only did he not want to think about being penned by the tree and storm damage, he didn't want to think about how hot, how mind-blowingly terrific Amy's kiss was. Or about how easy it would be to capture her mouth again and forget the crushing worries and frustrations that had taken over his life in the past twelve months.

What he needed to focus on was rescuing Peyton. Or getting a message to Connor. Or finding a way to free them from the gnarl of storm damage. Or doing something about—

"Hey," she whispered, and he glanced up at her. She stroked his cheek. "You okay? I probably shouldn't have done that, huh?"

He realized he was breathing too fast again. He made himself smile for her sake. "Did I complain?"

"No, but your expression says—"

"It was nice," he said quickly. *Nice?* What kind of lame-o word was that to describe an earthshaking kiss? He cleared his throat. "It did what you intended." *At least for a few moments...*

Amy cocked one eyebrow and twisted her mouth in a bemused moue. "Wow. Stop, I'm blushing," she said flatly. "Look, let's just forget I—"

And suddenly he was framing her face with his hands and pulling her close for another kiss. He kept this kiss more restrained, but the sizzle of attraction and heat wasn't any less intense as he gently caressed her lips and savored the tug of her mouth drawing on his. If he shut out the clamor of his guilty conscience, he found that kissing Amy was more than nice. More than electrically hot. Her kiss was…centering. Stabilizing. She helped him put the brakes on the unproductive fury and frustration that seethed in him when he thought about Peyton's kidnapping. She helped him tamp down the ghosts of his past and the stressors in the present and focus on what mattered—getting Amy safely out of the storm and recovering his daughter.

He felt his knotted neck muscles relax as she combed her fingers through the hair on his nape, and he deepened the kiss, relishing the taste of her and cherishing the fragile bond he felt growing between them. When her tongue teased his bottom lip, a tingle of pure pleasure tripped down his spine…followed by a pinch of guilt. Though he could enjoy Amy's kiss and acknowledge the difference she made in his frame of mind, that didn't mean he could ignore all that Tracy had meant to him. With a sigh of regret, he pulled away and turned his head.

"See?" Amy grunted, and gave a small head shake. "There's the expression again. Like you feel as if you're kissing your sister."

Grant scoffed a laugh and gave her a lopsided grin. "Oh, no. Certainly not like kissing my sister—if I had one." His expression sobered as he stroked her jaw, tracing her cheekbone with his thumb. "Just not…kissing my wife, either."

"Oh," she said, then with her eyes widening in understanding, "Oh!"

"I know she's gone, but I still love her."

"Of course you do. You always will."

"I just have to find a way to let go of the guilt I feel. I still feel like I'm cheating on her."

"It's too soon. I get it." She shifted slightly, clearly trying to make the alignment of their bodies less…sexual. But her wiggling and sliding across him only served to do the opposite.

Nerve endings already sparking and crackling, fired all the more. His groin tightened until it ached. Finally he grabbed her wrist with one hand while tightening his other arm around her waist. "Stop. Just…be still. You're okay. We just…need to do something else. We need to think of a way out of here. We need to figure out a way to call for help."

And find a way to get Peyton back from William Gale.

"Yeah, help getting outta here would be good. What are you thinking?" she asked.

Grant frowned. No phones, no neighbors close by. "I think our best chance is if my family or the cops check up on us, either because of the tornado or about Peyton's kidnapping."

"You never said what happened when you talked to the police after the ransom call. Is Officer Smith coming?"

His scowl deepened. "I didn't talk to him. I left a message on his voice mail. With this bad weather, Lord knows when he'll get back to me." He swiped at a tickle on his forehead and drew back bloody fingers.

"Yeah, you have several nicks from flying glass and splintered wood." Amy touched her own face gingerly. "I'm guessing I do, too?"

"Yep." He swiped a drip from her cheek, and she winced.

"Ow. That one still has the shard in it."

Squinting in the dim light available, he plucked the sliver of glass from her cut. "We're lucky minor cuts and bumps are the worst we got."

"True that. I don't think I've ever heard anything as terrifying as that twister roaring past. And I've heard some pretty scary things Mother Nature has to offer. A wildfire has a pretty scary soundtrack. Trees explode when the sap in them boils and expands. Powerful whirl-winds get kicked up. It can get ugly."

Imagining Amy on the scene of an ugly wildfire didn't help his state of mind, so he stubbornly shut it out. "So…back to our plan to get outta here…"

"I think we've determined the plan is to wait for help to arrive—" She paused and groaned as the hard rain returned, dousing them. "And pray it's soon."

Irritated by the truth in her assessment, he blinked and turned his head as rainwater dripped in his face. He shoved down memories of the fear he'd known as a kid, stuck in the old refrigerator, waiting to be found and knowing he could die. But when his thoughts returned to Peyton and the delay their entrapment meant to find-ing her, his impatience and panic flared again.

He needed a diversion—and not one that betrayed Tracy and fed his infatuation with a woman who was quite clearly unsuited for him. Not only did Amy have a high-risk career, she lived half a continent away. She'd be leaving as soon as her car was repaired. Excellent kisser or not, he'd be nuts to pursue any relationship with her.

"Do you want to talk about why you were so upset when I found you out here? Something about a T-shirt?" Amy said, twisting and obviously struggling to reach a hand behind her and rub a spot between her shoulders.

He bumped her hand out of the way and massaged the muscles around her spine. "Better?"

"Definitely. Thank you. Something smacked me there and…" With a grunt, she rolled her head and stretched her shoulders as far as she could in the confines of their prison. "So, the shirt?"

He sighed. "Apparently Peyton had a secret collection of things out here that I'd stored in the attic. Things from her babyhood and things that were Tracy's. Things clearly designed to comfort her, make her feel close to her mother. I had no idea."

"Oh, Grant…"

"I've been failing Peyton. I should have known how much she still hurt, and done something before now."

"Don't be so hard on yourself. You've had a boatload to handle and if she—"

"Don't make excuses for me. I'm her father. It's my job to know these things and…" He huffed his disappointment with himself. "Can we talk about something else?"

Something that didn't heap onto his sense of loss and defeat. His worry for Peyton, his grief over Tracy… Damn it, he was a mess!

Forcing himself to take a slow deep breath, he stroked a hand down Amy's back. "Earlier, when you found me in the living room, you had something to tell me, but you said it would keep. Since we've got nothing but time now, why don't you tell me what was on your mind?" Grant suggested and felt her stiffen.

Was it his touch that bothered her, or was the subject of what she'd had on her mind the stressor?

She shook her head. "No. It's…nothing."

"It's not like we're going anywhere anytime soon." Feeling her muscles tightening, he gave her shoulder a light squeeze. "It must have been at least a little important if you were going to tell me earlier."

"Really, Grant." She flashed him a quick, unconvincing smile, then averted her gaze. "It's not relevant to finding Peyton or the storm or any of that."

But the more she dismissed his concern, the more curious and uneasy he became. He kept his tone as light as he could, prodding her. "All the better. I need something to distract me from *my* worry."

"Grant, I—" Her voice broke, catching on a sob, and his concern spiked.

"Amy, please. Talk to me. Don't you trust me?"

"Of course, but…"

"I want to help. You've done nothing but help me since you got here, and now I want to return the favor."

Her brow beetled to match her tensed body. "There's nothing you can do. It's over, and I'm dealing with it."

"Are you? It seems to me whatever it is still upsets you." He thumbed the moisture that was forming on her eyelashes.

"You can't change the past."

"True, but I can listen. Empathize. Offer comfort."

"Grant…" she groaned, putting him off again with her tone. The distance she put between them chafed. He'd thought they were closer than that, that they were connecting on some level other than the purely physical.

But if she didn't feel safe opening up to him about her past, whatever that entailed, then where were they really?

He covered his hurt with a sigh of surrender. "Okay. I won't push. But later, if you want my help, need me just to listen, or—"

She groaned softly, then blurted in a hushed tone, "My stepfather sexually abused me when I was in high school."

At first he wasn't sure he'd heard her correctly. He froze, listening to the echo of her confession in his head, replaying her hurried mumble to double-check his memory. But the second and third times the words rang in his mind, they were just as stunning and terrible as the first. "Amy, I…"

"You wanted to know." She heaved a shaky sigh. "There it is. My deep dark secret."

He fumbled through the fog of shock for the appropriate response. *I'm sorry? That sucks?* Both of those replies popped into his head, but they seemed lame and woefully inadequate.

What he wanted to say was "I'll kill the bastard." That was his gut reaction. Even without knowing the gory details, he wanted to hunt down the man who'd dared to hurt Amy, and rip him limb from limb. And how was that for possessive caveman instincts? Violence was not what Amy needed in response to her intimate share. What she needed was—

"Grant? Did you hear me?"

What she needed was for him to stop lying there like a log and say…*something.* "I'm so sorry. That…sucks."

He winced as the lame platitudes tumbled out. *Bravo, genius.*

She grunted quietly, and he sensed her pulling away, emotionally. "Yeah. Sucks."

Gritting his teeth, he dug deeper. He could do better. He *had* to do better. He cared about Amy, and she deserved more than his trite condolences. He needed to give her the love and support and encouragement that her raw, difficult confession merited.

He curled his fingers in her hair and brought her head down on his chest. He kissed her forehead and whispered, "Tell me about it. I'm listening."

She hesitated at first, but slowly began telling a heartbreaking story of a teenage girl whose stepfather went from being inappropriately affectionate to criminally molesting. The progression had caught Amy in a quandary of her culpability. If she'd told him how uncomfortable his excessive hugs and kisses made her, could she have kept him from coming into her room to "tell her good-night?" If she'd stopped him from lingering in her bedroom when her mother was home, could she have prevented his visits when her mother was out of the house? Could she have stopped his predatory behavior before he'd stolen her innocence?

What if she'd worked up the courage to tell her mother the truth sooner? What had she neglected to do to make her mother believe her? What if she'd gotten mad enough, brave enough to go to the police before the abuse escalated?

Grant's fingers tightened on Amy's shoulder. "No, no and no. Geez, Amy. Stop doubting yourself or taking any blame. What happened is *all* on him. Should you have gone to the police sooner? Maybe so. But you were forced into an untenable position that no one, especially not a minor, should have to face. Your mother should have listened, should have believed you. She bears some blame, too, for not protecting you."

"Her disbelief hurt, for sure. Still does."

He clenched his teeth, a marrow-deep anger gnawing him. "If I ever get five minutes alone with this guy, I'll—"

"No. You won't." She curled her fingers against his chest and sighed. "Thank you for your gallant wrath on my behalf, but I don't want anyone to go to jail avenging me. Besides, if anyone gets to rip a piece out of him, it's me. Lord knows I've imagined doing that enough times. But it wouldn't change the past, so…"

"Wait a minute. When I found you and Stella on the side of the road last week, you said something about your stepfather being at your mom's house. That was why you'd left."

Another groan. "Yeah."

"Why the hell isn't he in jail? Didn't you say that you went to the cops, and he was convicted?"

"He got paroled."

Grant muttered a not-child-approved word he'd tried to banish from his vocabulary.

"Exactly. He's out, my mother is defending him again, and so I left. I couldn't stay under the same roof with him. Not that I think he'd try anything now. I'd emasculate him if he did. But I just can't stomach the sight of him."

"I can understand that." His own stomach was churning at the thought of this child molester being out of prison, walking around in the community again. "Amy, I…don't know what to say. I hate that—"

She pressed a hand to his mouth. "No. You don't have to say anything. I don't want you to say anything. I didn't tell you in order to get sympathy or advice. As much as it infuriated me and shamed me at the time, I'm dealing with it. I've talked to a counselor. I've gotten far away from him, and I'm putting the past firmly behind me where it belongs."

More pieces started falling into place. "That's why you moved so far away after high school?"

"Yeah."

He threaded his fingers through her hair, idly twisting the damp strands around his fingers. "Is any of it behind why you went into such a high-risk job?"

"Huh? No. I got into smoke jumping because I love the challenge and the adrenaline and the reward of making a difference. I love my job."

"Oh."

"All right, yes, it is therapeutic to rise to the challenge of beating a wildfire. It makes me feel more in control of my world, my environment. But ironically, sometimes it reminds me, too, that there are some things you can't control. Sometimes the wildfire wins. Mother Nature is one powerful bitch when she wants to be."

"Case in point." He motioned to the tree surrounding them.

She hummed her agreement, tapping a finger to the tip of her nose.

They fell silent for a minute, the patter of rain a steady cadence around them. Grant's mind whirled with the new information, unsure what to do with it. It changed everything. And nothing. Amy was still Amy. She'd said she wasn't looking for sympathy from him, that she'd moved on with her life. But having grown to care for her in the past several days, it shook him to his roots to know what she'd endured. He wondered how her past affected her current relationships with men. Seeing as he had no intention of starting a long-term relationship with her, he decided that was a too-personal question. Besides that, he didn't want to think about Amy with another man.

Ironic jealousy prodded him, and his mind scrambled away from that visual, even as his hold on her tightened.

"I've never told anyone about it," she said quietly.

"No one? But…"

"Well, I mean, none of my friends. I told the cops and my counselor, of course, but my identity was protected in those cases so none of my friends found out. And I told my mom, of course, but…like I said, she didn't believe me. Or she chose to ignore me to save her marriage. Either way, I can't forgive her for betraying me. For abandoning me."

Grant gritted his back teeth. "I can't imagine a mother not wanting to protect her daughter. What was she thinking?"

Amy lifted a shoulder. "Self-preservation maybe? I can't figure it out, either. I still love her. She's my mom after all, but…God, her denial hurts."

Grant mulled her confession another moment then asked, "So…why did you tell me?"

She snorted a laugh. "Because you were badgering me!"

"No, I was going to let it drop." He paused, rewinding his thoughts. "And isn't that what you were coming to tell me earlier? When I got the ransom call?"

"Uh…" She exhaled slowly. "Yeah."

"Why?"

"I thought…" She cleared her throat. "I was afraid David had taken Peyton."

Grant tensed. "Based on what?"

"I…called my mother, and she said—"

"Grant!" a frantic-sounding male voice called. "Grant, Amy, where are you?"

"Grant!" Another voice joined the first.

Relief flooded him, and the release of tension left his

muscles shaking. He was *so* ready to be out of that tomb of tree limbs and storm debris...

"Oh, thank you, Big Ernie," Amy whispered on a sigh. "I think our help has arrived."

"That's my dad and brother. Hold your ears. I'm about to yell back." He shouted their location to his father and Hunter, and soon the men and Hunter's wife, Brianna, were digging them out of the tornado's refuse.

"Big Ernie?" he asked as he waited impatiently to be freed.

"A superstition. He's the smoke-jumping god. He's got a twisted sense of humor. Not sure he had anything to do with *this* situation, but...I like to stay in his good graces when I can."

Hunter needed a chain saw to cut away the large branches of the oak, and what had taken seconds to bury them took closer to a half hour to remove. When at last a hole big enough for them to shimmy through had been cleared, Grant helped Amy climb free of the debris. He followed her out, taking a cleansing breath of fresh air. *Free.* Eyes closed, he savored the moment. But when he opened his eyes he received his next shock as he surveyed the damage to his yard and home.

Chapter 14

After greeting her former football teammate and his new wife, Amy shifted her attention to the storm damage. In the time it had taken Hunter to cut them free, the worst of the storm had passed, but Amy's heart sank as she cataloged the destruction with mixed emotions. Like the oak that had trapped them, numerous decades-old trees had been taken out, twisted like pipe cleaners or snapped in half like twigs. Bits of building material, trash and twigs littered the lawn.

But Grant's house was intact. Mostly. Roofing shingles lay scattered across the lawn and a few windows had been broken. A treetop had fallen on the master bedroom side of the house, creating a gaping hole, but the destruction seemed contained to the one room on the top floor.

Amy's chest tightened, seeing the damage to the home that had once belonged to his grandparents. Around them Stan, Hunter and Brianna muttered softly about cleanup and calling the insurance company and starting stop-gap repairs.

With a gasp, Brianna suddenly cried, "Sorsha!" Grant's sister-in-law cut her glance toward Amy and Grant. "Do you have any idea where the cats are?"

His expression still shell-shocked, Grant shook his head silently.

Amy's pulse pattered with new concern for the cats. "They were all safe inside when we went out to the playhouse. I saw Cinderella run and hide after the thunder grew loud."

Hunter took his wife's hand and started into the house. "Don't worry, Bri. I'm sure they're all right."

As Brianna and Hunter went in search of the three cats, Amy gave a sidelong glance to Grant, who was staring bleakly at his tree-punctured roof, clearly imagining the extent of damage to his waterlogged and wind-damaged belongings. She sidled closer to him and slid an arm around his waist. His body was taut and trembling. Resting her head on his shoulder, she wished she could shoulder some of the grief and worry he carried. This man she was growing to care for had borne too much pain in his life and still faced an uphill battle.

How was it fair that he should suffer tornado damage to his family home on top of all his other tragedies?

"I'm so sorry, Grant. I know the damage must hurt all the more since it was your grandparents' home." She rubbed his back and gave his shoulder a squeeze.

"Yeah." He blinked red, weary eyes but gave no further response.

After another minute of staring at the destruction together, letting the significance of the loss sink in and how the damage to his home would complicate his life and the search for Peyton, Amy stepped in front of Grant. Facing him, she cupped his cheeks in her hands. "Grant, as much as losing the house hurts, you can be thankful that—"

"Thankful?" He yanked free of her touch and stepped back, shoving both hands through his hair, his face rigid. "Amy, I don't care about the house. It's just a *thing*. My family owns a construction company, for God's sake. We can fix the stupid house!"

Amy opened and closed her mouth, his anger leaving her speechless.

He jabbed a hand toward the wreckage. "The damage sucks, but it means nothing." He drew a tremulous breath, and his eyes filled with fear and doubt. "What matters is that my little girl is still missing. Still in the hands of a sick, vindictive man. For all I know, the tornado hit the house where he's holding her. She could be hurt. She could be *dead.* And I know for damn sure, wherever she is, she's *scared.*" His voice cracked, and the sound arrowed through her heart. Grant paused long enough to compose himself and take another deep, shaky breath. "If I don't get her back—" His face crumpled, and Amy closed the distance between them.

"You will. You have to believe you'll get her back safe and sound." Wrapping her arms around him and pulling his head down to hers, she kissed his cheeks and held him tight. "We have to believe Peyton is fine, and she'll be back here soon. Try to stay positive."

"Stay positive? Why? Because the rest of my life proves karma is on my side? I don't think so." He gave a short, bitter laugh. "I must have been a real ass as a kid and done some horrible things earlier in life, because I'm sure as hell not getting any breaks lately."

What could she say to that? He was right. Life had been downright crappy to him in the past year. "You don't deserve any of what's happened to you, Grant. It is horribly unfair. But hear this and believe it." She fisted the front of his shirt in her hand and yanked him closer, sticking her face in his to draw his full attention. "I am here for you. I care about you and your girls, and I will stand by you and do anything I can to get you through this. You are not alone. You have my full support."

She felt the shudder that rolled through him just before he captured the back of her head and sank his fingers into her hair. "I'm sorry I yelled at you. I'm just... so scared. So worried about my baby girl. And this..." He glanced past her to the tornado's destruction. "This was just the last straw." He stepped back, scrubbing his stubble-dusted, stress-lined face with both hands. "I'm through with the self-pity. I promise."

He twitched a weak smile and directed his attention to the other destruction on his property. Hail had dented his truck and shattered his windshield.

He blew out a sigh. "Guess I should have parked in the barn, huh?"

"Actually...not," Stan said, crossing the yard to peer around the side of the house. The senior Mansfield sighed and shook his head. "The barn is gone."

Amy blinked, stunned. "Gone? You mean..."

"I mean *gone*," Grant's father said, his brow dented with concern. "There's nothing left but the slab."

Amy's pulse spiked. "But...Stella was—" She didn't bother finishing. Breaking into a hobbling semblance of a run, she hurried across the debris-strewn lawn to the side yard.

The barn was, in fact, gone. As was any sign of Stella. Amy gasped, her heart wrenching.

Grant and his father jogged up behind her, and Grant muttered a curse word under his breath.

Amy scanned the area, especially the gap in the woods where the tornado had broken trees and uprooted saplings. She saw the glint of blue metal at the same time Grant pointed and said, "There's the car."

Stan put a solicitous hand under her elbow as they

made their way through the mud and tangled brush. Bits of fiberglass insulation and roofing shingles dotted the path cut by the tornado. A chill shimmied through Amy, seeing the destructive power of the storm and knowing their situation could have been much worse if the house had taken a direct hit. All things considered, she was counting her blessings. But as they drew closer to Stella, her heart sank further. More and more damage was evident as they neared the wreckage. Twisted metal, crumpled panels, broken glass, shredded seats. Stella was a complete loss.

Spotting the back bumper with her father's Colt .45s bumper sticker twisted around the base of a nearby tree, a pained gasp escaped her before she could catch it. Seeing the outdated sticker on the demolished bumper felt like losing her father all over again. She pulled free of Stan's supporting grasp and limped to the crumpled metal. With a ragged sigh, she slumped to the ground and bent her face to her hands. She tried to jam down the tears that rose in her throat and stung her sinuses, but her grief was for more than a machine. The loss of her father's prized possession represented the end of an era to her, dragged her back to the lonely, frightened little girl mourning her father's untimely passing.

Grant crouched beside her and rubbed her back. "I'm sorry, Amy."

"I know, I know! It's just a *thing*. Like your house. But…it was the only thing I had left from my father. He was so proud of Stella, and I felt close to him when I drove her. Losing Stella brings back…" She hiccuped a sob before battling to regain her composure. "I just miss him so much."

"I understand."

She glanced over her shoulder to him. Of course he

understood. He fought a daily war with grief for his wife. She took the hand he offered and laced her fingers with his. Even after he'd helped her stand up again, she clung to his hand, treasuring the connection to him. She'd been crazy to think she could keep an emotional distance from Grant, and in the wake of the tornado and Peyton's disappearance, she knew they would need each other's emotional support all the more. Where that would leave them when she had to return to Idaho, she didn't know. She didn't want to go down that mental path right now. Leaving Grant and his girls would hurt, and she had quite enough pain on her plate at the moment.

Leaving Stella's crumpled carnage in the woods, the trio headed inside to regroup, dry off and check on the condition of the three cats. Once Brianna reported she had all three felines safely accounted for, if a bit frightened still, and Sorsha was in her carrier ready to go home, Grant headed straight for his cell phone to see if Officer Smith had returned his call. Now that he was free from the storm-damaged playhouse, he had to redouble his efforts to get Peyton back. He knew who had her, damn it. The cops should be able to do *something*.

But the only calls he'd missed were from his parents. Irritation and impatience fueled him with restless energy. He stalked his living room like a caged tiger and keyed in the number for Officer Smith's cell again. The call went to voice mail. Next he called the main police switchboard. If Officer Smith wasn't available, he'd talk to anyone who could help him recover Peyton. He wasn't picky. He just needed someone in authority to answer his call.

The operator at the police department politely and firmly told him that because of the storm, no one was available at the moment to talk to him, but if he had an emergency he needed to call 911. She warned him, however, that given the storm, 911 was currently being flooded with medical emergencies, destroyed homes, life-and-death rescues from rain-swollen streams.

Growling, he disconnected the unsatisfactory call with a flick of his thumb. If he'd had an old-fashioned rotary phone, he'd have slammed down the receiver. He needed to hit something, take out the hot ball of frustration chewing his insides.

Amy limped in with Hunter and their dad. "What did Officer Smith say?"

"Couldn't reach him." Grant paced the floor, rubbing the back of his neck and rolling the kinks from muscles made stiff by stress and the long period of entrapment under the tree.

"So now what?" Amy finger-combed her damp, tangled hair back from her face and lowered herself into a stuffed chair. "We can't just sit here and wait for Officer Smith to call back."

"I don't intend to." Grant clenched his back teeth as his thoughts darted one direction then another, like a football player weaving through defenders toward the goal line. "If the cops are too busy with the tornado to help me, I'll find Peyton myself, my way."

"Grant," his father said darkly, worry heavy in his tone, "Don't do anything foolish."

He sent his dad an agitated look. "Foolish would be to sit here and do nothing, knowing my daughter is being held by a convicted felon with a penchant for violence and a grudge against our family! I've got to do something!"

"And just what are you planning to do?" Stan crossed

his arms over his chest. "You don't know where he's holding her."

Grant flashed to the day he'd sat in court watching William Gale hug his son, then to Tracy's funeral when James Gale had confronted Connor. "No, I don't know, but I bet I know who does."

Chapter 15

"Wow. And I thought jumping out of an airplane into a wildfire was the riskiest thing I'd ever do," Amy muttered as she limped beside Grant up to James Gale's front door. "But here I am confronting a man with known connections to organized crime at his house."

"You can wait in the car if you want," Grant said as he banged on the door, then also rang the bell. His body hummed like a wood sander, and his heart hammered his ribs like his novice summer hires pounded nails.

"What? And miss all the excitement?" She buzzed her lips and flashed a nervous smile.

Stepping closer to him, she slipped her hand in his and squeezed. Her unspoken support meant the world to him, and buoyed him for the task at hand.

They'd learned the local businessman's unlisted address thanks to a few white lies and a call to a local pizza delivery store asking why the Gale family's pizza hadn't been delivered. And yes, the address on file was correct.

While Amy and Grant paid William Gale's son a visit, Hunter and their father had stayed at the house to begin repairs to Grant's bedroom roof and to receive Officer Smith should he come by the house.

Grant rang the bell again, and finally the front door

opened. An attractive brunette greeted them with a stiffly polite smile and curious look. "Can I help you?"

"Is James Gale home?" Grant asked.

"And you are?" The brunette divided a suspicious glance between them.

"In a hurry." Grant straightened his spine and raised his chin. "Is he home?"

"Honey, who is it?" a male voice called from inside the house.

Having his answer, Grant pushed past the startled woman, who tried to block their path. Failing that, she hit the panic button on the security system pad and cried, "James!"

Despite the blare of sirens, he towed Amy with him as he burst into the grand country mansion without invitation. He scanned the living room to his left and the long corridor stretching in front of him. "Where is he?"

"Sir, you can't just—"

"James Gale!" He had to shout full voice to be heard over the whooping alarm.

Within seconds, a man in dress pants and button-down shirt appeared at the top of a curved staircase to the upper floor. James Gale glowered down at the foyer. "Heather, shut that infernal thing off!"

Grant strode toward the stairs, his hands balled at his sides. "Where's your father? Where does he have my daughter?"

"Stop right there, Mansfield." James gave weight to the command by raising and aiming a gun.

Amy gasped and took Grant by the arm. "This is getting off on the wrong foot. Can we take it down a notch? Please?"

"William set the tone when he took Peyton," he returned, without moving his eyes from James.

A sour look twisted James's face as he marched down the steps and met Grant at the base of the staircase. "You have a lot of nerve barging into a man's home and making accusations." James's chest puffed up, and he pulled his shoulders back as he leaned close to Grant, breaching his personal space. "I have no idea where your daughter is. Or my father for that matter. He's a free man. Free to do as he pleases without checking in with me."

"Yeah? Well, he checked in with *me*," Grant said through gritted teeth, the memory of the phone call with William bringing a bitter taste to his mouth.

Heather Gale hurried to her husband's side and placed her hands around his gun hand, reaiming the weapon toward the floor. "James…" she said under her breath, in a tone that said, *calm down*.

Amy also hobble-stepped closer to Grant's side, reminding him of her warning for civility with a raised-eyebrow glance and standing with him in a united front as they faced James.

James's expression reflected squinty-eyed skepticism, and he cocked his head. "What do you mean, he checked in with you?"

"He called me," Grant started, his tone venomous, until Amy squeezed his hand. Hard. He paused and drew a deep breath of composure before explaining. "Earlier today, before the worst of the storm hit, he called my cell. He's taken my seven-year-old daughter—" he paused briefly when his voice cracked "—and is holding her until he gets a face-to-face meeting with Connor."

Heather made a soft noise of concern, but James remained unconvinced. "You're sure it was my father, that he really has your girl?"

"Yes, I'm sure. He put Peyton on the phone for a moment. She was crying and scared and—" Again he had to steady is voice before continuing.

James swore quietly, and his countenance modulated. Hostility morphed into frustration.

Grant shoved down the ache that split his chest open and left him raw, filling the void with hard-edged anger and resentment toward William Gale. He touched the side of his balled fist to his mouth for a second as he swallowed the bile rising in his throat. "He's got Peyton, and he's demanding a confrontation with Connor."

He shook his head as he struggled to hold himself together. Grief, panic and fury played tug-of-war inside him, and he felt ready to shred into rough bits like a blown tire. Only Amy's palliative presence kept him from flying apart. "But I don't know where Connor is. I swear to God I don't. And if your father harms one hair on my baby's head—" His throat closed, and he couldn't draw a breath.

Heather gave her husband a worried look. "James?"

James Gale's jaw worked, and his nostrils flared as he inhaled. Pain and disappointment flickered in his eyes. "I haven't talked to Pop since the day of his appeal. I don't know where he is."

Grant studied the crease in James's brow, the reluctant acceptance and discouragement that softened the set of his shoulders. Everything about the man's body language stood down and stepped back from his earlier hostile posturing. He held the lowered gun in a relaxed grip at his side. His unspoken truce was enough to make Grant believe him.

Frustration sucker punched Grant, and his own stiff-backed posture wilted.

"You don't have any idea where he might be holding her?" Amy asked. "He gave you no clue he might do something like this to manipulate Grant's family?"

"No." James huffed a sigh. "And yes."

Grant twitched, his heartbeat tripping. "What does that mean?"

"James," Heather said, hitching her head toward the end of the hall where a little girl peeked around the corner from the kitchen. "Maybe you should take our guests into your office to finish your conversation?"

His gaze darting to his daughter, James cleared his throat and nodded toward a heavy wooden door to their right. "If you would…this way."

Grant fought for patience, even if he understood James's desire to protect his little girl from an ugly confrontation. The door had barely closed behind them before he repeated his question, his muscles torqued with growing tension.

James raised a splayed hand in a silent request for patience. "As I said, I don't know where my father is. He did make comments after the appeal about seeking retaliation for my brother Victor's death. I urged him to give up his quest for vengeance. I explained to him again that Connor didn't pull the trigger when Victor died. I did. I told him that Victor left me no choice. He'd lost it and wasn't acting rationally." A dark sadness filled James's face. "I told Pop that it was self-defense. But he didn't listen. His whole life has been built on settling scores and seeking revenge. That's what he taught me and my brother, but I can't buy into that mentality any longer. I've found that path leads only to hate and pain and loss. I want to be around to see my children grow up and give me grandchildren." James gave Grant an earnest, level look. "I told your brother all of this that day on the hospital roof."

Amy rubbed Grant's arm as if to say, *See? He's not the enemy.*

But Grant had focused on another point James had made. "What plans for retaliation did your father mention after the appeal hearing?"

James tugged on the cuff of his dress shirt and moved to sit behind his massive walnut desk. "He wasn't specific. Only that he intended to hold Connor accountable for Victor's death. When I pointed out that Connor was in Witness Security, Pop said he'd find a way to get Connor to come out of hiding."

"By kidnapping my daughter, terrorizing her." In his gut, the coils of animosity twisted tighter. Fresh waves of panic and fear for Peyton filled him with a weighty cold that burrowed to his bones.

James scrubbed his face with a palm. "He didn't say what he had in mind. And I tried to talk him out of acting rashly, but my father's always been stubborn, convinced might makes right, and that allowing an insult or injury to go unchecked is a sign of weakness."

Amy waved her hands, calling for a halt to the current track. "All that aside, we need to focus now on finding Peyton and getting her back before anything happens to her."

James jerked a nod. "Of course." He placed the gun in a desk drawer and slid his cell phone from his pants pocket. After thumbing the screen, he raised the phone to his ear. His gaze locked with Grant's, his eyes hot with displeasure. Despite his cooperation, James was clearly still unhappy about their barging into his home.

After a moment, he said, "Pop, it's James. We need to talk. Call me." He lowered the phone from his ear and repocketed it. "Went straight to voice mail."

"Look, I have to find my daughter. Do you have any

idea where he might have taken her?" Grant stepped to James's desk and braced on the edge as he leaned toward the other man. "Do you know any place he might hole up if he was looking to lie low for a while?"

James's mouth contorted as he thought. "Not with certainty. But…I have a few ideas where he might have gone, starting with our old hunting camp. I don't think anyone's been out there in years, but it's worth checking out."

Grant straightened, new hope flaring in his chest. "Take me there. Now."

"I still think we should have brought the police with us," Amy whispered to Grant as they pulled in the tree-lined dirt road leading to the rural camp.

Heavy wind damage was all around them, branches down and full trees twisted and toppled. Anxiety buffeted Grant with gale force.

"You heard his conditions." Grant squeezed the steering wheel of his father's SUV as he followed James down the rutted road, weaving around storm debris and splashing through giant puddles. "If the price for having him show us the hunting camp and other unlisted properties the family owns is leaving the cops out of the equation, I'm willing to take that chance. These properties are the most likely places the bastard is holding Peyton. I need to check them."

"And how do we know he's not leading us into an ambush? That he's not going to march us into the woods and shoot us in the back of the head?" Amy glanced at him, and Grant's stomach churned harder.

The same possibility had occurred to him, but he'd followed his gut instincts about James. All indicators were that William's son truly wanted a truce between the families and an end to the violent vendetta that had caused both families such strife in the past year. But just in case...

"When we get to the camp, I want you to stay in the truck. Have your finger on the button to dial 911 in case there's trouble."

Amy's eyes widened. "Then you do think there's a chance..."

"Just a precaution. My dad keeps a 9 mm in his glove box. Do you know how to shoot a gun?"

She blinked as if stunned they were having this conversation, then nodded slowly. "Yeah. I have a little training with handguns. We're allowed to carry up to a .357 Magnum in case of bear attacks on our fire jumps."

Bear attacks? Geez, and he'd thought parachuting into wildfires and wielding chain saws in chaotic conditions were the worst dangers she faced on the job. He swallowed hard, and as they reached the storm-ravaged camp, he parked his father's SUV next to James's Jaguar. He exhaled and jerked a nod to Amy. "Good. Stay here, then, and stay alert. Okay?"

She seemed ready to protest, but she glanced down at her walking cast and frowned. "Okay." She caught his sleeve as he turned to get out. "You be careful, too." She grabbed the front of his shirt, tugged him closer and leaned over to smack a kiss to his mouth. "For luck."

His lips tingled, and his body hummed, charged with adrenaline and heightened senses. With one quick kiss, Amy had zapped him onto a higher level of alertness and energy, jolted him from the tight ball of worry that had his brain locked in an infinite loop.

As he emerged from the SUV, he cast a dismayed glance around the property. The cabin itself was still standing, but windows were shattered, roofing materials were missing and a chuck of siding had been ripped away. The yard was littered with glass and roofing shingles, branches large and small, and a tumbled picnic table and grill. A late model sedan sat parked toward the rear of the property with a small pine tree across the hood.

Grant aimed a finger toward the car. "Is that your father's?"

James jerked a nod, his expression as dark and dire as the gunmetal gray clouds roiling overhead. With long, stiff strides, James headed toward the front door. "Pop!"

As difficult as it was not to yell for Peyton or go charging into the cabin, Grant had agreed to let James approach the situation first, without giving William or Peyton warning that Grant was with James. Their theory was that, while Grant would likely rile William and cause an escalation of tensions, James might be able to mediate a resolution to the standoff.

Grant hung back letting James enter the house first and take stock of the situation. Restless energy and anticipation vibrated to his core, winding his nerves springtaut. While James went inside, Grant stalked around the perimeter of the small house, the ground squishing around his work boots.

He glanced in the windows of the smashed sedan. On the backseat, lying among shards of glass, he spotted a pink Hello Kitty backpack. His heart squeezed so hard he couldn't draw a breath. Peyton *was* here. Or she had been in this car at some point. "My little squirt..." he whispered, the words a ragged sigh.

The squeak of the cabin's screen door hinges brought him around quickly. James stood on the front porch, scrubbing his hand on his cheek and scowling. He looked upset.

Grant's stomach swooped. Where was Peyton? He

jogged toward the sagging porch, his throat closing with dread. James met his gaze as he approached, and Grant raised a palm in query. "Well?"

"The cabin's empty." James stepped down from the porch and scanned the property, turning his body slowly as he searched the tangled trees.

"What do you mean, it's empty?" Grant snapped. "The car's here. They have to be here!"

James glared at him, then swept a hand toward the front door. "Check for yourself if you don't believe me. No one is there."

Disbelief and frustration body-slammed him. If they weren't in the cabin then where—?

Amy climbed out of the SUV and stood in the V of the open passenger door. "What's wrong? Aren't they there?"

"No." James braced his hands on his hips and continued scanning the property. "Pop! Pop, are you there?"

Grant could hold his tongue no more. Cupping his hands around his mouth, he shouted, "Peyton!"

"I'll try calling Pop again. Maybe they hiked out after the storm hit."

While James thumbed his cell phone, Grant peered far into the woods, noting every shadow, every sign of color or incongruous shape. "Peyton!"

He walked a few steps away from the cabin, and Amy joined him. She'd put a plastic bag around her walking cast and gave Grant a quick wry grin as she neared him. "Think this look will catch on in Milan?"

He gave the bag a cursory glance before returning his attention to the woods. "You can stay in the car, if you—"

"Hell no! Do you really think I want to sit on my duff if I can help find Peyton?"

"He's still not answering," James said, the phone pressed to his ear.

Grant grumbled a curse, and Amy hushed him.

"Don't you think the situation calls for something stronger than *skunk*?" he asked.

"No…I mean, yes. I mean…listen!" She pointed a finger toward the treetops and turned slowly, her head tipped as she listened for…something.

Grant fell quiet, straining to hear what Amy had heard, but only the drip of rain from the leaves and low rustle of branches in the breeze stirred around them.

Amy spun toward James. "Call his phone again."

James's brow dented, but he tapped his cell phone as she requested. All three of them held perfectly still, listening…

Then he heard it. The distant trill of a cell phone.

Grant's pulse leaped, and he pivoted, trying desperately to pinpoint the sound. Pegging the ring as coming from behind the cabin, he hurried that direction. "This way."

James followed close behind him, with Amy, encumbered by her cast, trailing them.

"Peyton!" Grant panned his gaze around the gnarled forest, straining to hear a reply, or footsteps in the underbrush, or a whimper from his daughter. Anything to tell him Peyton was out there in those storm-ravaged woods. "Hello? Peyton, can you hear me?"

"Pop!" James called.

Not hearing the phone trill anymore, Grant slowed to a stop, uncertain which direction to head. "Call him again and keep calling until we find them or the phone."

James nodded and dialed again. As they listened for the trill, Amy hobbled up to them.

They turned in the direction the ringing came from,

but before they could set out again, Amy gasped and grabbed Grant's arm. She pointed into the woods twenty degrees farther to the left. "Over there! What's that?"

With his heart climbing into his throat, Grant squinted into the mottled shade of the trees and scrub brush. On the ground about one hundred feet further into the woods, Grant could just make out a white-and-red form. Whatever the form was, it wasn't moving.

His body stilled, frozen with dread, while his insides thrashed and screamed denials. *Please, God, let it be trash. Let it be something inanimate and not my baby girl.*

A tiny moan slipped from his throat unbidden. He had to brace a hand on the nearest tree in order to stay upright. Bile rose in his throat, and he shuddered as he swallowed the bitter taste.

On some level he acknowledged Amy's hand on his back, her attempt to comfort and support him. But his head felt thick, muzzy. The ground tipped, and he wobbled.

"Grant, are you okay? Do you need to sit?" Her voice reached him as if coming up from the depths of a well.

If he didn't walk over to the unknown object, he could pretend for a little while longer that his daughter was fine, that soon he would find her and take her home and tuck her safely into her bed. *Oh, God, pleasepleaseplease don't let it be my baby!*

"James!" Amy called when the other man continued following the trill of the phone. She pointed toward the crumpled form. "There's something on the ground up there."

As Grant fought to control his shallow breathing, James redirected his gaze, and his expression darkened. Then, looking down at his feet, James bent and picked up an object that had been hidden in the debris. A cell phone.

Fresh waves of distress rippled through Grant, and he tensed to stem the tide.

Amy rubbed his shoulder and squeezed the tendons corded in his neck. "Don't assume the worst. All this means is that William lost his phone. Anything could have happened."

Grant exhaled a long shuddering breath as he tracked James's progress, picking his way through the forest's thorny vines and branches toward the red-and-white object.

In a heartbeat, the dread that had immobilized him gave way to a pounding urgency. The need to know the truth fueled his feet and sent him running toward the unknown form. With each staggering step, each slap of a wet branch in his face, each thud of his heart, a plea drummed in his head. No! No! No! Nononono! *No!*

As he neared the form, he made out a hand, a sock... blood. He reached the body seconds ahead of James. Even before Grant rolled the body over, the unnatural position of the body's limbs left no doubt the man was dead. Even before they found the jagged limb protruding from his gut, evidence showed the man was a victim of the brutal storm. Even before James groaned and collapsed on his knees, choking on a sob, Grant knew the mud-splattered and bloody man was William Gale.

Two emotions, polar opposites, seized Grant back to back. Relief that the body wasn't Peyton's, and stark fear that if William had been killed by the storm that Peyton's body could be lying nearby, just as broken and bloodied. Just as dead.

Amy caught up to them and gasped her horror when she saw William's body. Casting a side glance to Grant, she met his eyes with a stricken gaze, then pulled him into her arms for an embrace, silently lending her support.

Grant stood there, his head feeling a bit numb. Having had his emotions jerked in so many directions in the past day, the past hour, even the past minute, he was reeling. All he knew for sure was he still hadn't found Peyton. He still needed to get his daughter back. And he still had no idea where she might be.

Chapter 16

Amy rubbed Grant's back, trying to bolster him in the face of their gruesome discovery—and the ill it might portend concerning Peyton's fate. Grant's eyes were bleak as he turned without saying anything and wandered away. Zombielike.

She started to follow him when a ragged sigh stopped her. James Gale knelt beside his father's body with his head down, his shoulders hunched inward and one hand on the dead man's shoulder. Sympathy stabbed her. She knew the pain of losing a father, and her own pain nudged her as she studied James's back, stooped with grief. She listened to the tremor of his indrawn breath.

Torn, she glanced back at Grant for a moment before deciding compassion dictated she console James first. She awkwardly lowered herself beside James, the seat of her shorts getting soaked as she sat on the forest floor and stretched her cast out in front of her. When she put an arm around James's back, he flinched, clearly startled by her touch. He whipped his head around, sending her a puzzled look and swiping his eyes with his thumbs.

"I'm sorry for your loss," she said. "Can I do anything for you?"

He blinked at her, as if stunned she was showing him this kindness. Then schooling his face and clearing his throat—all evidence to her that he, like so many men she'd seen do the same thing, was shoving his emotions down, down, down—he sat back on his heels and scrubbed his face with both hands. "No. No, I'm just… It's just a shock." He drew a deep breath and blew it out slowly. "Thank you." He pushed to his feet and held out a hand to help her up. "I'll…call an ambulance. Or the coroner. Or…whoever. I—" He stopped abruptly as his breath caught, and Amy again reached for him, offering condolences with her touch, her expression, her gentle tone.

"I lost my father when I was young. I can't imagine it's any easier later in life. I'm truly sorry."

James gave her an appreciative nod and strained smile. "You're kind. Thank you." He tightened his jaw and turned, sweeping the woods with his gaze. "But a little girl is still missing. After I call the authorities about Pop, we need to search the surrounding woods and pray that she's all right."

Amy dusted the seat of her damp shorts and located Grant rambling through the dense trees, his head turning back and forth as he searched the landscape and called for his daughter. Her heart twisted. Losing a parent, a spouse was devastating enough. She couldn't stand to think of the pain Grant would suffer if he lost Peyton.

Ninety minutes later, the police had photographed the scene, and the coroner had carried William Gale's body away. Despite spotty communication due to the remoteness of the hunting camp and limited cellular service due to the aftermath of the storm, Grant, Amy and James had called friends and family, spreading word of the crisis. A small search party of neighbors and family had been scrabbled together, directed to the Gale's hunting camp and instructed in search procedures. The sheriff's department, stretched thin because of the tornadoes—three had reportedly touched down in and around Lagniappe with one at the Gale camp being a possible fourth—had only been able to offer one deputy to lead and advise on the search.

Amy kept a close eye on Grant, who seemed to be holding himself together by sheer force of will. She'd offered him supportive hugs while they waited for his family and friends to arrive, and his worry for Peyton was palpable. But as the search volunteers gathered, a collective energy, anticipation and hope, hummed in the air and filled Amy with an optimism that she prayed Grant could feel, as well.

"We want to cover the area in a grid fashion, thoroughly covering the woods in an organized and thorough manner," Deputy Hanford explained, as water bottles, two-way radios and flashlights were passed out. "Be meticulous. Sift through leaves and look under debris for any scrap of clothing, any sign of footprints, or… human remains."

A murmur of distress rose from the group, and Amy, her arm around Grant's waist, felt the shudder that rolled through him.

"Don't disturb any evidence you find, but report it immediately to me. Stay within sight of the other searchers…"

Familiar with search procedures because of her job, Amy's attention drifted to the grim faces around the circle. Grant had a large support network of family, coworkers and friends. But all the friends in the world could never erase the pain if Peyton wasn't found.

She sent up a silent prayer as the group dispersed. *Please, God. Please!*

The skeletal search party was just about to head out when one more car pulled up the rutted drive to the Gale's hunting camp—a familiar silvery-blue sedan. David and her mother climbed out of the car, and as they headed toward the assembled group, fresh tension scraped up Amy's spine.

She intercepted them fifty yards shy of the search team's circle and blocked David's path. "What the hell are you doing here?"

David cast her mother an I-told-you-so look, and Bernice jutted out her chin. "We're here to help Grant look for his daughter, of course. We got word of the search party forming from Sue Anders and wanted to help." Her tone held a note of scolding, condemning Amy for not having informed them herself.

Amy squared her shoulders and folded her arms over her chest. "We don't need your help." Cutting a narrow-eyed glance at David, she added, "And since we passed the parish line a mile up the road, I'm betting you're outside the geographic limits of your parole. So you might as well go home."

The crunch of tiny branches and storm debris announced Grant's arrival, even before her mother and David shifted their gazes to him. "What's going on? Are you folks here to help?"

"We intended to help, but Amy seems to think you don't need us."

Grant moved up beside her and sent her a querying look before offering his hand to David and her mother to shake. "I'm Grant Mansfield. It's my daughter that's missing. Thank you for coming."

"David and Bernice Holland," David said, gripping Grant's hand.

Amy pitched her voice lower as she faced Grant. "Grant, they're my mother and stepfather."

A flicker of polite interest and the understanding of someone making connections in their mind crossed Grant's face an instant before a darker countenance, like a black cloud eclipsing the sun, hardened his expression. "I see."

David grunted as he withdrew his hand. "Your expression tells me that Amy has poisoned your head with her lies."

Keeping a level stare on David, Grant placed a hand on Amy's shoulder, so that his arm draped across her back. "She told me about you and what you did to her, if that's what you mean."

Warmth tingled on her neck where Grant's arm brushed her skin, and his possessive and supportive gesture made her head spin, helium-light.

"Amy!" Her mother's expression of horror and petulant tone said she didn't appreciate her daughter sharing the family's dark secrets.

Amy had to bite her tongue not to snap out a waspish retort. She swallowed the bitter words that swelled in her aching chest, knowing an argument with her mother and David wouldn't serve any purpose now other than to cause an unnecessary scene. She and Grant had bigger problems facing them.

Instead she took a cleansing breath. "That's right, Mother. I told Grant. And now, if you'll please leave, we have to start our search for Peyton."

Her mother's mouth opened and closed, and her gaze darted from Amy's to Grant's to David's as if grappling with their dismissal. David shoved his hands in his pockets and tilted his head. He stared at Grant, apparently waiting for Grant to contradict Amy's verdict.

But Grant said nothing. His body remained rigid, his mouth grim as he glared at David. Grant's dark stare said he wanted to tear a piece out of David's throat and watch him bleed.

A frisson of something sweet and strong swirled through Amy while they stood there shoulder to shoulder, facing down the man who'd hurt her and the mother who'd turned her back on her. She felt a sense of unity with Grant that encouraged and empowered her. For the first time in her life, someone outside of law enforcement believed her and supported her.

A giddy little trill of victory danced in her chest when David twisted his mouth in disgust and hitched his head toward the car. "Fine. Come on, Bernie." He reached for her mother's arm as he turned away. "If we're not wanted—"

"Wait." Grant's voice was low and tense.

Amy shot him a curious look.

His brow furrowed, and he rubbed his closed eyes with the pads of his fingers as he released a deep sigh. "Don't go. We can use your help."

He angled an apologetic look at her, and icy betrayal shattered the newly minted bond of solidarity and affirmation.

"Grant?" she said under her breath, trying to hide the quiver of hurt in her voice, "he's a child molester! You can't seriously want a convicted felon anywhere near Peyton?"

"I'm sorry." The hand he'd put on her shoulder slid away, and he gripped her arm as he faced her, his own voice pitched to a whisper. "I know you disagree. But… finding my daughter is my priority right now, and I'll take any help I can get."

She shook her head. "You can't trust him."

A muscle in Grant's jaw jumped as he clenched his back teeth and cast a quick side glance to David. "We can assign someone to stay with him the whole time, to watch him."

She couldn't believe what she was hearing. Acid puddled in her gut, and a too-familiar pain pierced her chest, making it hard to breathe. "He sexually abused me, Grant. For three years."

Grant flinched, and his mouth tightened. "I'm sorry. I can't turn my back on any chance of finding my baby."

No, but clearly he could turn his back on the pain he knew David had caused her. The cold truth slapped her with an open palm. She staggered back a step, drawing her shoulders square and shrugging out of his grip.

"Is there a problem, Grant?" Stan Mansfield called from the circle of searchers. "We're ready to head out."

"Coming!" he shouted back. He waved a hand, directing David and her mother toward the staging scene. "This way. I'll have Deputy Hanford fill you in on the search procedure."

As Grant turned his back and walked away from her, Amy tried to channel her disappointment and shove her resentment into the recesses of her heart. For a few brief moments, she thought she'd found an ally, a refuge from the storms of her past. But Grant's decision to include David on the search party decimated that illusion as surely as a twister through her heart.

"What about dogs?" Grant asked Deputy Hanford as they trudged through the woods, making slow progress in the grid search. "Couldn't we get a couple of dogs out here to track her scent?"

"I've put in a request for a canine team, but our resources are stretched thin due to the tornadoes. There were a lot of houses destroyed and dozens of people missing. The dogs are working overtime already."

Amy kept one ear tuned to the conversation Grant was having to her left and another on the mumbled discussion between her mother and David to her right. They'd been searching for two hours and had made frustratingly little progress. The deputy insisted they be thorough as they searched, so the process didn't have to be repeated. To Amy, moving fast and covering more ground quickly, before Peyton had a chance to wander too far away seemed the better plan, but she deferred to the deputy.

David left his appointed search zone and walked over to confer with Amy's mother. Amy slowed her step and watched him closely.

"What about hiring a private search organization? I'll pay whatever expense is incurred," James Gale said.

Amy whipped her head back to the men on her left. James's generous offer surprised her. Given the history between the families, James's suggestion was the clearest indicator yet that he meant to call a truce, that he truly wanted to help find Peyton.

Grant stopped walking and faced James. "You'd do that? Really?"

"I have a daughter almost the same age as Peyton. If she were kidnapped, then went missing after a tornado, I know how crazy I'd be with worry." James jutted out his chin and pulled his shoulders back. "And because my father is responsible for her disappearance, I feel it's my duty to provide the resources and cover the cost of recovering her."

A hard anger crossed Grant's face before his expression modulated. The fight seemed to drain from him, as if he finally accepted that James wasn't the enemy. "I'd appreciate that. Very much."

"The department has information about private search teams, but even the private operations are likely deployed now. Perhaps you could…"

Amy tuned the deputy out as she glanced back toward her mother. David was gone.

Her heart lurched, and she left her search zone as she stormed toward her mother. "Where is he? He's not supposed to leave the search alone!"

Her mother scowled and shook her head. "Settle down, Amy. He had a headache and went back to the car to get an aspirin from my purse. He'll be back in a couple of minutes."

Amy peered through the shadowed forest and could just make out David's blue shirt as he wended his way in the direction they'd just come. "Someone should go with him. I don't trust him."

Her mother gave an exasperated huff as she waved a hand toward David's retreating back. "Feel free. If dogging your stepfather and indulging in your paranoia is more important to you than finding that little girl, go. Leave your post and follow him."

Amy fisted her hands at her side. "I would if I thought I could catch up to him. I'm a little encumbered, though. Remember?" She raised her casted foot and waggled it. "You should go. I asked you to stay with him, Mom."

Bernice continued walking the search path, using a large stick to look beneath leafy plants and push aside thorny vines as she moved forward. "And I've told you I will not listen to your hurtful accusations anymore. You've caused enough harm to my marriage. I'm done with your delusions and hatefulness."

"Delus—" Amy gasped, fury slamming her. But she cut off her retort. A shouting match with her mother served no purpose other than to cause a spectacle. Finding Peyton needed to be her focus now. Her priority. She'd spent enough of her time, emotions and energy fighting her mother and David. She was done, done, *done*! She couldn't wait to leave Lagniappe once and for all and never look back. No more awkward Thanksgivings with her mother, pretending they still had a viable relationship. No more frustrating attempts to convince her mother of the truth. No more disappointing phone calls where nothing was resolved.

With Stella destroyed by the tornado, she no longer needed to hang out at Grant's house waiting for repairs to be finished. As soon as Peyton was found, Amy would be on the next plane out of town. She would go back to Idaho and forget about her life in Louisiana.

She hobbled back to her search zone, her back poker straight and her body taut with determination. But as she resumed her careful examination of the ground, the trees, the scrub brush around her for clues to Peyton's location, her vision blurred, and her chest drew tight. She blinked away the tears and struggled to take a breath. This decision shouldn't be so painful. She'd been on the brink of a separation from her mother for years. So why did the idea of leaving town hurt so much?

Her gaze lifted to Grant as if pulled by powerful magnets. Sensing her gaze, he turned toward her, and their eyes locked. His brow dented, and stark concern washed the color from his face.

She shook her head, silently reassuring him that the ruckus between her and her mother wasn't due to a morbid discovery. She was fine, she lied with a forced smile.

But he didn't look away. For several long seconds, they simply stared at each other, communicating their mutual frustration, anxiety…apology—and silently drawing strength from each other for the task at hand

and the hours ahead. The squeezing tension in her lungs eased, and in place of that pressure, a swelling fullness expanded inside her. But rather than suffocating her as the stress of her broken relationship with her mother did, the blossoming sense of saturation filled her with warmth. Calm. Direction.

Amy marveled at the stillness that settled in her soul as she held Grant's gaze. She hadn't known this comforting feeling of assurance and acceptance—of *home*—in a long time. Not since before her father died.

A couple of hours earlier, she'd been so hurt by his choice to allow David to join the search team. But deep down, she understood his reasoning. She didn't for a minute believe Grant had sold her out easily. The look in his face now said he'd hated hurting her, hated the situation that had forced his hand. He was her ally, just as she was his, and she'd miss that alliance when she returned to Idaho.

Idaho. Her stomach dropped. How could she think of leaving Grant and his family? For the first time in years she felt connected to someone. She had a family she wanted to be part of and people she wanted to give her love to.

Her breath stuck in her lungs. So how in the world did she reconcile this new yearning—her desire to be part of Grant's family—with her career? She'd worked too hard to get on the smoke-jumping team. She loved the thrill of her job, the other jumpers, the service she provided. She couldn't imagine walking away from the life she'd built in Idaho. But neither could she bear the thought of giving up on Grant. Not that Grant had said he wanted her to stay, that he had feelings for her or any intention of remarrying. He was obviously still grieving his first wife.

"Over here!" Hunter said, and Grant tore his gaze from hers to see what his younger brother had found.

Amy plodded over to the spot Hunter pointed out to the other searchers, grumbling under her breath about her encumbering cast. What she wouldn't give to be free of the darn thing so she could cover ground more quickly, be of more help finding Peyton.

"What do you have?" Deputy Hanford asked.

Hunter crouched in a lower-lying area where rainwater had collected and left the ground muddier than other parts of the woods. He pointed out broken stems and small indentations in the mud and leafy debris. "These look like footprints."

Amy leaned to see past the circle of searchers to the undelineated impressions on the ground.

"How do we know those weren't made by a deer or a dog?" one of Grant's neighbors asked.

"Wrong size for animal tracks. Plus, look." Hunter, who according to Grant had served in the military and had tracking experience, pointed farther up the muddy patch. "Skid marks. Then what look like knee impressions and—" he shifted the aim of his finger "—hand prints."

Sure enough, two distinct small hand prints had been left in the less-boggy mud. Amy's heart pattered, and without questioning why, she sidled closer to Grant, grasping his hand.

"Looks to me like she was running, slipped and fell to her knees. Pushed up and kept going." He pointed deeper into the woods. "That way."

"What's that direction? How far are we from any sort of homes or businesses?" Grant asked, his grip tightening on Amy's hand.

"Highway 212 is not too far that way," Deputy Hanford said, consulting a paper map and a handheld GPS. "But we are still a couple of miles from the closest business district."

"But we are going in the right direction. That's a good sign. Right?" Stan Mansfield said, clearly trying to boost his son's spirits. Facing the direction Hunter indicated, Grant's father cupped hands around his mouth and shouted, "Peyton! Call if you can hear us!"

"If we're close to her, why isn't she answering?" Grant asked, aggravation lining his face.

"Lots of reasons," Deputy Hanford said. "We don't know what condition she is in. Considering the storm and her kidnapping, it's quite likely she's in shock, dehydrated, disoriented, injured—"

Grant groaned, and beside her, she felt his body sag. She rubbed his arm and murmured, "That doesn't mean she is. But even if she's disoriented or confused, we'll still find her. Have faith."

He cast her an appreciative side glance for her efforts to bolster him, even as Hunter said, "There are plenty of cases on file of lost hikers fleeing from search parties due to confusion brought on by stress and dehydration." Hunter gave his brother a level look. "But she's near here. I know she is. And we will find her, Grant."

"All right," Deputy Hanford said, "let's regroup and concentrate our efforts to the west, toward Highway 212. Spread out this direction—" he motioned with his hand "—and continue searching in the same grid pattern moving this way." Another slash of his hand to guide the search party.

Amy gave Grant one last encouraging squeeze then headed back to her place in the search line. She cast a glance toward her mother, making sure she and David had heard and complied with the new directive.

Her mother stood facing the ground they'd already covered, back toward where the cars were parked. "I'll just wait here for David."

Amy's gut pitched. "He's not back yet?"

"No. But he will be." Her mother craned her neck as she scanned the woods, biting her lip. "He will be. Soon."

Amy watched the other searchers head out, closing in on where they'd determined Peyton had fled, then turned back toward her mother. A sick suspicion gnawed at her. She gritted her back teeth, deciding to wait with her mother. Just in case. "He'd better be back soon."

"He will," her mother repeated, her chin high and her lips pursed.

But thirty minutes later, the rest of the search party was out of sight, and David had not returned.

Peyton stopped running when she reached the highway. She was out of breath. Her legs were tired. Her elbow was bleeding.

And she was scared. So scared. Even though the horrible storm was over, the bad man was dead. Would people think she'd killed him? She shivered, remembering how she'd had to squirm out from under his body. The yucky blood. His spooky eyes.

What if the dead man became a zombie and chased her? Bobby Hamilton said zombies ate people. She didn't want to get eaten, so she'd run away from the dead man. Then she'd heard voices. People yelling her name, chasing her. And she'd got more scared, more confused. She ran and ran until her legs hurt. She was so hungry her tummy growled and felt hollow. Her throat ached from crying, and she wanted a drink of water really bad.

She should never have run away. Daddy was going to be *so* mad at her. He'd probably spank her and send her to her room for a month. Maybe a year. But she still wanted to go home. She missed Daddy and Kaylee. And Amy. Amy was nice. Maybe Amy would be her new mommy.

Thinking that made her feel bad. As if she'd forgotten about Mommy. Tears trickled down her cheeks, and her nose got runny when she thought about Mommy. She missed Mommy most of all. Amy said Mommy was still with her. Amy felt her Daddy's love like a hug.

Closing her eyes, Peyton tried to feel Mommy's love. A hug should be warm, but she was wet and cold. A hug should make her happy, but she was sad and scared and lonely. It was starting to get dark, and that scared her, too. She didn't want to be in the woods alone at night. Mean animals lived in the woods. And zombies.

With a whimper, she left the cover of the woods and jumped the ditch at the side of the road. She looked both ways, trying to decide which way led back to her house. The day was ending, and already the sky was turning dark. She wouldn't be able to see much longer. How was she supposed to find her way home?

The mean man had driven a long time. She didn't think she was near her house anymore, but she had to try. The voices in the woods were still yelling, still chasing her. Her steps wobbled a little as she started down the road. Her head felt dizzy, but she was scared to stop. If the people in the woods caught her, would she ever get back to Daddy? Were the voices zombies?

Wiping her eyes, she started running again. The dead man was chasing her, and he'd eat her if he caught her!

She heard a rumble behind her, and a car whizzed by on the highway. She remembered how the bad man had grabbed her. Maybe she should get off the road. She glanced behind her, crying harder now. She was trapped.

There were cars on the road, where bad men could grab her. But there were zombies in the woods.

"Mommy, I'm scared," she whispered, even though she knew Mommy wasn't there.

Another grumble of tires made her look behind her. Headlights were coming down the road. Run! She scrambled down into the ditch, trying to get in the woods. She hid behind the closest tree and crouched down. Her knees were shaking. Hard. Please don't let the car see her!

But the car stopped. Backed up. And a man got out.

Her heart beat so hard she could feel it against her chest. A whooshing noise filled her head. Was he a *zombie*? She covered her mouth trying to muffle the sound of her crying.

"Peyton?" he called.

A chill raced through her. He knew her name? But how? She didn't recognize his voice, and couldn't see his face because of the bright headlights behind him. Was it a zombie trick?

He walked closer. "Peyton Mansfield, is that you?"

Daddy only used her last name when he was mad. Was this man mad at her? She bit her bottom lip trying hard not to make a noise.

"Don't be scared. I'm a friend. Come on out, honey."

A friend? She wrinkled her nose and squinted as she tried to see his face. He stopped a few feet short of the trees, and his body blocked enough of the headlights that she could see a little of his face. He did look kinda familiar.

"We've all been looking for you, Peyton. Why don't you come on out, and I'll help you get home."

He moved closer, and her chin trembled. "A-are you a zombie?"

He laughed. "A zombie? No. Not a zombie. I'm a real man. My name's David."

She couldn't remember any friend of hers named David. But as he got closer, she could see his face better, and he didn't look like a zombie.

But then she thought about what Amy said about stranger danger. The bad man had been a stranger, and he'd kidnapped her.

"I'm not supposed to talk to strangers."

"Oh, I understand. But I'm not really a stranger. I'm a friend. I've been helping your daddy look for you."

She sat straighter. "You know my daddy?"

"Yes. I met him today. And I know Amy. I'm her stepfather."

"You are?"

"Yep. Don't you remember meeting me the other day when you got off the bus? I was in my car in your driveway, talking to Amy. You waved at me."

She did remember a guy waving at her last week. She looked at him hard and decided he was the same man.

He put his hands on his hips and sighed. "Honey, your daddy is real worried about you. Why don't you come on out, and I'll take you to him."

"Is he mad at me?"

"No, baby. He's just real worried."

But she still wasn't sure.

"Don't be scared, Peyton. I won't hurt you."

She did want to go home. If this man was really Daddy's friend, Amy's stepdad, she could trust him. She stood up on shaky legs and crept out from behind the tree where she'd hidden. "You'll take me home?"

He smiled at her, but the shadows from the headlights made his smile look spooky. "Sure."

She walked toward him, and he took her hand. Her

stomach felt jumbly—half scared, half happy to be going home. Her legs were so tired that they shook as he helped her climb in his backseat. "Can we call my daddy? I want to talk to him."

He winked at her. "We will soon. I left my phone at home, but we'll call him first thing when we get to the meet-up spot." Amy's stepdad closed the car door and got in the front seat. The doors all locked as he pulled out onto the road, and her heartbeat jumped. The bad man had locked her in, too.

"I want my daddy." She started crying again, having second thoughts about whether she should have gone with Amy's stepdad. What if he lied? What if he wasn't really Amy's stepdad? What if he wasn't really a friend of Daddy's?

"I'll take you to him. Don't cry, sweetie."

Peyton tried to be brave, tried not to cry, but the longer he drove, the more her stomach hurt. "When will we be at my house?"

"Soon. But your dad wanted me to take you to our special rendezvous place. We can order a pizza and have ice cream, and he'll come pick you up there in a couple of hours."

She didn't know what a *rondeepoo* place was, but she didn't like the idea of waiting for daddy. Her tears came harder, and she started getting scared again. Really scared. "I don't want pizza. I want my daddy! I want to go to my house!"

David smiled at her again, but it didn't make her feel better. "Soon, Peyton. First, you and I can have some fun."

The search for Peyton was called off when darkness fell, and a new band of strong storms passed through the region. Hurrying through the slashing rain and flicker of lightning, the search party made their way back to the hunting cabin where they'd left their vehicles.

But David wasn't there. Amy noticed her mother's puzzled look and stalked over to her.

"Where'd he go?" she called over the drumming of the wind-whipped rain. "Why did he leave without you?"

Her mother wiped rain out of her eyes and shook her head. "I don't know. I don't get it."

Amy gritted her teeth and hitched her head toward Stan's SUV, which Grant had borrowed. He had the engine running, waiting for her. "Come on. Get out of the rain. You can try calling him from Grant's car."

Her mother followed her to the SUV and climbed in the backseat. Once they were inside, wiping their hands and faces on the clean T-shirt Grant pulled from his dad's gym bag, Amy's mother fished her phone out of her pocket. One of the volunteer searchers had had the forethought to bring sealable plastic baggies, which saved everyone's cell phones from the rain.

Amy turned on the front seat to face her mother, waiting impatiently while her mother listened to David's cell ring without response.

"I got his voice mail," her mother said, then looked away and lowered her voice. "David, it's me. The search has been called off for the night because of the lightning. Where are you? I'll ask Amy to drop me at home. Call me."

Bernice thumbed the disconnect and raised her eyes to Grant. "Could I impose on you for a ride to my house?"

"Sure." Grant pulled out on the rain-drenched highway, and they rode in silence toward home. The patter of rain and swish of the windshield wipers seemed to punctuate the lonely sense of defeat that went unspoken.

Peyton was still missing, and the fresh round of spring storms threatened to wash away any footprints or other clues to her whereabouts.

When he let Bernice out at her house, Amy's mother gave Grant a sad smile. "I'm sure she's fine. You'll find her just as soon as this weather clears."

Amy tensed, ready to chastise her mother, but she bit her tongue. Anything could have happened to Peyton during the tornadic storms that had blown through town. Her mother's stiff assurances fell flat in the face of such grave circumstances.

But Grant managed a weak smile and a nod. "Thanks for your help."

Before Bernice climbed out in the driving rain, she scanned the empty driveway and frowned. David's car was not there.

The tingle of apprehension that had been growing in Amy's gut spiked. "Call me when you find David. If you find him."

Bernice drew a weary breath. "I will."

Amy watched her mother dash through the rain to the side door and into the house. She prayed she was wrong about David's sudden disappearance, but Amy didn't believe in coincidence. If she was right, Peyton had escaped one monster, only to be caught by another.

Chapter 17

After dropping Amy's mother off, Grant reluctantly returned to his house. Going home felt like giving up on Peyton, but the lightning made any further searching now dangerous. He cut the engine but didn't leave his truck. Hands still gripping the steering wheel, he stared, without really seeing anything, into the storm-ravaged landscape of his yard. His chest ached so much it stole his breath, and he fought the despair that threatened to drown him. First his friend Joseph, then Tracy, now Peyton. Connor was alive but gone from his life. Was he destined to lose everyone he cared about?

Amy reached over and curled her hand around his. Her fingers were cold from the chilly rain, but her comforting gesture, her presence, her help with the search all filled him with a warmth he hadn't known in a long time. In more than a year. Not since Tracy had offered the same unflagging love and support.

His heart squeezed, and he raised her hand to his lips. "I appreciate your help more than you could know."

She tightened her grip on his fingers. "Let's go in, get dried off."

He nodded, and they darted into his house together. But he wouldn't stay in. As soon as this bad weather moved out of the area, nighttime darkness or not, help from a search team or not, he would be back out looking for his daughter. They'd covered two square miles around the Gale's camp and found little to indicate which direction Peyton had gone, but he wouldn't give up. He would cover the same ground, move deeper into the woods, stay up all night if he had to, until he found her.

Grant held the door for Amy as she limped inside, more dragging her casted foot now than walking on it. Her shoulders drooped, and her face was drawn with fatigue, a reflection of the difficult day they'd both had.

His mother had driven to his house as soon as the search was called off and was waiting there now with Kaylee. He took his baby from her and snuggled her close, treasuring the feel of Kaylee in his arms. Would he ever hold Peyton this way again?

His mother greeted Amy with a brave smile, then faced Grant. "I really think I should keep Kaylee with me at our house tonight, honey. You two are obviously exhausted and need to concentrate your energies on finding Peyton."

He hugged Kaylee and fought the rising panic inside him. Peyton had been in those woods. He knew it in his gut. So why couldn't they find her? Why didn't she answer their shouts?

When the notion that she could have been caught up by the tornado and carried miles from the Gale's cabin entered his mind, his brain recoiled. He simply couldn't bear losing Peyton.

Burying his nose in the sweet baby shampoo scent of Kaylee's hair, he gave his head a small nod. If he was going back out looking again, his mother's offer made sense. He wanted to be free to move out at a moment's notice when this storm cleared or should the authorities find anything. He blanked his mind to what that *something* might be.

His mother rubbed his back and gave his cheek a kiss. "We'll find her, Grant. Keep believing that."

Grant didn't say anything. He wished he had his mother's faith and optimism, but his spiritual life had taken a hit when Tracy died. He found it harder to believe in happy endings and the power of good over evil. If he lost Peyton, too…

He slammed his eyes shut, and his stomach lurched. Fate couldn't be that cruel, could it? Deep down he knew it could. Life gave no guarantees. He kissed Kaylee on the head and passed her back to his mother. "Thanks, Mom. I need to go change clothes now."

"Can I fix you a sandwich? Maybe heat up some soup?" Julia offered.

He started to refuse her, but he knew he'd need fuel for the night ahead. Somehow he'd choke down some food before he left again. "Sure."

"Amy?" she asked. "A sandwich?"

"Thank you. That'd be great."

While his mother headed into the kitchen, Grant went upstairs to change into dry clothes. He heard the thump of Amy's cast as she followed him up the steps. As tired as he was, Amy had to be twice as worn out. For every step he'd taken in those woods today, she matched his pace, dragging that heavy cast with her.

He paused at the top of the staircase and murmured, "Thank you…for all your help. You got more than you bargained for when you decided to stay here. And to top it off, a tornado wrecked your dad's car." He exhaled slowly. "I'm so sorry."

His limbs were weighted with sandbags of worry and fatigue as he dragged himself to the door of his bedroom—and pulled up short. The tarps and plywood patches his father and Hunter had employed to patch the tornado damage to this corner of his house provided temporary protection from the ongoing storm, but water and wind had damaged much of the room's contents, including his bed and dresser top.

He released a groan, and his shoulders slumped as he sagged against the door frame. He muttered a curse word he rarely used anymore, in deference to young ears. Then, slapping the wall with his open palm, he shouted the earthy word. But all the cursing in the world would never restore his bedroom, or bring Peyton home, or ease the raw grief that consumed him.

He jerked in surprise when Amy wrapped her arms around him from behind and rested her cheek on his shoulder. For several moments, neither spoke. He simply absorbed the comfort and support she offered with her silent embrace. Amy had no real ties to his family, no obligation to give so much time and energy to the search for Peyton. She just had a good heart. A generous nature. A loving warmth and inner strength that he appreciated more than he could say. When she left, he would miss her. Deeply.

He furrowed his brow, realizing Amy's reason for staying in Lagniappe had been nullified when the tornado wrecked Stella. She had nothing keeping her here any longer. Disappointment and sharp regret pinched his heart. "Don't feel like you have to stay. If you need to get back to Idaho—"

"Seriously?" she interrupted, her tone sharp. "You think I'd leave before we find Peyton?"

"I only meant—"

Her embrace tightened, cutting him off. "For your information, I've come to care a great deal for your daughters." She exhaled a tremulous breath that tickled his ear, and her voice dipped. "And their father."

Beneath the heavy grip of his anxiety-tight lungs, his heart performed a tuck and roll. He raised a hand to the arm she had tucked across his chest and gave her forearm a squeeze. "The feeling's mutual. We'll miss you when you do go."

She loosened her grip and sidled around until she faced him. "Are you trying to get rid of me?"

He snorted a dark laugh. "Hell, no." Plowing his hand into her damp hair, he cradled the side of her face. "In fact, I wish I knew a way, short of criminal restraint, to keep you here a little longer."

She bit one side of her bottom lip and arched an eyebrow. She eased closer, her body canting against his and her arms looping around his neck. "You can start by kissing me."

Grant's muscles tensed, and his fingers tightened against her scalp. Despite the heat that surged through him, he balked. He thought of the kisses they'd shared earlier today, while trapped beneath the playhouse rubble. Had that really been today? So much had happened since then. And yet so little had changed.

He thought of Tracy, as he did so often every day, but instead of guilt tingeing the memory, he sensed that Tracy would have liked Amy. Had they known each other, they would have likely been fast friends. And he knew Tracy would have been grateful for the help Amy had been to him, not just today, but throughout the past weeks.

He stared into Amy's green eyes, her gaze expectant, bright with desire. And—God help him—he wanted her. He *needed* her. He needed to lose himself, even just for a few moments, in the comfort and raw passion she offered.

But he hesitated a bit too long, and her expression darkened. "Okay. I get it." She pulled away, her eyes downcast, her cheeks flushing. "I read things wrong and—"

He gripped her hand hard before she could slip away and hauled her back against him. "You read nothing wrong."

Anchoring her body against his with a splayed hand low on her back, he cupped the base of her head with his free hand and captured her lips with a searing kiss. He surrendered to the need he'd been trying to suppress the past two weeks. The crush of her body against his and the velvety softness of her lips was more than he could fight. Maybe his defenses were down, or maybe he'd just decided Amy was worth any regrets he'd have later. Either way, she tasted like a piece of heaven, a momentary reprieve from the hell his life had become.

Stepping toward her, he pressed her against the wall, trapping her with his body and savoring the feel of her generous curves. Her toned muscles and soft breasts were a sexy combination, a physical manifestation of the complex woman in his arms. Both tough and tender. Softness and steel. Unique—and everything he wanted in one beautiful, confounding, terrifying package. Yes, terrifying—because he didn't know how she fit in his life, how he could live with the risks she took for her job, or if she even wanted the life he could give her.

Amy threaded her fingers through his hair, then slid her hands down his back to cup his buttocks. She made an erotic purring noise as she angled her head and deepened their kiss. Her tongue flicked against his lips and he answered the invitation by tangling his tongue with hers.

His body blazed to life, every cell in him waking from his year's celibacy and greedy for fulfillment. He indulged himself with the crackling energy that hummed through his veins and heated his blood. For just a few moments, he wanted to feel alive, he wanted to forget his pain, he wanted to relish the pleasure that he found in her kiss, her touch, her welcoming warmth.

But a harsh buzzing cut into his bliss, a stark tone he tried to ignore. A phone. Not his. If something had happened with Peyton they'd call his phone, not hers. But the intrusion of reality still dampened the fire flaring inside him.

When her phone continued to buzz, she finally pulled away from his embrace and checked the screen. "It's my mother." She thumbed the screen and lifted the cell phone to her ear. "Please tell me you found David and he has a good alibi for his disappearance."

"I…no. Oh, Amy…" Her mother's voice carried from the receiver. "You need to come over. I…found something. Something terrible."

Amy's eyes darted up to meet his, and the color in her face drained. Grant's stomach plummeted to his toes. Dread left him cold and numb.

"I…I don't know what to do—" Her mother's voice cracked.

"What is it? Mom!"

"Can you come?"

Grant managed a small nod, and dug deep for the strength to face whatever Bernice had found.

Amy looked ready to be sick, but she started for the stairs. "We're on our way."

Chapter 18

Amy drew an audible breath as Grant pulled in at her mother's, screwing up her courage to face whatever waited inside. Sitting there, staring at the front door of her mother's house, filled her with an uneasy déjà vu. "How many times have I sat in this driveway dreading going inside this house?"

Grant looked at her across the front seat, and his forehead creased. "I've been so caught up in my worry over Peyton, I ignored how hard this must be for you, facing your stepfather and what he did to you. Forgive me." He laced his fingers with hers and raised her hand to his lips. "You up to this? I can go in alone if you'd rather wait in the car?"

She sat straighter and jutted her chin out. "Hell, no." She softened her expression and squeezed his hand. "Thanks for the offer. I appreciate the thought, but I refuse to cower or hide from David and what he did to me anymore. That only gives him the power."

Grant's expression shifted, lighting briefly with a quick grin of pride. "You're right. Good for you."

Still clutching his hand, she rubbed her thumb over his knuckles, wordlessly thanking him for his support. "I decided long ago not to let him rule my head or my life any longer. I won't let my memories of what happened hold me back or dictate my life any longer."

Her mother appeared at the front door, her face wan, and Amy groaned. "Let's go see what this is about."

She shouldered open the passenger door and slid off the seat of the truck into the steady rain. Her ankle throbbed a protest for the long hours of walking she'd put the healing joint through today, but she soldiered on. She couldn't let her aches and pains hinder the search effort for Peyton. Grant's daughter was all that mattered.

She was surprised by how much Peyton mattered to her. As if she were her own daughter. She couldn't deny that she'd formed a bond with the girl in the past weeks that went beyond casual interest. She'd become emotionally invested in the lives of Grant and his girls.

When she thought of leaving town, returning to her lonely apartment in Boise, her chest ached with regret. She'd miss Grant and his family more than she had any right.

She and Grant hurried—as much as her hobble would allow—to the front porch, getting drenched again by the rain. Bernice ushered them inside, wringing her hands and gnawing her bottom lip.

"Show us," Amy said without preamble. "Whatever you found, just show us."

Her mother nodded, her expression dark and shattered. Her eyes were rimmed in red, and her face was blotchy from crying. "When I didn't find David at home and he still didn't answer his phone, I got worried about him. I thought maybe he'd gone to the pharmacy to refill his migraine medicine or gone out to pick up dinner for us and had car trouble."

Amy bit the inside of her cheek, trying to be patient with her mother's explanation. "And?"

"Well...I thought I could check our credit card bill online to see if he'd made any purchases this afternoon."

"And had he?" Grant asked, the tone of his voice indicating his impatience.

"I didn't get that far. I...got sidetracked." More hand rubbing. "You see, David spends a lot of time in here alone while I'm at work. I asked him once what he did all day, and he said he watched TV and piddled on the computer. He bought some supplies the other day to start woodworking again in the old shop behind the house, too, but he hasn't—"

"Mom! What did you find?" Amy asked, curling her fingers into her wet hair.

Bernice pressed her lips in a taut line and gave a small hitch of her head, telling them to follow her. She led them into the living room where a laptop was set up on the desk where Amy's dad had always paid the bills. "His access to the laptop was password protected, which surprised me." She wet her lips and sat down at the desk. "After all, he and I are the only ones who use the laptop." Her mother put a shaking hand on the wireless mouse and rolled it to wake up the screen. "It took me a few tries to guess his password, but I finally guessed it and..."

Beside her Grant stood silently, his face grim, his muscles taut. Amy's gut knotted, somehow knowing what was waiting for them. She swallowed hard to force down the bile that tried to inch up her throat.

Her mother cast a mournful glance over her shoulder at them before finally clicking through to a file of photographs.

Amy's breath caught, and Grant groaned in disgust.

David had a file overflowing with kiddie porn. Still photos and video clips captured images of children in horribly lewd and compromising positions.

Rage surged through Amy, and her stomach rebelled with a lurch of nausea. "Damn it, Mom, didn't I tell you? I've been telling you for years the man's sick, and you wouldn't listen to me!"

Grant turned away, plowing both hands through his hair as he started pacing.

Bernice closed the file of graphic images and buried her face in her hands. "Oh, Amy, I'm sorry. I should have listened to you, but…" Her mother's shoulders shook as she sobbed.

"But you didn't," Amy snarled, unwilling in that moment of vindication to cut her mother any slack. "You believed that monster over your own daughter! You let him back in this house and enabled him as he continued his filthy hobby."

Balling her hands, her mother dropped her fists to her lap and sent Amy a sharp glare. "I know what I've done. Believe me, I am every bit as disgusted and angry about this as you are. More so, I'd wager! I've been sleeping with this man. Trusting him. Loving him unconditionally for fifteen years, only to be betrayed—"

Her mother's voice cracked, and Grant used the lull in the arguing to step forward.

"Ladies," he said, putting a hand on Amy's shoulder. She hadn't realized how hard she was trembling until she felt his steadying grip. "Can we put a pin in the accusations and regrets for a minute and focus on the bigger picture? David has disappeared at the same time my daughter is missing. That could be a coincidence, but…" He huffed a harsh sigh. "We need to find them. Both of them. We need to report David's nasty little hobby to the police and use any other clues on his computer to find my daughter."

Bernice shook her head and swiped at her cheeks. "I

know what you're thinking…but even if he has her, he wouldn't hurt her. I know he wouldn't."

Amy growled her frustration. "Do you know that, Mom? Maybe he wouldn't cause her physical pain, but I'm proof that he knows how to inflict emotional pain. Those pictures he's saved are proof he doesn't care about the psychological suffering or exploitation of children!"

"I know it looks bad for him, but I can't believe he'd—"

Amy threw her hand up to interrupt. "Save it. We'll debate your blind faith later. Right now, we have to get Peyton back." She glanced to Grant, who'd already pulled out his cell phone and was dialing. Facing her mother again, she squared her shoulders. "You said you never made it as far as checking the credit card activity. Can you do that now?"

Bernice swiveled back to the computer and looked at it as if it were a viper. "Oh, David," she muttered, her voice anguished. "What have you done?"

"He may not be answering his calls, but maybe we can track his phone's GPS. Most phone companies have apps that let you trace a phone in case it is lost or stolen."

Bernice nodded. "I have that on mine. I think we had it added to David's, too, when I added his line to my plan last month."

"Good. Let's do that." Amy waved a hand toward the laptop, but her mother looked at the computer as if it were a snake. Amy huffed. "If you don't want to do it, slide over and let me."

Her mother raised her chin and put on a determined face. "I can do it."

Bernice tapped the keyboard and navigated to the website where she could track David's cell phone. After entering passwords and answering security questions, she finally entered David's mobile phone number and took a deep breath before clicking Enter.

Amy held her breath as the web page refreshed and brought up a map of a fifty-mile radius around Lagniappe. An icon showed David's cell phone location with a small green star. Her mother zoomed the map to better read the location of the phone.

The green star was centered over—her mother's address.

Amy groaned her disappointment.

"That can't be right," Bernice said, scrunching her nose in confusion. "He's not here. I looked for him all through the house and garage when I got home."

"It doesn't mean he's here. Just his phone." Amy shuffled away from the computer, giving a side glance to Grant, who was across the living room in conversation with the sheriff's department. He sent her an inquisitive glance as she headed into the hallway and shook her head.

She clomped into her mother's bedroom, Bernice at her heels, and sent a careful glance around the clutter. After rummaging through dirty clothes and old newspapers, she found David's phone in the nightstand drawer... turned off.

Her mother sighed. "Well, that answers one question. He's not used to carrying a cell phone. He forgets it a lot."

"Or he doesn't want people to be able to call him, track him," Amy said, tossing the phone back in the drawer, with more force than necessary.

Her mother opened her mouth as if to defend David, then seemed to think better of it. An expression of disillusionment crossed her mother's face, and Amy could guess Bernice's thoughts had returned to the horrid porn David had password protected in his computer. "I *am* sorry, Amy. I should have never doubted you. I just… couldn't let myself believe such a terrible thing about that man I loved."

"But you could believe I was a liar? That I'd drag my family through criminal proceedings out of misplaced anger or vindictiveness?"

Tears welled in her mother's eyes. "I know. I was wrong. But…yes, it hurt less to think you were a bitter teenager who didn't get along with her stepfather. David hid his sickness from me well. He was convincing with his denials, and I wanted to believe him. I…" She released a shuddering sigh. "I have no excuses. I let you down, honey, and I'm ashamed of myself."

Amy's eyes stung, and she blinked hard to force back the tears. "There'll be time for apologies later. Right now, we need to concentrate on finding Peyton. Let's check your credit card and see if he's made any purchases this afternoon."

An excruciating hour later, Amy and Grant were out of ideas for finding her stepfather when a sheriff's deputy finally became available from storm-related calls to answer their summons. The deputy filled out a report, called in a request for a warrant to take the laptop as evidence and collected photographs of David to be issued with a "be on the lookout." Bernice's joint credit card with David had shown no purchases and given no clues where David was.

Grant rambled restlessly through Bernice's house, feeling useless. They had no proof David had Peyton. Perhaps his best move was to go back out and keep searching the woods as he'd planned before Amy's mother called. Darkness had fallen outside, which would hamper his efforts dramatically, but when he thought of his baby girl spending a night alone in the woods, scared, hungry, possibly injured, nausea gripped his gut and dread choked him.

"Come on," Amy said, stepping in front of him and squeezing his shoulder. "Let's go home. There's nothing left to do here."

He agreed with a silent nod and watched the awkward parting between Amy and her mother before trudging through the rain to his dad's SUV.

As he opened the passenger-side door for Amy, she gave him a lingering look and touched his cheek. Damn, but he would miss her support when she left. She'd been an anchor for him in this most recent storm.

She settled in the SUV, and he hustled around to the driver's door. How likely was it he could offer Amy a life that would persuade her to give up smoke jumping? Disappointment jabbed him, and he gripped his keys so tight the metal bit into his palm.

Amy had worked hard to be selected for the smoke jumping team. It had been part of her therapy, her personal recovery plan from her abuse. Who was he to ask her to give up that achievement?

He glanced across the front seat at her as he cranked the engine, compunction drumming in his chest. She'd said she wasn't the motherly homemaker sort. She didn't cook, claimed not to be good with children—though what he'd witnessed in her interactions with his girls disproved that. And she could learn to cook. Tracy had.

He craned his head to look out the rear window as he backed out of the driveway. If Tracy learned to be a homemaker, Amy could—

He braked hard, a jolt of dismay slashing through him. He jerked his gaze up to Amy, clenching his jaw in regret when he recognized where his train of thought was traveling. He could deny it all he wanted, but the truth was obvious. He was trying to fit Amy in Tracy's mold. He was trying to fill the hole Tracy's death had left in his soul. But Amy wasn't Tracy. She would never be the right shape and size to plug the empty spot Tracy had left. No one would. "Skunk…"

Amy's brow dented with worry. "What?"

He slammed his eyes shut and shoved down the raw ache that accompanied the reminder of his loss. Nothing and no one would bring Tracy back or replace her. *Deal with it, Mansfield, and move on.*

He shook his head. "Nothing."

Amy's frown said she was skeptical, but she didn't press him. Instead she brought him back to the subject that mattered most at that moment. Finding Peyton.

"I know you were planning to go back to the woods tonight, but I'm wondering…" She nibbled her lip, her expression pensive.

"Go on." He cast side glances at her as he pulled onto the state highway and headed back to his house.

"Maybe our time would be better spent tracking David down. I don't believe in coincidence, and the fact is that he disappeared the same day, near the same time and place Peyton did."

Acid filled Grant's stomach, accepting the harsh truth that his daughter could be with a known pedophile. He swallowed the bitter taste that inched up his throat and groaned. "You're right. I didn't want to admit it before but…you're right." He curled his lip in a sneer and gritted his back teeth. "God help him if he touches her—"

"Grant, I…" She rubbed her palms on her damp shorts. "We need to think about where he could have taken her. An abandoned house, a secret room somewhere, an unused campground or cave…"

He shook his head. "No caves in this part of the country. You should know that. You grew up here."

She waved a hand. "I'm just throwing things out there. But maybe I've watched too many B-grade thrillers." She turned toward the window and twisted her hair around her finger as she thought. "Maybe on short notice or simply for ease, he took her somewhere like an amusement park or the zoo. They'd be pretty empty today with all this bad weather." She motioned toward the drizzle that continued to fall and the storm-damaged trees that lined the road. "Or a motel…if he was thinking of keeping her for a while."

Grant gripped the steering wheel tighter. "What do you suggest?"

Amy pivoted toward him on the seat. "We have pictures of David and Peyton. We could pick a few kid-friendly places and flash their pictures around. Maybe someone has seen them. If he were trying to earn her trust, he might take her someplace to have fun and eat junk food. You know, to win brownie points with her."

"As good of a place to start as any." He gave the SUV more gas, driving past the turn to his house. He handed his cell to Amy. "Call my mom. Ask her to stay at my house until we get back. Just in case Peyton shows up there by some miracle."

"Got it."

While Amy dialed and talked to his mother, Grant talked to God for the first time in months. His faith may have taken a hit after Tracy's death, but he needed all the hope, all the help he could get. *We could use a miracle here,* he prayed. He blinked back the sting of moisture in his eyes then added, *Please.*

Chapter 19

Amy and Grant spent the next three hours checking every pizza shop, ice-cream parlor and toy store. They worked in motels as they came to them, flashing the pictures of David and Peyton to the employees, and got exactly nowhere. Frustration clawed at Amy as they returned to the parking lot after trying Mr. Gator's to no avail.

Grant slammed the door of the SUV, mirroring her sense of futility. He loosed a loud, tense growl and pounded his fist against the steering wheel. "This is a waste of time!"

"Is it?" Amy countered, trying to stay positive for Grant's sake. "It's only a waste until we find someone who saw her. We're crossing off possibilities, narrowing the search."

He sent her a weary, defeated look. "My little girl needs me, and every minute that passes is another that I've let her down. All I've ever wanted was to protect my family, and I've failed." A shadow flickered in his eyes. "Twice."

She sat taller, a prickle walking down her spine. "Grant, do you…blame *yourself* for Tracy's death?"

He didn't answer for a moment. Neither did he crank the truck's engine. He stared blankly out the windshield, while rain dripped from his hair onto his cheeks like tears. "No…not exactly. I know the Gale family and their thugs planted the car bomb."

"Good."

He drew a slow breath and continued, "But as her husband, it was my job to keep her safe, and I didn't." He paused, his brow furrowing. "I was older than my friend Joseph. I should have known better than to play in that refrigerator, but I didn't. And Joseph died. And it was my job as Peyton's father to protect her, and I let her be kidnapped."

Amy shook her head, aghast that he could blame himself. "You didn't *let* anything happen. That presupposes you knew what would happen and didn't stop it. Okay, maybe you were careless as a kid, but so was Joseph. Kids make mistakes. You need to forgive yourself!"

He sent her a skeptical glance.

"And while I respect your belief that it's your job to keep your family safe, you're not a superhero or a god. You're not magic or all-powerful."

His expression grew irritated. "I know that. What's your point?"

"My point is bad stuff happens. Terrible, horrible stuff happens, and it sucks! Wives get murdered. Children die in freak accidents. Fathers die too early. Tornadoes destroy homes. Stepfathers steal your innocence. Ankles get broken. People have heart attacks. People lose their jobs."

He shot her a confused frown. "Who had a heart attack?"

"Plenty of people. Thousands every year. And lots of people lose their job in a bad economy."

He huffed an irritated sigh and cranked the engine.

"So life sucks and then you die. Is that your point? Real helpful, Amy. Thanks."

She reached for the key and turned the ignition back off. She needed his full attention and wouldn't share it with the traffic. "My point is you don't have a monopoly on the bad stuff that happens in life. You're not responsible for it, and you're not alone in it. You are only responsible for how you respond to it."

He gave her a patient look. "Listen, I appreciate what you're trying to do, but—"

"I'm not done."

He groaned and rested his head on the seat back.

She grabbed his forearm and shook him. "Do you know what happens after a wildfire ravages a mountain?"

"Go on. Tell me."

"New growth. Wildflowers and shrubs that had been choked out because of the dense forest can get the sunlight they need to grow. In fact, the heat of a wildfire ruptures hard-shelled seeds, allowing them to receive moisture and sprout. The flowers bloom because of the fire, Grant. Raspberries, plum, chokecherries—food for the wildlife—grow as a result of the fire. New seedlings emerge. Life goes on. The environment *prospers*."

"So wildfire is good." He flipped up his palm, his tone sarcastic. "Then why put them out?"

Now she growled her frustration. "Don't be purposely obtuse. *Wild*fire is bad. Obviously. That's why I have a job. But *controlled* fires are part of a normal wilderness management plan, and—"

"Thanks for the environmental lesson. Can we get back to looking for my daughter now?" He reached for his key, and she grabbed his wrist.

"I'm saying you have a choice. You can stay stuck

in your pain and let it control you, or you can cherish the blessings you still have and make every day count."

He gave her another false grin. "Make lemonade. Got it."

"Grant, I just want to see you happy. From the day you stopped to help me with Stella, I've seen the pain in your eyes, the grief that is holding you back from appreciating life and enjoying your family. I know you miss Tracy, but do you think she'd want you to stop living because she's gone?"

"So…get over it," he said raising his hands and his voice. "Is that your advice?"

She was startled by the bitterness in his tone, the anger he directed at her.

"Grant, I'm just trying to—"

"What do you know about my pain? What I face *every day*?"

"I've been there, Grant. I know—"

"You know nothing!" He jabbed a finger toward her, his face hard. Bleak, raw emotion blazed in his eyes and creased his face. "You've suffered setbacks, sure. But you *ran away* from your pain. When things got tough at home, you ran away to Idaho and put it all behind you."

His accusation stung. How dare he compare her abuse, her choices with his!

"Well, news flash, Amy. I don't have that luxury. I can't run away from my grief, because I'm a father. I see my wife in my daughters' faces every day. I live with the fact that she is not going to see them grow up." His voice cracked, and he fisted his hand, clenched his teeth, seemingly angered by the evidence of his rising heartbreak. After drawing a deep breath, his nose flaring while his mouth stayed pinched closed, he added, "But there is something I can do to avoid more pain down the road."

An uneasy tremble stirred in her belly as he started the truck and sent her a dark, even stare. "What does that mean?"

"First thing tomorrow, I want you to leave. You have nothing keeping you here anymore, so it's time you ran back to Idaho and your wildfires."

Her mouth dried. She knew he was reacting to the stress of the search for Peyton, the lack of sleep and hot buttons she'd poked with her attempts to shake him out of his malaise. But his rejection hurt. "I want to stay until Peyton—"

"She's *my* daughter. Finding her is my problem, not yours."

"But I care about her." She drew a shaky breath. "And I care about you, Grant. I thought we had—"

"Feelings for each other?" He looked away as he backed his truck out and cruised slowly through the parking lot toward the road. "Yeah, well, maybe we could have, if you'd stayed. But frankly, I can't let myself fall in love with someone who jumps out of planes and puts herself in the path of wildfires for a living. So that's a nonstarter."

Amy rocked back in the seat, her lungs contracting as if sucker punched.

"I don't need more worry or stress in my life. Sitting by the phone waiting for the call that I've lost someone else I loved." He gave a short derisive laugh. "Oh, hell, no. Not happening. So whatever you thought we had…"

Whether she understood the source of his bad mood or not, his words hurt. The sentiment had to be rooted in truth. Grant didn't have the same investment in their relationship, the same hopes for a future that she had. Speechless, she squeezed the armrest, her heart breaking.

He shook his head and pulled the truck into traffic. "Just not happening. And I think the sooner you go home, the better it'll be for everyone."

Grant rubbed a hand over his breastbone. He knew heartburn wasn't the only reason for the gnawing in his chest. He suffered from a bad case of regret, remorse and heartache.

One glance across the front seat of his truck told him how Amy had received his harsh brush-off. The hurt and disappointment in her eyes contradicted the proud lift of her chin. She wouldn't say as much, but his cold tone and abrupt delivery of his edict had wounded her. Which had been his intent…to a degree.

He knew if he'd been gentle in his delivery of his decision, she'd have argued with him, and he simply didn't have the strength or will left to debate what was already difficult for him. He taken a hard line to make his position clear, but the biting cruelty of his words had been overkill. He ground his back teeth together, hating himself for the sharp edge he'd wielded in his tone.

Perhaps it had been a product of his own pain, his frustration with all the spinning wheels in his life, but he had no excuse for hurting Amy. She'd been nothing but good to him.

But when she'd started in on him about needing to deal with his pain, count his blessings and get his life in order, she'd cut too close to the truth. He *had* allowed himself to wallow in his grief, paralyzed by his fear of losing anyone else. And when he felt himself falling in love with Amy, he'd panicked.

Loving Amy meant accepting Tracy was gone. Loving Amy meant risking his heart again. Loving Amy meant facing his fear of loss every day that she left home to report for work. How could he live with—

"Grant, stop!" Amy cried, jolting him out of his deliberations.

He slammed on the brakes, realizing he'd been dangerously inattentive in his driving. His heart thundered as his gaze darted left and right, seeking the hazard Amy had seen. "What?"

Twisting in her seat, she tapped her window as she pointed to a parking lot they'd just passed. "Back there. I think I saw David's car in that motel parking lot!"

Without questions, he whipped the SUV into the nearest driveway—that of the hamburger joint next door to the motel, and pulled into a parking spot. A fresh dose of hope and adrenaline flooded his veins as he gathered the photos they'd been showing about town. "Where?"

Amy had already slid out the passenger-side door and aimed a finger toward the side lot. "I didn't see it at first. It's kinda hidden toward the back, by the trash bin."

Together they hurried to the sedan, and Amy circled the vehicle while Grant peered inside the locked car.

"This is it. I'm sure. The decal on the back is Mom's employee parking sticker for the hospital."

Grant pivoted toward the long row of doors, two floors' worth of motel rooms. Peyton was here, somewhere. He'd bet his life on it. His body hummed with anticipation and rage, spoiling for a fight. "So what… do we just start banging on doors?"

Amy headed toward the front of the building, giving her head a brisk shake. "No. The commotion might alert David. He could hide her or slip out and get away. Let's show the front office manager the picture. He should be able to tell us which room David's in."

A tiny bell clinked as they pushed through the office door and pounded the counter to call the clerk out from the back.

"Hello? Anyone back there?" Grant shouted, his impatience mounting. *Hang on, squirt. Daddy's coming.*

Amy loosed a shrill whistle, and a sloppily dressed college-age guy stumbled out from a back room, a slice of pizza in his hand. "Coming. Keep your pants on."

Grant muffled a growl, and Amy placed a hand on his wrist. "We need your help."

"Smoking or nonsmoking?" the guy asked as he chewed. "Second floor all right?" He started tapping computer keys with one hand while he took another big bite of his pizza.

"We don't want a room." Grant slapped the photos onto the counter. "Have you seen this guy? His car's in the lot. Maybe you rented a room to him a few hours ago?"

The desk clerk shuffled closer and glanced at the photo. Shrugged. "I don't know. Don't remember."

Grant slapped the pizza from the guy's hand and shoved the picture closer. "Look again."

"It's important," Amy added, her tone calmer. "What about the little girl? She might have been with him."

The guy wiped his mouth on his sleeve and gave Peyton's photo another glance. "Yeah, maybe. Why? What's it to you?"

Grant tensed. "She's my daughter. What room are they in?"

The desk clerk glared at Grant. "I ain't allowed to give out information on guests. I could get fired."

"What room are they in?" Grant repeated, barely holding on to his temper.

"We believe his daughter is in danger. This guy has no right to have her with him. Just tell us what room they are in. Please?" Amy's tone said she was losing her patience, as well.

When the guy still hesitated, his arms folded over his chest, Grant drilled the counter with his finger and leaned threateningly close to the clerk. "I'm this close to banging on every door out there until I find them."

The clerk scowled back. "Try it, and I'll call the cops."

Amy lifted the receiver of the landline on the counter. "Please do. It will save us the call when we find them. Did we mention he's a convicted felon? Did we tell you the charges you could face for harboring a criminal?" Amy threw in the last bit just to rattle the guy's cage. She didn't know whether the cops could charge the clerk with anything or not.

It was worth the shot, though, because the clerk edged back to the keyboard and tapped a few keys. "What did you say his name was?"

"David Holland," Amy said.

The clerk shook his head. "Nope. No Holland."

Grant glanced at her. "Does David have an alias?"

"Does 'Dirtwad' count?" She sighed and flattened her hand on the counter. "Just tell us the rooms you rented in the last five hours. Can you do that?"

The clerk scratched his mop of hair and screwed his mouth sideways. "Well…"

Grant growled under his breath and paced in a tight circle. "Dude, I'm five seconds from pounding an answer out of you."

Amy caught Grant's hand, pulling him up short from his restless shuffling, and laced her fingers with his. Her silent support and calming presence spread through him, taking the edge off his agitation—probably saving the kid behind the desk from major dental work.

The clerk banged a few keys on the computer and brought up a list. "Only rented two rooms this afternoon. A lady named Hinklebaum and a guy named John Smith."

Grant snorted. "Creative."

The desk clerk glanced at Amy. "Mr. Smith paid with cash."

Amy wiggled her fingers at him, egging him on. "Smith's room number?"

The guy cut a glance at Grant, then back at the screen, muttering, "I'm so fired." Then, "Room 210."

Chapter 20

Grant spun on his heels and charged out the door without waiting for Amy to follow.

She dug a twenty-dollar bill out of her purse and slapped it on the counter. "For what it's worth, we won't rat on you. Thanks for your help."

She limped out of the front office and hobbled onto the elevator with a housekeeper just before the door closed. "Which way is room 210?"

"To your left. All the way to the end."

Amy thanked the woman and hurried off the elevator the second the doors opened enough for her to scoot through. She spotted Grant mid-walkway, jogging toward the end of the row of doors. He flexed and balled his fists as he reached the door, and for the first time, she feared what he might do to David. Not that she minded David being taught a painful lesson before returning to jail, but she didn't want Grant landing in lockup with her stepfather. "Grant, wait. Take a breath. Don't go crazy if she's there."

He hesitated just long enough for her to join him at the door to 210. "Are you kidding? If he's touched her, I'll rip him apart."

"And join him in jail. Is that what you want?"

"Fine." He rolled his shoulders and took a deep breath

before banging on the door. "Holland, open up! We know you're in there."

Amy saw the curtain over the window move slightly at the edge, just enough for someone to peek out. "David, give yourself up. Open the door."

Grant banged his fist again. "Now, Holland! Open this damn door!"

David opened the door a crack, the security chain in place. "What do you want, Amy? Can't a guy get away for a while and think?"

"Think?" She chortled. "Is that what they call kidnapping and child molestation these days?"

Grant craned his head trying to see past David into the motel room. "I want my daughter. Where is she?"

"What?" David sounded truly offended. "I don't have her. I just needed some space, some—"

"Daddy?" a tiny voice called from inside the room.

"Peyton!" Grant shoved on the door, which went nowhere thanks to the chain.

"Daddy!"

David tried to slam the door, but Amy stuck her cast in the way. Pain shot up her leg from the jolt, and she chalked up one more grievance against her stepfather.

"Open this door, you son of a bitch!" Grant snarled, ramming the door with his shoulder.

"Amy, I can explain. It's not how it seems—" David said through the thin door.

Pushing Amy out of the way, Grant stepped back and kicked the door with the flat of his heel. Wood splintered around the chain mounting. Another kick sent the door swinging open.

David backpedaled from the door, standing between his visitors and the little girl in the far bed.

Amy quickly sized up Peyton's condition. Grant's

daughter was still dressed in muddy clothes, and as she sat up, she rubbed her eyes sleepily.

Grant gave his daughter only a cursory glance before charging David and pinning him against the wall with his hand around David's throat. "You sick monster!"

"No…" David gasped. "I—"

Grant reared back with his fist and smashed it into David's jaw.

Amy rushed over to the men and grabbed Grant's fist before he could land another blow. "Grant, stop!"

"Like hell! He took my daughter! God knows what perverted things he did to her!" He was trembling with rage, his face contorted with misery and a thirst for vengeance.

"Please, Grant—" Amy wedged herself between the men and framed Grant's head with her hands. "She's safe, Grant. Look at her!"

He angled a quick glance to his daughter, and his expression shifted to one of unfathomable pain. His Adam's apple bobbed as he swallowed. "Peyton, baby, are you okay? Are you hurt?"

Peyton's eyes were round with fear and confusion, but she shook her head. "I wanna go home."

Amy curled her fingers against Grant's scalp, her throat tightening with emotion. "I know you want to beat him to a pulp, but Peyton doesn't need to see her father bloody another man."

She felt the shudder that raced through Grant as he sucked in a breath and closed his eyes. "Take her to the truck. Call the cops. I'll wait here with David."

Grant's nostrils flared as he gave David a last glare. "I will see that you rot in prison for this."

Amy signaled to Peyton. "Come on, sweetie. Your daddy's going to take you home now."

Grant gave David an angry thrust as he pushed away, then shook out his hand as he turned toward the bed.

Peyton's eyes filled with tears as she scooted across the mattress and flung herself into her father's arms. "I'm sorry I ran away, Daddy."

"Oh, baby, I'm not mad. I'm just so glad you're okay." He pulled her into a bear hug and scrunched his eyes closed. "I love you, Peyton. So, so much."

His shoulders shook as he carried her toward the door, and when he gave Amy a querying look from the door, his eyes were red and damp. "You sure you're all right?"

She jerked a nod. "Yeah. David and I are gonna have a little talk while we wait for the police. I'll catch up with you later."

Grant stared at her, obviously still calculating, but with a small nod, he disappeared outside.

Amy turned back to her stepfather, her gut sour with loathing.

"Thanks," he said, rubbing his jaw.

"For what?"

He moved his hand to his throat, where a red hand print marked where Grant had grabbed him. "Keeping that guy from beating the tar outta me."

"Save your thanks. I just wanted the honors for myself." Swinging an arm up, she smashed the palm of her hand into David's nose.

He howled in pain and clutched at his bleeding face.

"That one was for the pain you've caused my mom today. She found your sick little photo collection on your computer."

She followed the punch with a swift, hard knee to his groin—not easy while balancing on her casted foot, but oh, so satisfying when she saw his eyes bulge in pain.

He grunted as he doubled over in agony and crumpled on the floor.

"And that was for teenage me, who always wanted to kick you in the jewels but never had the courage. Well, I've found my courage, David, and you will never hurt me or the people I love again!"

He angled a defiant glare at her and struggled to his hands and knees, sucking in shallow breaths. Blood dripped from his swelling nose, and he dabbed at the flow with his fingers.

She slipped her cell phone from her pocket and thumbed the voice recording app.

"What did you do to Peyton?" Her gut roiled, imagining Grant's little girl being subjected to the depravity he'd put her through years before.

"Nothing," he muttered.

She barked a laugh of disbelief. "What did you do, David? Tell me!"

"Nothing! I found her wandering along the highway, and I was taking her home!" he ground out. "Ask her."

"Oh, we will. But I want to hear it from you." She showed him the phone with the recording graphic shining from the screen. "Confession is good for the soul, they say."

His expression darkened, and he held Amy's stare. "I was taking her home. I swear, I never touched her."

"If you were taking her home, why did you stop at this motel and register with a fake name?"

He lowered his head, groaning. "She was tired. She needed sleep."

She goggled at the lunacy of his response. "She could sleep anywhere. Why not go to her house and wait for

Grant? Or call us? Or take her to the sheriff's office? Or take her to Mom's house?"

"I would have." He started to push up off the floor, his voice stronger now. "But she—"

Bracing one hand on the wall for balance, she planted her good foot in his back and shoved him back onto the floor. "Stay down."

"I need a rag for my nose," he grumbled. "I think you broke it."

"I'll get it. You stay put until the cops come." She started toward the sink at the back of the room, but only made it two steps before his arm snaked out and wrapped around her good foot. He yanked hard, leaving her unstable, off balance.

Her hand flailed, grabbing for something to catch herself. But she found only air. She landed on the floor. Hard. Her head snapped back and cracked against the thin carpet. She blinked, stunned and disoriented.

"You bitch!" David crawled to her and used his legs to pin hers. "I will not go back to prison because of you!" With one hand, he held her shoulder against the floor. His other hand smacked her across the cheekbone, making her ears ring. "You've been a thorn in my side from the day I married your mother. Now your meddling is gonna cost you."

Stunned by the shift in David's demeanor, she shook off the throb in her skull and focused on the maniac glowering at her. David reached into his pocket with his free hand and pulled out a hunting knife. With a flick of his thumb, a five-inch serrated blade unfolded from the handle. The ominous flash of silver sent a chill to her marrow.

"If you take me down," he growled, "I'm bringing you with me."

* * *

Grant clutched Peyton to his chest as he carried her across the parking lot, bombarding her with questions. "Are you okay, squirt? Do you hurt anywhere? What did that man do to you? What did he tell you?"

"Can I go home now?" she said, sniffling. "I'm sorry I ran away. I won't do it again."

He stroked Peyton's tangled hair as he wove through the parked cars toward his dad's SUV. "It's all right, honey. You're safe now," he said, as much to reassure himself as his daughter. He was still shaking from the inside out. *Thank you, God, for leading me to my baby.* "We'll go home in a minute. Are you hurt?"

He wondered if the kid in the front office had called the cops like he was supposed to. The sooner the cops came, the sooner he could take his daughter home where she belonged.

"No, I'm not hurt. I'm hungry, Daddy. I want French fries."

"Of course, Pey. Whatever you want. We'll get it soon." Grant shifted Peyton in his arms so he could open the truck door. After lowering Peyton on the passenger-side seat, he glanced back toward the second floor of the motel. A prickling premonition told him Amy needed him. He'd hated leaving her alone with David, knowing her painful history with him, but he'd wanted Peyton out of harm's way. Gritting his back teeth, he weighed his options. He couldn't leave Peyton alone, but his gut said he needed to get back to that motel room, needed the cops...

"Peyton, honey..." He leaned in the front seat and motioned his daughter back to his arms. "C'mere. I know where you can get something to eat."

She obediently wrapped her arms around his neck,

and he headed back to the motel office. Shoving through the front door, he marched behind the desk and into the back room where the scruffy college kid was watching NASCAR on the TV.

"What the hell—?" the desk clerk said, rising from his seat.

"I need your help." Grant put Peyton in a vacant chair and walked to the television to change the channel to cartoons. "If you haven't already called the cops, do it now. Send them to room 210." He motioned to Peyton. "This is my daughter Peyton. The guy in 210 kidnapped her. Give her a piece of your pizza, and be nice to her until I get back. Don't leave her alone or let anything happen to her until I get back. Can you handle that?"

"I'm not babysitting your kid!" the guy groused.

Grant pulled money from his pocket and thrust thirty dollars at him. "Yes, you are." He drilled the desk clerk with a no-nonsense glare. "She'll eat pizza and watch cartoons. Easiest money you ever made."

As he turned back to Peyton, he liberated a slice of the pizza from the box in front of the clerk. "Squirt, I have to go back and help Amy. You stay here and eat pizza with this nice man."

"No, Daddy! I want to stay with you!" Panic filled her eyes, tearing at his heart.

"Please, Peyton. I need to help Amy. I promise it's just for a few minutes." He pointed to the TV. "Look, it's Bugs Bunny, the silly rabbit Daddy used to watch as a kid. You'll love it. Eat this pizza, and be sweet for him. Okay?" He pulled out his cell phone and gave it to Peyton. "Here, squirt. Call Grandpa and Uncle Hunter. Tell them where we are—the 6th Street Motel. Tell them to come. Stay on the phone with them until I get back."

She sent the desk clerk a dubious glance but didn't argue anymore.

Grant sighed his regret and frustration. Pausing at the exit, he aimed a finger at the scruffy clerk. "Now call the cops." He flexed his fist which still throbbed from smacking David's face, and the prickle of premonition escalated to a shrieking warning siren. A chill crawled down his spine. "And tell them to send an ambulance."

Chapter 21

Amy froze as David pressed the knife against her throat.

"You should have stayed in Idaho," he said with a sneer.

"Agreed," she rasped.

Except that if she'd not returned to Lagniappe, she'd have never met Grant and his precious daughters. She'd have never fallen in love. A keen ache slashed through her, remembering Grant's rejection just moments earlier.

I can't let myself fall in love with someone who jumps out of planes and puts herself in the path of wildfires.

"I should cut you, just to even the score for how you've ruined my life." David angled the blade, and she felt the jagged edge scrape her skin.

So Grant was scared to love her because of the dangers of her job, yet here she was, about to die in her hometown, at the hands of the man she'd fled Louisiana years ago to escape. The thought of dying was almost as abhorrent to her as the notion of leaving Grant and his family without putting up a fight.

"You've been no picnic for me, either." Despite his weapon against her neck, she met his glare with a challenging glower. She wouldn't cower for this man ever again. He'd stolen enough of her soul. She hadn't made the smoke-jumping team by quitting after her first defeat. She hadn't sent David to jail as a teenager by giving up when her mother doubted her. She'd fought against the odds before, and she would again. She would fight for her life—and for a future with Grant.

David's fingers dug into her shoulder, and he shook her. Waving the knife in her face, he railed, "That snotty attitude of yours is gonna get you killed. And, know what? I'll enjoy it. You've been nothing but a pain in my ass for years."

"The cops will be here soon," she said, praying it was true. "Don't add murder to the charges against you."

"Shut up!" David's eyes glinted with a feral intensity, and his face grew florid. His temper was spiking, a side of David she was unfamiliar with. But whether he had a violent side or not, even the most well-adjusted person acted unpredictably when pushed to rage. Even a docile animal could become dangerous when cornered. "I don't plan to be here when the cops arrive. But how can I pass up the opportunity to thank you properly for destroying my life?"

He poked the tip of the knife under her chin, and she winced at the prick to her tender skin. He rested his wrist against her collarbone, and she felt a tremble shake him. A similar rush of adrenaline left her insides quaking.

A warm tickle told her blood had seeped from the puncture wound. His hesitation was telling. He did have *some* reticence about killing her. But his resolve could harden in a heartbeat. He could dispatch her with a flick of his wrist.

She needed to regain the upper hand. Quickly.

In the kickboxing class Amy took at her gym in Boise, she was known for her agility and speed. But the weight of her walking cast left her slow and clumsy. She scrolled through the self-defense aspects of the kickboxing class, scrambling for an action plan.

Sirens wailed somewhere beyond the door Grant had left open when he took Peyton to the truck. Following the sound, David's gaze flicked away from her for an instant. And she seized her chance.

Cupping her hands, she clapped her palms against David's ears as hard as she could, attempting to burst his eardrums.

As he yelped in pain and surprise, his hand flinched. The tip of his knife jerked and sliced along the upper arc of her throat. He recoiled, ducking his head and clutching his ears as he roared in agony. His knife thumped onto the floor.

Ignoring the sting of her cut neck, she landed another blow, plowing stiff knuckles into his Adam's apple. She didn't get a clean lick on him, but his gasping sound said she'd caused enough damage. Moaning, he curled his body inward in self-defense as he rolled off her.

Freed from his weight, she struggled off the floor. Amy staggered to the bed where she dropped wearily on the edge, panting for breath. She clasped a hand to her neck and palpated her wound. It seemed to be a shallow cut, but *damn*! It stung like fire.

Mere seconds passed before David pushed to his hands and knees. She spotted his target lying a few inches from his grasp. The knife.

"No!" Lunging from the bed, she dived for the blade. Her skull cracked against David's as he surged toward the same prize. Pain ricocheted in her head, but her fingers closed around the knife handle.

David grabbed her wrist, squeezing her arm with a viselike grip. He battled her for the knife. Amy struggled, not only to keep possession of the hunting blade, but to stay on her feet. David's every yank and twist of her arm shifted her tenuous balance. Her cast dragged at her, but adrenaline fueled her fight. She tried to knee David in the groin again or stomp his foot, anything that would give her an advantage, but he managed to dodge her moves.

Fear and determination fed her endurance. But rage lit his face and gave him a frightening strength. Seizing the front of her shirt, he growled and flung her aside like a rag doll.

Amy stumbled and fell onto the bed. David pounced, landing so hard on her chest that air whooshed from her lungs. Still, she held the knife out of his reach, though her palm grew slick with sweat. She clawed at his eyes, thrashed her good leg, praying she could disorient him. If she could distract him, could she free her arm from his grip? She only needed to land one debilitating strike with the knife...

But David squeezed harder on her wrist, until the pain of his crushing grip sent spots of light flickering in her peripheral vision. He smashed her hand against the headboard until the knife slipped from her numb hand. Her saving grace was the clattering sound that said the knife had fallen behind the bed rather than on the pillows.

David's rage didn't ease when she lost the knife. Instead he shifted his fury-powered grip to her throat. Her heart raced, and a fresh wave of panic swelled in her as his hands crushed her windpipe. She gasped for a breath, but little air reached her lungs past the pressure of David's chokehold.

Desperate to save herself, she flailed her numbed arm at him. Her throbbing hand slapped at him futilely. Squirming to roll free of him proved equally fruitless. Amy's energy quickly waned. Her lungs burned. She scrabbled, clawing at his hands, fighting to break his grip, to loosen his hold enough for even a small breath. As her strength drained, her sight dimmed, narrowed to the wrathful determination contorting David's face.

The hoarse rasp of too-little air wheezed in her throat, in her ears as she struggled. She was losing. Fading…

Grant. A sharp pang of regret pierced the muzziness that enveloped her. If only she'd told him she loved him…loved…

Grant gulped air as he sprinted up the motel stairs. The clang in his head, the sense of urgency that had swept through him telling him Amy was in danger, propelled him up the steps three at a time. God had answered his prayer in bringing Peyton back safely, but would the price be losing Amy?

He'd been gone from the motel room too long. If anything happened to Amy, it would be his fault. Icy dread speared his heart. If he lost another woman he should have protected, another woman he loved…

His breath caught as he topped the stairs and bolted down the second floor walkway. His step only faltered a fraction of a second as the truth rattled through his head. He *loved* Amy. He loved her, and he could lose her.

"Not on my watch," he muttered as he sprinted to the door of room 210. As he swung through the open door, he spotted David straddling Amy. And Grant saw red.

He charged toward the bed and planted his hands on David's back. "Get away from her!"

Grabbing the neck of David's shirt and the waist of his pants, Grant hauled Amy's attacker off her. With an angry roar, Grant flung David to the floor. Storming to the spot where David landed, he gave the known child molester a hard kick in the jaw and another in the ribs.

While David cradled his gut, groaning, Grant rushed back to Amy.

She'd sat up on the bed, coughing and sucking in raspy breaths. She fingered the bright red marks that stood out on her neck from where her stepfather had choked her. A thin cut trickled blood from under her chin as well, and Grant's gut swooped at the sight of the garish crimson smears.

He dropped onto the bed beside her, brushing her hair away from the telltale marks and carefully pulling her into a gentle hug.

"Grant…" she murmured breathlessly.

"I'm here. You're okay." He kissed her forehead and examined the injuries to her neck as guilt snowballed in his soul. He'd failed her, because he hadn't correctly judged the risk David posed. "I shouldn't have left— "

Her sharp gasp stopped him. "Grant, look out!" she croaked.

He turned just as David swung a lamp.

Grant dodged the threat—almost. The heavy base clipped his temple hard enough to make his ears ring. Head throbbing, Grant surged to his feet, assuming a fighting stance as David, clearly still suffering from his injuries, struggled to heft the lamp for another offensive swing. When the lamp arced toward him again, Grant ducked.

The weight of his makeshift weapon made David stumble, even as he snarled. "Come on, lover boy. Bring it!"

Grant lowered one shoulder and rushed David, backing him against the nearest wall. His opponent dropped the lamp and lobbed a punch to Grant's gut. Grant shook off the hit and reared his fist back for a satisfying jab in David's sneering lip.

"Grant, stop!"

Amy's voice was stronger, and as he pulled his arm back for another punch to David's face, her warm hands grabbed his wrist.

He cast a startled look over his shoulder and needed a moment to cool his temper before he spoke. "What are you doing, Amy? Stand back. I can handle him."

"You've already handled him. Look at him."

The raw hoarseness of her voice scraped through him, a ready reminder of how his failing had hurt Amy. When she hitched her head, he directed his gaze toward the man in question. David's eyes drooped, only semiconscious. Grant's fist, twisted in David's shirt, seemed to be the only thing keeping the man on his feet.

"Self-defense is one thing," she said quietly, prying his fingers off David's collar. "Revenge is another. Don't stoop to his level. Don't do something that could take you away from those precious girls."

He drew a long, calming breath and blew it out slowly. A shudder rolled through him as he shoved the anger and vengeful wrath from his lungs. One by one he uncurled his fingers, releasing David. Groaning, Amy's stepfather slumped to the floor.

Grant rolled his shoulders as he stepped back and shook the tension from his hands. "Where the hell are the cops?" He moved to the open door and craned his neck to check the parking lot, the road. "That punk in the office had better have—"

Hearing a scuffling noise, he spun back toward David. Amy's stepfather had crawled toward the bed and pulled himself to his knees. Amy turned as well, just as David shoved to his feet and stumbled toward her.

"Seriously?" she croaked and easily tackled him to the floor. "Give it up, David! You're finished."

"No!" David moaned, fighting her. "Won't go back to prison…can't go back!"

Grant hurried over and grabbed the lamp that had been used against him as a weapon.

"Grant!" she said, her tone a warning.

Much as he'd have liked to beat David over the skull with the light, he shook his head. He raised the power cord and offered it to her. "Maybe this will hold him still until the cops come."

She sent him a lopsided grin and began looping the cord around David's feet, while Grant used the sheet from the bed to tie their captive's hands. After knotting the binding, Grant had only enough time to pull Amy into a fierce hug and whisper, "We need to talk," before two Lagniappe PD officers burst through the door with weapons drawn.

Grant sank onto the bed his hands out for the police to see he was unarmed. "Glad you could join us, officers. It's been a long day."

Chapter 22

Hunter came to the motel to take Peyton home while Grant and Amy dealt with police reports and stopped by the emergency room for a quick check of their injuries. By the time they were finished, dawn was breaking, and they were both too tired and emotionally wrung out to have the conversation Grant wanted.

Rather than returning to Grant's house, Amy asked to be dropped off at her mother's, knowing Bernice's revelations about her husband and David's arrest would have left her mother distraught. While Grant understood Amy's concern for her mother, he couldn't help but feel Amy's refusal to even retrieve her toothbrush from his house was a bad omen for their relationship. Not that he could blame Amy for pulling away, shutting him out. He'd said some harsh things, drawn a proverbial line in the sand between them.

The hell of it was, he hadn't changed his mind. He still couldn't see himself having a future with Amy, much as he wanted it. It would be too hard. There were too many complications, too much difference in their lives, their goals. How he would tell her goodbye, though, was anybody's guess. Already his heart felt smashed. The grief and pain of a second lost love was already tearing him apart.

His only consolation was finding Peyton sleeping peacefully in her bed. Given that Hunter was dozing on the floor beside Peyton's bed, reaching up to hold his niece's hand as they slumbered, spoke to the fact that peaceful sleep had not come easily for his daughter.

Grant's chest contracted, twisted by the rush of gratitude and love for the two people in that frilly bedroom. His sweet girl, safe at home, an answer to his prayers. And Hunter…for all the guff he'd given Hunter, the baby of the Mansfield brothers, growing up, he wouldn't trade him for anything. Hunter came through for him time and again. Even Cinderella and Sebastian were curled on Peyton's bed, as if protecting their friend, or comforting her, or simply glad to have her home. Cinderella lifted her head and chirped a meow before curling in a tighter ball to return to her catnap.

Next he checked on Kaylee and found his youngest was in her crib, her diapered butt adorably poked in the air as she snoozed with her thumb in her mouth. He kissed his fingers and pressed them softly on Kaylee's head, careful not to wake her. His next stop was the guest bedroom, where he found his mom and dad, asleep, on top of the made bed, fully dressed as if ready to charge off at a moment's notice. The baby monitor on the stand beside his mother hummed with Kaylee's gentle snores.

Standing there, knowing how his brother and parents had been ready at a moment's notice to help and support him, knowing his daughters were both safe in their beds, a wave of emotion washed through him. Joy, love…humility. He was blessed. No matter what losses he'd suffered, what pain he'd endured this past year, he had a family that was second to none. Unconditionally embracing him and standing by him. Amy's words from the evening before filtered through his head, convicting him.

You can stay stuck in your pain and let it control you, or you can cherish the blessings you still have and make every day count.

She'd been right. He'd known it then as he knew it now. But he'd been so blinded by his concern for Peyton, his stubbornness, his pain that he'd shut her down, sniped at her and—*hell*—thrown away the possibility of true happiness with her.

Grant's gut roiled, and he grabbed the door frame as his knees buckled. He'd told her to take a hike. Told her he had no room for her in his life. That she wasn't *worth* the worry and potential pain her career would cause him.

Amy had bravely faced her fears, her dark past for him, and he'd tossed her aside. She'd given her all to helping him, trudged through the woods, dragging that chafing cast without complaint, stood up to her stepfather, and he'd repaid her sacrifice and generous support by ushering her out of his life. Regret rolled through him. He was an idiot.

A tiny creak from the bedroom door had his mother wide-awake and sitting up in an instant.

"Grant?" She blinked and rubbed her eyes.

His father stirred then, quick to reach for his wife and assure himself she was safe.

"Hey," Grant whispered. "Sorry to wake you. Just wanted you to know I'm home. Thanks for holding down the fort while I was out."

Stan was on his feet, rounding the end of the bed. "Everything all right? What happened with the police?"

"Everything's fine now. I'll fill in the details when I've had some sleep."

His mother pushed off the bed. "Come sleep in here. Your bed is still wet from the storm damage."

"No. You go back to sleep. I'll take the couch."

He fended off his mother's protests and was turning to go downstairs when his mother asked, "Is Amy with you?"

A sharp ache sliced his chest, and he shook his head.

"No? Is she all right? What—"

"That explanation will keep until morning, too." His reply silenced his parent's questions, but their worry and doubts were obvious in the slant of their respective brows.

Grant made his way to the living room and collapsed on the couch, virtually unconscious before his head hit the throw pillow. Until a high-pitched shriek woke him a couple of hours later.

Heart thundering, he bolted into the kitchen, where the sound had originated. Peyton was at the back door, fumbling with the lock, tears pouring down her face.

"Peyton, baby!" Grant scooped her into his arms and clutched her close. "Daddy's here. You're safe."

"Daddy, m-my h-h—" Peyton hugged him for a moment, crying and choking on her tears. Finally she twisted in his arms and pointed out the window to the backyard. "M-my house!"

Grant followed her gaze to the pile of rubble that was Peyton's playhouse. A tremor rolled through him as he remembered the terrifying moments when the tornado raced over and trapped him and Amy. They could have been killed. Peyton could have been killed by the twister that claimed William Gale. He kissed the top of her head and exhaled the stress that those near misses stirred inside him. "I know, squirt. The storm squished it."

Peyton raised a tearful gaze to him and wiped at her nose. "B-but I loved m-my house."

"I know you did, sweetie."

Hunter came skidding into the kitchen in sock feet,

his hair rumpled and his eyes wide with alarm. When he saw Peyton in Grant's arms, he visibly relaxed.

"She saw what happened to the playhouse," Grant explained.

Hunter strolled over to ruffle Peyton's hair. "Hey, no problemo, kid. Your dad and I will build you a new playhouse. A better playhouse."

She blinked and glanced back at Grant. "You will?"

"Absotively, posilutely," he replied with gravitas. "A bigger, better house."

Peyton swiped her cheek and tipped a grin. "With real windows and curtains?"

"Yep. Curtains, window boxes, bookshelves…anything you want. And enough room for all your friends to play with you."

Reassured that her treasured play spot would be restored, Peyton gave Grant another big hug and a smile that filled his heart with sunshine. *His daughter was home.* Thank you, God!

"Now, how about pancakes for breakfast? I bet we can talk Grandma into making her clover-shaped flapjacks."

Peyton gave an enthusiastic nod. "Can I wake Amy up to eat with us?"

Grant's pulse lurched. "Um…Amy's not here, squirt."

His daughter's face fell. "She's not? Where is she?" Peyton's eye grew large and troubled. "Did the bad man hurt her?" Her breathing grew rapid and panicked. "Is she killed like Mommy?"

The tears puddling Peyton's eyes and the tremble in her voice grabbed his heart. "No. No, no, sweetie. She's fine. She's at her mom's house."

He exchanged a loaded look with Hunter. His brother was clearly worried by Peyton's assumption, her lingering fear and pain as obvious as Grant's.

"I thought she was mad at her mommy. That's why she was staying here."

"They made up. And she wanted to make sure her mom was okay last night. We were all pretty upset about the stuff that happened yesterday, huh?"

Peyton nodded. "Is she gonna be my new mommy?"

Grant swallowed hard and caught the raised-eyebrow curiosity Hunter sent his way. His mother entered the kitchen with Cinderella meowing at her heels.

He took a deep breath and tweaked Peyton's chin. "No, honey. She was only staying with us until I fixed her car. But the storm smashed her car, so…she'll probably be flying home to Idaho soon."

Peyton looked crestfallen. "Oh."

Grant scratched is chin. "Why did you think she was going to be your mommy? I never said that she was."

Peyton lifted a shoulder in feigned nonchalance, but the disappointment in her eyes spoke louder. "Cause you were all kissy with her that day. And you smile at her like you used to smile at Mommy."

Grant's heart somersaulted. "I do?"

Hunter backed away, wearing a smug Cheshire-cat grin.

Peyton nodded, and her chin trembled. "I like Amy. I want her to be my new mommy."

Grant took Peyton's hand and led her with him as he moved to a kitchen chair. "Squirt, it's not that simple. Adult relationships are…complicated. Difficult sometimes."

She scrunched her nose. "Like math?"

"No…" He rubbed his chin as Hunter snickered and his mother swatted his brother's arm. "A different kind of hard."

"Doesn't Amy like us?"

"She does, but…" He fumbled and glanced toward his mother, who was feeding Cinderella. "I'm gonna need coffee if I'm going to do this now."

"Coming up," she said, but her expression said she was not happy with the course of the conversation.

"Peyton, last night while we were looking for you, I was scared and worried and…I said things to Amy that I shouldn't have. I hurt her feelings. And even though I said the wrong things, the ideas behind the things I said were true. I don't know if Amy and I could ever have the kind of marriage I had with your mommy."

His mother sighed, and Hunter snorted. Grant glanced over his shoulder at the peanut gallery and silenced them with a glare.

"You had a fight with her because you were scared about me?" Peyton asked.

His stomach sank knowing how his daughter had misinterpreted his explanation.

"Um…"

"I won't run away again, Daddy. I promise."

He stroked her hair and hugged her again. "That's good to know. We were really worried about you." He held her at arm's length again and met her gaze. "But I want you to know, as worried as I was, I don't blame you. You aren't the reason I said the wrong things to Amy. I'm not mad at you."

Peyton tipped her head and raised her eyebrows. "You're not?"

"I don't want you to run off again, but…no, I'm not mad. I'm just happy that you are home with me again. I don't know what I'd have done if I'd lost you, squirt. You and Kaylee are my most important people. My treasures."

Peyton threw herself against him, and he hugged her tight.

After a moment, Julia cleared her throat and said, "Peyton, honey, why don't you get dressed, and I'll make you a special breakfast."

Raising her head from Grant's shoulder, Peyton brightened. "Clover pancakes?"

"Sure."

"With chocolate chips?"

Grant ruffled her hair. "Why not?"

Grinning, Peyton took two steps away from her father before turning back for another quick hug. "I love you, Daddy."

Sucker punched by his daughter's simple profession, Grant squeezed her back, his throat so clogged with emotion he could only rasp, "You, too."

Peyton scampered upstairs, and the silence in the kitchen lasted only a few seconds before Hunter tapped the table with his finger and groused, "Don't be a moron."

Grant lifted a startled look to his youngest brother. "Excuse me?"

"Hunter," their mother said in a warning tone. Julia cracked an egg in the bowl of pancake mix and beat with practiced finesse. "What your brother is trying to say is it's obvious to the rest of us how much you care for Amy. Whatever complications you think exist don't matter nearly as much as whether you love her or not."

"Mom…"

"Do you love her?"

"I…think I do."

Hunter grunted.

"Okay," Grant said and sighed his irritation with his brother. "I do. I love her. Okay?"

Hunter turned up a palm. "Was that so hard?"

"She lives in Idaho. She's a smoke jumper up there."

Hunter whistled. "Impressive. Well done, Amy."

"Does Amy feel the same way about you?" Julia set the pancake batter aside and pulled out the chair next to Grant. He felt a bit like a football receiver being double-teamed.

"Mom, the point is she has a life somewhere else. She's not like Tracy. She doesn't—"

"Whoa." His mother grabbed his wrist and squeezed. "Hold it right there, buster."

Grant shook his head. "I know what you're going to say."

"Amy is not and will never be Tracy," his mother said, just as he'd expected.

"I only meant—"

"We all loved Tracy and miss her. But you can never fill her shoes with someone new."

Grant nodded patiently. "I know."

"You say you do, but…you're about to let a special woman walk out of your life because of some perceived complications." His mother pinned him with a no-nonsense, talk-to-me look. "What's so hard to figure out that it trumps your love for her?"

"Seriously, man." Hunter rocked back in his chair, tipping it up on the back legs. "Look at the complications Connor and Darby overcame to be together. And don't you think Brianna and I had some issues to work out what with her son being heir to a foreign throne? If you love Amy, do something about it. And what's not to love? She's hot. And tough enough to be a smoke jumper and the first girl on our football team. That's cool."

"She's good with the girls, and they love her," his mom added.

"She's smart, too, if I remember right. Honor roll in college prep classes…" Hunter said, twisting his mouth in thought. "And she obviously cares about you and the girls if she was willing to trek all over creation in that heavy cast, and she was brave enough to take on her stepfather to save Peyton. That says a lot about her character."

"You don't have to—"

"Surely there's a way to work around the long distance with her job situation," his mom interrupted. "Honey, you've always overthought decisions that should be so black-and-wh—"

"It's not the distance, Mom." Grant gritted his back teeth and pinched the bridge of his nose. He'd not had nearly enough sleep to be having this conversation. "It's the danger involved. I can't deal with the risks she takes. Smoke jumping is full of risk, as her broken ankle illustrates. I lost one wife, and it nearly killed me. I can't lose anyone else I lo—"

He stopped short when his voice cracked.

His mother pushed out of her chair and drew him into a hug. "Oh, darling. I know this year has been hard on you. I know how losing Tracy devastated you. But any one of us could walk out that door and get hit by a bus."

Hunter scoffed a laugh. "Way to cheer him up, Mom."

She pulled back enough to send her youngest a scowl. "Let me finish." Cupping Grant's face between her hands, she continued. "If you knew someone you loved had a genetic predisposition to get cancer, would you · let that stand in your way of spending every minute you could with them?"

"I—"

"If you'd known, before you married her, that Tracy would be killed so young, would that have stopped you from marrying her?"

Chapter 23

Grant jerked his spine straight, his heart lurching.

Before he could answer, he heard his father's voice at the front door, followed by Amy's. The foyer floor creaked as his father showed Amy in and waved to the kitchen table. "Here they all are. Amy needs to pick up her stuff. I invited her to have breakfast with us."

"Great! The more the merrier." His mother nudged him as she returned to the bowl of pancake batter on the counter.

Hunter rose and waved Amy toward his chair. "So Amy, my brother was just telling us that he loves you, but he's too stupid to act on it. No, wait…it was that he's too scared of his feelings to risk his heart again. Understandable perhaps, but still a lame reason to pass up happiness, in my opinion."

"Hunter!" Julia fussed.

Grant shot Hunter an I-can't-believe-you look, followed by a you-are-so dead glare.

Hunter only flashed a smug grin.

Amy met Grant's gaze and tugged up a cheek in a melancholy smile. "I know."

She knew? Grant forgot his pique with his brother and narrowed a puzzled look on Amy.

"Maybe you can talk some sense into him." Hunter

sauntered toward the door. "It'd be a shame for a couple as right for each other as you two to screw up a good thing."

"I can try," Amy said, "But your brother's got a thick skull."

"True that!" Hunter laughed.

"Scram!" Julia said flapping her hands at Hunter. "Go help Peyton with her shoes. I'm ready to start cooking pancakes."

"How is Peyton this morning?" Amy asked.

Grant held Amy's gaze, hoping to see some indication of where things stood between them. He knew he had no right to be hopeful after his harshness last night, but… "Shaken, but recovering. David didn't hurt her."

Amy nodded. "That's what he told the police, but I've learned not to believe him. Good to know Peyton corroborates. What about earlier? What happened with William Gale?"

"Turns out Gale saved her life in the storm. She told Hunter and my dad that she tried to run away when the storm distracted Gale, and he chased after her, covered her with his body when the tornado hit. He died protecting her."

Amy flopped back in the chair, clearly as amazed as Grant had been when Hunter told him the story. "Wow."

"So she was pretty traumatized by the time we showed up calling for her. A tornado, a dead man on top of her, the whole kidnapping…she ran from us because she thought we were going to hurt her. She thought we were zombies."

Amy coughed a short laugh. "What?"

"Some kid in her class has been filling her head with horror stories apparently."

Threading her fingers through her hair, Amy blew

out a sigh. "Well, at least she's home now, and her healing can start." She pushed away from the table. "Mind if I tell her hello before I get my things and head out?"

"You're not staying to eat with us?" Julia chimed in.

"Thanks, but I won't intrude on the family. I have to arrange a plane ticket and get ready to head back to Idaho."

"Don't," Grant rasped, then cleared his throat to continue. "Don't leave, Amy."

She blinked and sent him an uncertain frown. "What?"

He sucked in a shuddering breath. *Don't blow it.* "The arrangement we had was that you would stay here until your car was ready."

She barked a wry laugh. "Kinda moot now, seeing as how the storm turned Stella into a pretzel."

"I can fix her." He had no reason to believe he could, but if it would buy him time, he'd figure out a way to do just that. "It will take a while…a lot of body work obviously and replacement parts, but my dad and I have rebuilt cars before. We can rebuild Stella."

His father turned a stunned gaze to him from his post by the sink. "We can? Grant…"

His mother hushed his dad with a subtle head shake.

Amy narrowed a skeptical look at Grant and beetled her brow. "You would do that? Why?"

"That was our deal. I know how important that car is to you because of your father. I want to do this as a gift. To say thank you for all you've done to help us bring Peyton home. And because I promised—"

"I release you from the arrangement." Amy gave him a wry smile. "Let's be honest. Stella will never be the same."

"Honestly? No. She won't. But…neither will I."

Amy's uncertain frown returned.

"And more honestly…I'm looking for a way to keep you here. I don't want you to leave. I know I said some things last night…cruel things about you and me…selfish things about—"

"Grant…"

"Hunter was right. Irritating and smug but right. I was scared to love you because…losing Tracy hurt so much, and I—"

"Grant!" She leaned across the table, stretching her arms out to grab his wrists. "I know."

He paused long enough to take a cleansing breath. His heart hammered against his ribs, and his entire future felt like a glass ball teetering on the edge of a high ledge. "You know?"

"I've seen your pain in your eyes from the day you stopped to help me with Stella. I understand your loss and the struggle it has been for you. I know you've felt things for me, and it fed a guilt inside you. But I don't want to replace Tracy. I never could. Just like no one will ever replace my dad." Amy shifted her grip, releasing his wrists to lace her fingers with his. "Here's the thing…I don't cook. I'm playing it by ear when it comes to taking care of your girls. I'm not especially good with domestic stuff, and usually ruin at least one article of clothing every time I do laundry."

Grant's pulse slowed a bit, expectantly. What was she saying? Did he dare hope?

"But what I lack in housekeeping skills I make up for in other areas. Tops among those areas is my determination and dedication. When I set my mind on something, I see it through to the end, no matter how much work it takes."

Grant lifted the corner of his mouth. "Good to know."

"Somewhere along the way, about the time you juggled a teething baby, a first grader's homework, feeding cats and cooking dinner after a day at the office, without snapping, I knew you had the same kind of dedication for the things in your life. And I set my mind on loving you. Despite all your pain, the hardships life has dealt you, you are a giving, compassionate, loyal man. You give your all to your family and hold yourself to a high standard…perhaps too high. You're a protector and a provider bar none, and have a warm, loving soul. I don't know how I'll fit in your life, but I want to try. If you want to fix Stella, knock yourself out. I'd be thrilled to have her running again. But if you don't want me to leave, you need only do two things. Tell me you love me, the way I've fallen in love with you, and ask me to stay."

The air in Grant's lungs stilled. He tried to draw a breath, but relief and joy, love and anticipation clogged his throat.

The clatter of running footsteps on his hardwood floor forestalled his reply.

"Amy!" Peyton cried happily as she hurried into the kitchen.

Turning and scooping his daughter into a bear hug, Amy smiled broadly as she squeezed Peyton. "Hey there, sweetheart. Am I glad to see you!"

"Grandma's making pancakes. Are you going to eat with us?" Peyton raised a hopeful look to Amy, and Amy sent Grant a querying glance.

Rising from his chair, Grant rounded the table and pulled Amy to her feet. Brushing her caramel hair away from her face, he framed her cheeks in his hands. "Amy Robinson, I love you. I want to grow old with you. I want to raise a family with you and share my heart with you until death—" His voice cracked but he forged on. "Until death do us part."

Amy caught her bottom lip in her teeth and moisture puddled in her eyes. He heard his mother gasp, then sigh happily.

"Stay with me? Please? I can't lose you."

Amy wet her lips. "And my smoke jumping?"

"Will always be a source of gray hair for me, but I can't let my worries rule my life anymore. Your job is part of who you are and the woman I fell in love with. I respect the courage and skill and toughness it takes to do what you do. I can't ask you to give it up."

She draped her arms around his neck, smiling through her tears. "In that case, Peyton…" She glanced down at Peyton, who followed their conversation with excitement dancing in her eyes. "Yes, I will stay for breakfast."

"Yea!" Peyton cheered and scurried over to help her grandmother flip pancakes.

"And yes, I will stay. And I will grow old with you. And I will love you until my last breath…which I don't plan to take for a long, long time."

A spring of happiness welled inside him, and he pulled her closer. "You've got a deal."

Dipping his head, he seized her lips in a long, deep kiss. The first of many. Because fate had granted him a second chance at happily-ever-after, and he wouldn't let it go.

Epilogue

Two months later

Grant sat on the back deck early one morning in late July, before the sweltering Louisiana heat could get fully revved up, and sipped a glass of iced tea as he reflected on the twists his life had taken in recent months. He'd never fully get over the loss of Tracy, his first love, but thanks to Amy, he'd found a way through his deepest grief. He could breathe again and enjoy the sunshine on his face. And he'd found that he had more than enough room in his heart for new love—because love had a way of making one's heart bigger and one's life fuller.

A stack of lumber and nails and roofing shingles sat in the corner of the yard, waiting for Hunter and their dad to arrive. Peyton was getting a new playhouse today, one even bigger and grander than the last, to accommodate Kaylee when she was old enough for that sort of make-believe—and maybe more kids, if Amy wanted them.

Through the screened door to the kitchen, he heard the front doorbell.

He checked his watch. Hunter and his dad were early. Maybe they were hoping to get to work ahead of the day's heat.

"I'll get it!" Peyton called, and Grant heard the thump of running steps in the foyer.

"Look to see who it is before you open the door!" Amy warned, already getting the hang of being a mother.

With a last deep breath of dew-scented air, Grant pushed out of the patio chair and strolled into the house to greet his brother.

Peyton gave a long, loud squeal, and Grant's pulse spiked. What was—?

"Uncle Connor! Savannah!" Peyton cried, excitement raising her voice an octave.

"Hey, squirt!" a familiar voice answered.

Grant's step faltered, even as a wide grin spread across his face.

"How's my favorite oldest niece?" *Connor? But how...?*

More childish squeals—his niece's—echoed through the house as he stumbled around toys and hurried to the front door. Grant skidded to a stop and stared in disbelief when he spotted his younger brother, Connor's wife Darby and their daughter Savannah standing in his foyer. Peyton and Savannah were squeezing each other in an enthusiastic cousin hug. His heart squeezed when he noticed his niece, who'd battled cancer and had a bone-marrow transplant last year, now looked chipper and robust. Savannah's dark hair had grown in, she'd returned to a normal weight and her cheeks had a healthy glow.

Connor lifted his gaze from the giggling cousins and flashed his trademark, lopsided grin at Grant. "Well, you just gonna stand there, or are you gonna give your little brother and his family a hug?"

Grant laughed as he stepped into his brother's bear hug. "I can't believe it. How? I thought..."

Connor pounded Grant's back. "The US Marshals in

charge of our case heard about William Gale's death. With him gone, so is the threat to our lives. We don't need WitSec anymore, so…here we are. Back where we belong."

"In Lagniappe!" Peyton chirped.

"With your family," Grant said, feeling a swirl of emotion rise in his chest. He stepped back, giving his brother's shoulder a squeeze. "The lost sheep has returned."

"With news…" Connor said, turning to let Darby get a hug, too.

Grant noticed his sister-in-law's baby bump, and his smile widened. "Son of a gun. You're expecting?"

"In October." Darby wrapped him in a warm embrace and kissed his cheek.

"That's fantastic." Over Darby's shoulder, Grant saw Amy, now rid of her walking cast, appear at the entry to the living room with Kaylee in her arms. Kaylee clutched one of the doughnuts Grant had driven out for earlier as a Saturday breakfast treat. "I have my own news."

Connor arched a dark eyebrow. "Oh? What's that?"

His heart swelled as he crossed the foyer to Amy and took his daughter from her. Putting a hand at the small of Amy's back, he puffed out his chest with all the pride and love in his heart. "I'd like you to meet Amy Robinson, my fiancée. Amy, this is my brother Connor, his wife and daughter."

"Your fiancée?" Connor sputtered at the same time Amy gasped, "Connor? But—?"

Grant laughed. "Yes. And yes."

The crunch of tires on gravel pulled everyone's attention to the newest arrivals on the driveway. Hunter parked his truck behind Amy's Mustang—well on its way to being rebuilt—and circled the front fender to open the passenger door for Brianna and their young son.

"Uncle Hunter!" Savannah cried, bouncing on her toes.

"Go on," Connor told his daughter. "We're right behind you."

Holding Peyton's hand, Savannah ran outside, shouting to the young couple.

The adults followed the excited girls to the lawn, just as the senior Mansfields' car pulled in behind Hunter.

Hunter's grin wavered briefly as he stepped away from his truck, then lit his face to full wattage. "Connor? Holy smoke!"

Savannah launched herself into her uncle's arms. "We're back, Hunter!"

Julia Mansfield didn't even close her car door as she ran to her middle son and folded him into a teary embrace. "Oh, Connor, thank you, Lord! My prayers have been answered! Please say you are home to stay!"

"Grandma!" Savannah squealed. She wiggled away from Hunter and was swept up to share the hug Julia gave Connor.

"Oh, my precious girl, how are you?"

While Connor and Darby were introduced to Hunter's wife and son, more hugs and kisses were exchanged, and excited chatter swirled around Grant.

"Wow." Amy chuckled under her breath and nudged Grant. "I think we're gonna need more doughnuts."

"Forget doughnuts," Julia said, wiping happy tears from her cheeks. "This family reunion calls for my homemade waffles and bacon."

"Hear, hear!" Stan cheered, slapping Hunter on the back before getting his own hug from Connor.

A family reunion. Grant sent his gaze around his front

yard with a growing sense of joy and gratitude. His family had changed a great deal in the past several months. They'd survived numerous threats and battled to stay together. Loved ones had been lost, but treasured new faces had joined the fold. Through the trials and tempests, one thing had prevailed over all—the love of his family. The Mansfields were together again.

Grant smiled and drew Amy close for a kiss. He and his brothers were truly blessed.

* * * * *

Available January 6, 2015

#1831 UNDERCOVER HUNTER
Conard County: The Next Generation
by Rachel Lee

Two detectives must fake marriage while hunting a serial killer who's resurfaced in a small Wyoming town. But mutual disdain turns to explosive passion at the deadliest possible time—when they're about to reel in a murderer already on their trail.

#1832 BAYOU HERO • by Marilyn Pappano

Gruesome murders unravel shocking secrets in Landry Jackson's family. They also bring Special Agent Alia Kingsley to investigate him thoroughly. Together, they have to chase down answers—and face an unexpected, burning attraction.

#1833 HIGH-STAKES PLAYBOY
The Prescott Bachelors • by Cindy Dees

Movie pilot Archer Prescott is hunting a saboteur who may turn out to be his sexy camerawoman, Marley Stringer. Danger only intensifies, as do the emotional risks. Who will get him first—the girl or the killer?

#1834 THE ELIBIGLE SUSPECT
Ivy Avengers • by Jennifer Morey

Framed for murders he didn't commit, Korbin Maguire flees and finds himself stranded on Savanna Ivy's remote property. Though wary of each other—and dependent on their isolation—will they find redemption in each other's arms?

SPECIAL EXCERPT FROM

H HARLEQUIN®

ROMANTIC suspense

To bring down a serial killer, two detectives must pose
as husband and wife. They infiltrate a community, never
expecting love to intrude on their deadly mission!

Read on for a sneak peek of

UNDERCOVER HUNTER

by *New York Times* bestselling author
Rachel Lee, coming January 2015!

Calvin Sweet knew he was taking some big chances, but
taking risks always invigorated him. Coming back to his
home in Conard County was the first of the new risks. Five
years ago he'd left for the big city because the law was closing in on him.

Returning to the site where he had hung his trophies was
a huge risk, too, although he could claim he was out for a
hike in the spring mountains. There was nothing left, anyway. The law had taken it all, and the sight filled him with
both sorrow and bitterness. Anger, too. They had no right
to take away his hard work, his triumphs, his mementos.

But they had. After five years all that was left were some
remnants of cargo netting rotting in the tree limbs and the
remains of a few sawed-off nooses.

He could close his eyes and remember, and remembering
filled him with joy and a sense of his own huge power, the
power of life and death. The power to take it all away. The
power to enlighten those whose existence was so shallow.

They took it for granted. Calvin never did.

From earliest childhood he had been fascinated by spiders and their webs. He had spent hours watching as insect after insect fell victim to those silken strands, struggling mightily until they were stung and then wrapped up helplessly to await their fate. Each corpse on the web had been a trophy marking the spider's victory. No one ever escaped.

No one had escaped him, either.

He was chosen, just like a spider, to be exactly what he was. Chosen. He liked that word. It fit both him and his victims. They were all chosen to perform the dance of death together, to plumb the reaches of human endurance. To sacrifice the ordinary for the extraordinary. So he quashed his growing need to act and focused his attention on another part of his life. He had a job now, one he needed to report to every evening. He was whistling now as he walked back down to his small ranch.

A spiderweb was beginning to take shape in his mind, one for his barn loft that no one would see, ever. It was enough that he could admire it and savor the gifts there. The impulse to hunt eased, and soon he was in control again. He liked control. He liked controlling himself and others, even as he fulfilled his purpose.

Like the spider, he was not hasty to act. It would have to be the right person at the right time, and the time was not yet right. First he had to build his web.

**Don't miss UNDERCOVER HUNTER
by *New York Times* bestselling author
Rachel Lee, available January 2015 wherever
Harlequin® Romantic Suspense books and
ebooks are sold.**

HRSEXP1214

ROMANTIC suspense

Heart-racing romance, high-stakes suspense!

HIGH-STAKES PLAYBOY
by *New York Times* bestselling author
Cindy Dees

Available January 2015

**Who will get this Prescott bachelor first—
the girl or the killer?**

To help his brothers, marine pilot Archer Prescott goes
undercover to find out who's sabotaging their movie set.
But the die-hard bachelor isn't ready for what he finds
in the High Sierras: his doe-eyed girl-next-door
camerawoman is the prime suspect.

Marley Stringer isn't as innocent as she seems.
As Marley turns irresistible and the aerial "accidents"
turn deadly, Archer begins to wonder who's more
dangerous—the perfect woman who threatens his
heart...or the desperate killer who threatens his life.

Don't miss the first exciting installment from Cindy Dees's
The Prescott Bachelors series:

HIGH-STAKES BACHELOR

Available wherever Harlequin® Romantic Suspense
books and ebooks are sold.

ROMANTIC Suspense

Heart-racing romance, high-stakes suspense!

BAYOU HERO
by *USA TODAY* bestselling author
Marilyn Pappano

Available January 2015

One family's scandal is responsible for a rising body count in New Orleans's Garden District...

Even for an experienced NCIS agent like Alia Kingsley, the murder scene is particularly gruesome. A man killed in a fit of rage. Being the long-estranged son of the deceased, Landry Jackson quickly becomes a person of interest. But does Landry loathe his father as much as the feds suspect?

It's clear to Alia that Landry Jackson has secrets, but his hatred for his father isn't one of them. Alia feels sure Landry isn't the killer, but once more family members start dying, she's forced to question herself. What if the fierce attraction she has developed toward Landry has compromised Alia's instincts?

Don't miss other exciting titles from
USA TODAY bestselling author Marilyn Pappano:

UNDERCOVER IN COPPER LAKE
COPPER LAKE ENCOUNTER
COPPER LAKE CONFIDENTIAL

Available wherever Harlequin® Romantic Suspense
books and ebooks are sold.